JEWEL OF THE SEA

THE KRAKEN #2

TIFFANY ROBERTS

Cover Illustration by Marespinosa

Art by Sam Griffin

❦ Created with Vellum

*Dedicated to my true love. You are the **wind in** my sails, and the seagull screeching in **my** ear.*

*Special thanks to all our readers **who took** a chance on us!*

CHAPTER 1

361 Years After Landing

AYMEE SMILED as she walked along the beach. The sunlight warmed her skin, sand squished between her toes, and she knew *he* was watching.

Arkon.

Her mysterious, otherworldly admirer was out there, hidden in the undulating cerulean water.

She shifted the weight of the metal canister to her left arm and picked her way through a patch of rocky ground to the lower beach. It was a familiar place, little changed by the passage of time. The place she and Macy, her best friend since childhood, had called their own — before a tragic accident had taken the life of Macy's sister.

After that, Macy refused to go near the water. Aymee had little reason to go to the sea without her friend.

Now, the ocean sang to her, and she counted the days

between these exchanges. It was worth the wait just to get little glimpses of him.

She'd met Arkon only once, three months earlier. Their encounter had been hurried, and Arkon remained hidden throughout — except for the fleeting moment during which he'd shown her his face. She'd painted his violet eyes, with their alien pupils, many times since, had seen them in her dreams, but it wasn't enough. She longed for *him*, not his memory.

The wind flipped her hair into her face. She tucked it back and glanced up at the rock formation ahead. As a child, it had reminded Aymee of a krull, an animal native to the nearby jungle. They were tall, powerful beasts with long necks, slender horns, and purple fur. Stone stretched from the seaside cliffs here and dipped into the water, resembling a krull with its head lowered to drink.

Few townsfolk came to this beach, and fewer still to this part of it. That made it an ideal location for these supply exchanges.

A metallic glint caught Aymee's eye as she approached the cliffs. A second container sat nestled amidst the rocks. With anticipation thrumming through her limbs, she quickened her steps.

Settling onto her knees, she stood her canister in the sand beside her, and lifted Arkon's container from the recess in the cliffside. Something rattled inside.

Warmth blossomed across her chest.

She tucked her canister in the empty space, gathered the container Arkon had left, and stood.

The loose material of her blouse and skirt fluttered around her as she dragged her gaze over the restless, sparkling waves. He was out there, waiting, but she'd never spot him unless he wanted to be seen.

Why didn't he approach her? Why did he hide from her?

Releasing a wistful sigh, she went inland, giving the ocean —
and Arkon — her back. She paused near a rock and slipped her
sandals on before resuming her walk. Soon, soft sand gave way
to dirt and vegetation. The briny scent of the sea mingled with
the smell of plants and earth.

She followed the footpath leading back to town for fifteen or
twenty meters before stepping off. Weaving through tall,
vibrant indigo capeweed flowers, large, green-and-violet-leafed
bushes, and tangled vines of crimson creeper, she placed her
container down and knelt near the edge of the cliff.

Her heart raced as she reached forward and parted the vegetation in front of her.

The beach stretched out in either direction below her; to the
right, it snaked along the coastline, narrowing into a pale ribbon
with distance. To her left, it widened until it hit the bulge in the
cliffs that ended in the krull-rock, where the strand passed
beneath the hollow in the formation.

While the beach was finite, the ocean stretched into infinity,
incomprehensibly large. The water darkened to navy blue and
then to midnight as it neared the horizon. The evening sun
would be swallowed by the sea within a few hours. Its soft
orange glow met the blue of the sky in the beginning of a
nightly struggle against encroaching darkness.

It was beautiful, and that beauty would only intensify as
sunset neared. But it couldn't hold her attention now.

"I know you're there, Arkon," Aymee mumbled, sweeping
her eyes over the rolling surf. Beads of sweat trickled between
her breasts and down her back, the humid air made more suffocating by the vegetation around her.

Finally, her waiting paid off.

3

The incoming waves broke around a vague shape. A moment later, the form gained definition — Arkon's leanly-muscled arms and broad shoulders emerged, followed by his tapering torso, and finally...his tentacles.

"There you are," she whispered.

He grew more distinct as the water retreated and he moved inland. His skin changed to match the sand, but his camouflage was imperfect in open air and direct sunlight. She wished he'd revert to his natural color — the loveliest blue-gray she'd ever seen — but understood why he didn't.

There was no telling how the people of The Watch would react if they knew a kraken came ashore so close to their town once a week. The townsfolk gossiped incessantly about the night Jax — one of Arkon's kind — had broken free of a holding tank in the warehouse and escaped into the darkness of the sea with Macy. That only a handful of people truly knew what'd happened didn't stop anyone from talking.

Most were unable or unwilling to understand that Macy had *chosen* to go with Jax. All they'd seen was a monster. If only they knew of the intelligence, beauty, and prowess Aymee had witnessed. Would it have changed their minds, or instilled more fear in them?

It didn't matter. There was no reason to call unnecessary attention to the current arrangement.

Arkon stopped at the cliffside. He twisted, checking his surroundings.

She eased back, allowing the vegetation to close slightly, but she couldn't look away from him. Though they were impossible to see from this distance, her imagination filled in the rich violet of his eyes.

He turned back to the cliff and pulled the canister from the recess. Removing the lid, he reached inside the container and withdrew a rolled-up piece of paper, dangling it by the string around its middle.

It was a painting she'd done for him of the nighttime jungle.

Her heart thudded; she'd never cared much about what people thought of her art one way or another, though she couldn't deny her satisfaction at bringing smiles to people's faces. Her friends' opinions mattered, but Macy and Camrin were always kind.

She found herself wanting Arkon to like her painting with all her heart. She'd wanted to give him a little piece of the land to call his own, but she couldn't deny that she'd given a tiny bit of herself in the process.

Smiling broadly, Arkon returned the painting and resealed the container.

Aymee watched him return to the sea. Though it should have appeared awkward or unsteady, there was a strange grace to the way he moved on land. Within a few seconds, he disappeared in the waves.

Sitting back on her heels, Aymee dropped her hands, allowing the vegetation to close. She twisted around, dragged over the nearby canister, and removed the lid.

Within were three folded pieces of paper — one addressed to Aymee, one to Camrin, and one to Macy's parents. She reached inside and shifted the papers. Her fingers brushed over something small, hard, and smooth.

Aymee picked up the rock and held it in her palm. It was dark gray, the edges rounded. Thin, wavy lines, flowing like ocean waves, had been carved over its entirety.

She grinned and closed her fingers around it, pressing her hand to her chest. When she'd received the first such stone in their first exchange, weeks ago, she'd thought it a gift from Macy. But Macy said she hadn't sent it when Aymee asked in their following correspondence.

The stones were from Arkon.

Aymee's first glimpse of a kraken — Jax in his holding tank — had been breathtaking. The kraken were part human and part *other*, and wholly fascinating. She hadn't feared him, especially after Macy had spoken about her relationship with Jax.

Aymee had been intrigued. She hadn't thought it possible to be more enraptured...until Arkon.

One look into his entrancing, alien eyes, and her fascination had deepened into something more like obsession.

For the first time in her life, Aymee had been envious of her friend. Macy deserved happiness, but Aymee wanted that same happiness, that freedom, that...*love*. The guilt that followed her jealousy hadn't assuaged her desires.

Lowering her hand, she examined the stone again. They were gifts, perhaps even *courting* gifts, but why hadn't he come to her? Why did he always hide until she was out of sight?

"Stop being so mopey." She sighed, set the rock in the canister, and replaced the lid.

Rising, she brushed off her legs and skirt, tucked the container under her arm, and returned to the footpath. She followed it through a dense swath of shady, cloying jungle, grateful for the wider dirt road it led to when she emerged.

Sheep and cattle grazed in the fields and pastures on either side of the road, feeding on a purple and green mix of Earth and Halorian grass. She walked toward town without paying much attention to the animals; their lowing and bleating was part of the ambience, mingling with the sound of the leaves rustling in the wind and the ocean crashing ceaselessly against the shore.

She didn't give in to the brief but powerful urge to return to the beach.

The first part of The Watch to come into view — as always — was the lighthouse perched high on the promontory. Now that the wet season had come, the light was on more frequently, alerting townsfolk and fishermen of the sudden storms that were so common this time of year.

As she crested the final rise leading into town, the other buildings became visible — dwellings crafted of metal, concrete, and wood, many of them having stood since the first colonists touched down on Halora.

This was home.

And yet...

With Macy gone, Aymee felt disconnected from the people here — even from her parents and her only other close friend, Camrin. They encouraged her well enough when it came to her art, but none of them truly understood the compulsion to create, the joy of expression. The townsfolk appreciated her works, but most seemed to think her time would be better spent on more practical pursuits.

As though spending the majority of her days tending to their ailments wasn't contribution enough.

She huffed, blowing her curls out of her face.

She wouldn't give it up.

The smell of bread drifted to Aymee on the breeze as she approached her house. Unlike many of the other buildings, this one was adorned with brightly-colored paint — flowers of all shades, animals and birds, even a simplified portrait of Aymee and her parents she'd painted when she was young.

They hadn't minded her using the house as a canvas. Her

mother, Jeanette, had even encouraged her to decorate the interior walls.

Opening the door, Aymee stepped inside and inhaled the sweet aroma of freshly baked bread.

"Mom?"

"In here!" Jeanette called from the kitchen.

"Okay, I'll be there in a minute." Aymee hurried to her room, which had been added as an extension to the original building sometime in the past.

The room wasn't large — her single bed was shoved into one corner, leaving room for a small nightstand, a dresser, and a table cluttered with brushes, papers, bottles of paint, and an easel.

Setting the canister on her bed, she opened it and plucked out the stone. She ran her fingertips over its tiny carvings before adding it to the jar on her nightstand, which held the other gifts he'd given her — each stone a different size, shape, and color, and each with a unique pattern etched into it.

After removing the folded letters from within, she sealed the container and stood it on the floor against the wall to await the next exchange.

Seven long days to go.

"From Macy?" Jeanette asked from the doorway.

Aymee turned toward her mother. Jeanette's hair, skin, and eyes were darker than Aymee's, but the resemblance between them was clear; her youthful spark and natural beauty made them look more like sisters than mother and daughter.

In that moment, Aymee was overcome with thankfulness — her parents' easy demeanors meant she didn't have to keep these secrets from them. She'd always been close to her mother, and she'd adored her father since her earliest memories. He'd never pushed her into the *family business*; his work as the town's doctor had fascinated her from a young age, and she'd been the one to start following him and her brother to the clinic every day to learn all she could.

When their medical scans had revealed Macy was pregnant with Jax's child, it had been Aymee's father, Kent, who made sure there'd be no record of it for the other townsfolk to find. Somehow, though it seemed impossible, Aymee loved him a little more that day.

"Yeah." Aymee smiled. "She didn't write back last week, which isn't like her."

"I'm sure her parents are eager to hear from her then, too." Jeanette's returned smile quickly faded. "There are some strangers here from Fort Culver. They've asked the town council to hold a meeting this evening."

Aymee's stomach knotted with unease. "Why?"

"They haven't said anything yet. I was waiting for you to get home, so we could go together. Your father's already there waiting for us." Jeanette dipped her chin, indicating the letters in Aymee's hand. "You can bring those. I'm sure Camrin and the Sinclairs will be there."

"How long have these strangers been here? I hadn't heard anything about it until now." Aymee removed the letter with her name and tucked it beneath the jar of rocks.

"They came into town when you were on your walk."

"And they've already got a meeting set up?"

"You know as much as I do at this point."

"Okay." Aymee took a deep, steadying breath. There was no reason to be anxious. Strangers came into town from time to time; it was just a little variety sprinkled into the everyday routine. "Let's go."

They went outside and walked toward the town hall side-by-side. Many more townsfolk were emerging from their homes and heading the same direction.

"Evening Jeanette. Hi Aymee!" Maris Everett called as she approached. She was a few years older than Aymee, and, though they'd lived next door to one another all their lives, they'd never been more than acquaintances.

"Hello, Maris," Jeanette said. "Thank you again for the muffins this morning. I had to chase Kent out the kitchen when he tried to come back for a third within ten minutes of you dropping them off."

Maris laughed. "It was the least I could do after what he and Aymee did for my James."

"How is he?" Aymee asked.

"Better. He's still in a lot of pain, and he won't be back to work for a while, but thanks to you two he still has both feet — even if he's short a few toes." The woman's smile was at once grateful and sorrowful as she shook her head. "I don't know what we would've done otherwise, and if he hadn't..."

"I'm glad they got him to us in time. Vorix have fast-working venom," Aymee said. James had been extremely lucky. Vorix — long-bodied, rough-skinned creatures that used several sets of short, clawed legs to climb trees — injected deadly venom with their breakaway fangs. Had it not been for James's heavy-duty footwear, the fang would have been embedded in his foot and continued pumping poison into his bloodstream.

If the man had taken the bite anywhere else, he would have died. His screams of pain — which had only stopped when, exhausted and overwhelmed, he'd passed out — still echoed in Aymee's mind.

Maris caught Aymee's hand, gently bringing her to a halt.

"You and your father saved my husband. I keep thinking about all those *what-ifs*, and how I haven't had nearly enough time with him, or how our child would have had to grow up without his father, and I... I just can't imagine it." She squeezed Aymee's hand. "There's nothing I can give you that would repay what you've done for him, but I can tell you this: take what you want. Take it all. Do not hesitate, because it could all be gone faster than you can blink."

Aymee's mind went to Macy. Macy, who hadn't cared what others might've thought when she chose what she wanted — Jax.

Arkon's face rose to the surface of Aymee's thoughts, but she dismissed it. He was a fascination, a curiosity sparked by Macy's stories about the kraken. There was no future for Aymee with Arkon, especially when he was unwilling to emerge from hiding.

She'd laugh at herself if it wouldn't make her look insane; of all the men on Halora, the only one who held her interest so strongly wasn't even human.

"Thank you, Maris." Aymee gave the woman's hand a comforting squeeze in return. "My father and I don't want anything in return. It means everything that we were able to help him. But I'll take your words to heart."

Maris smiled and released her.

"We'd best hurry," Jeanette said. They quickened their steps toward the town center.

The meeting hall was one of the largest buildings in The Watch. It served as a gathering place both for meetings and recreation; because resources were too precious to leave such a space unused, it doubled as a pub.

Dozens of people filed through the open doors, from beyond

which the din of a hundred simultaneous conversations spilled out. Aymee kept beside her mother as they squeezed inside. She stood on her toes and searched until she spotted her father, who was waving his hand.

She tugged on her mother's sleeve and motioned toward her father. Maris smiled and shooed them away, going to her own family.

The heat and noise of at least two hundred people was overwhelming. Aymee clung to her mother's hand as they wove through the crowd, slowly working their way toward Kent. Whatever the meeting was about, the allure of newcomers had apparently piqued the town's interest.

The crowd's palpable curiosity did nothing to quell Aymee's unease.

When they reached Kent, he leaned forward and kissed them each on the cheek. Aymee took his arm and leaned against him, turning her attention to the front of the room.

Several members of the town council were on the small stage, but it was the unfamiliar faces alongside them that caught Aymee's eye. One of the strangers stood closer to the councilmen than the rest — a handsome man who looked to be in his early thirties with short, dark hair, a stern expression, and serious eyes. His gaze roved over the crowd as people funneled into the hall, but there was no restlessness in it, only alertness. His clothes were the deep purples and greens of the jungle, and he wore a large knife on his belt.

Six other rough-looking men in similar attire stood behind him.

Culver Hunters.

Though Aymee had never seen a Hunter before, their reputation was well-known in The Watch. The Hunters of Fort

Culver fearlessly battled the most dangerous beasts on Halora and always came away the victors. They were said to travel from town to town, thinning out the populations of such creatures to keep people safe.

That they'd come here now, so soon after the events involving Jax and Macy, boded ill.

By the time the influx of townsfolk stopped, everyone was crammed into the hall shoulder-to-shoulder. Aymee had only seen the place so packed once before — the day Jax arrived. Sweat beaded on her forehead and trickled down her back as the air grew stuffy. She wrinkled her nose at the stench of unwashed bodies. Many of the townsfolk had likely just come in from the fields.

Walter Bailiff, the head councilman, stepped forward and raised his hands. A hush spread through the crowd, leaving only the occasional coughs or whispers.

"Thank you." He ran a hand down the front of his shirt, smoothing the fabric. His cheeks reddened; despite his aptitude for organization and mediation, Walter had never seemed comfortable speaking in front of crowds. "In light of…recent events, we have some visitors who've come to The Watch. I don't want to put my foot in my mouth and explain it wrong, so…"

He stepped back, gesturing to the dark-haired man from Fort Culver. The stranger took Walter's place at the front of the stage. Despite his serious features, his smile was warm.

"Let me echo Mr. Bailiff and thank all of you for coming on such short notice. My name is Randall Laster. Me and my men have come all the way from Fort Culver, and let me tell you, your town is paradise after that long on the road."

Laughter filled the room.

"I think most folk call us Culver Hunters, or something along those lines. We call ourselves rangers, but that doesn't matter much. It's been a long time since any of us came this way, so I'd like to take a few moments to explain what it is we do, and why we're here."

"Excuse me," someone muttered.

Aymee turned her head to see Macy's father, Breckett Sinclair, carefully squeezing his broad-shouldered frame through the crowd. He stopped beside her, his mouth hidden in his thick beard.

"This can't be good," Aymee whispered to him.

He shook his head. Even if she couldn't see his mouth, his eyes were troubled.

She took Macy's letter out of her pocket and passed it to Breckett. "Here."

He tucked it away, and they both returned their attention to Randall.

"I'm sure, like in most places, everyone here has a job to do." He paced slowly along the stage, boots thumping on the wood, hands clasped behind his back. "Our job is simple. We hunt the creatures that give people trouble. Doesn't matter if it's a snatcher plant taking your babies or a pack of krull eating your crops. We control their numbers so humanity can thrive."

Aymee grabbed a handful of her skirt and pressed her lips together.

"I got a pemling problem! Want to come deal with that?" a woman called out.

The crowd laughed again. Pemlings were fist-sized vermin that could eat entire silos of food if they weren't kept in check.

Randall raised a finger, his smile tilting to one side. "That's a bit smaller than what we tend to specialize in, ma'am, but we'd be more than happy to come take a look. Afraid to say we didn't come all this way to deal with some pemlings."

"Then what are you here for?" Aymee asked.

Pausing, Randall turned his head toward her. When their eyes met, she saw an unsettling spark of interest in his gaze. "We're here to help The Watch, Miss...?"

"Help us how? We've been doing well."

"He's here for the sea monster," another person said from the left side of the room. "Aren't you?"

Aymee looked in the speaker's direction but couldn't tell who'd said it. Her stomach twisted. "He's not a monster."

"Aymee," Jeanette warned quietly, catching her daughter's hand.

The scrutiny — and interest — in Randall's gaze intensified. "We don't always follow rumors across Halora, but the story we heard from this town... Monster or not, this thing must be viewed as a threat until we know more about it."

"He is no more a threat than you or me." Aymee couldn't stand and listen to this in silence. "Jax had many opportunities to hurt people, but he didn't. He *let* himself get captured. He obeyed every instruction given to him without resistance. Even when he escaped, not a single person was harmed. How could you consider him a monster?"

Commotion erupted in the hall; everyone in town had their own version of those events, though almost everyone in town had been either in the comfort of their homes or here in the town hall, drinking, when Jax escaped. The only people who knew the truth would never betray Jax and Macy.

"He caused no trouble," shouted one of the men who'd guarded Jax.

Randall silenced them by lifting his hands in the same

manner Walter had. "I don't want everyone to argue about it. We've heard some stories, and we came to sort it all out. We might carry some big guns, but we're on your side. If this *Jax* is on your side, too, we won't have any problems. But until we know that, without a single doubt, we must treat him as a dangerous beast. Because *that* is what will keep people safe."

"He's not a beast!" Aymee snapped. "We've lived here in peace for years before he came, and we still live in peace months after he left. You're here for no one but yourselves!"

One of the other rangers — older than Randall, with short blond hair and a cruel grin — barked a laugh.

"Aymee!" Kent pulled Aymee back, and she stumbled into him.

Randall's smile faltered, and his brow creased. "I understand emotions are high in the wake of what happened here. I'm not going to take offense. We came to help, and that's what we intend to do. Our first goal is to determine what that will entail."

Breckett cleared his throat. "What she says is true. That *beast*, as you call him, brought my daughter back after we thought her dead at sea. She was badly injured, and he exposed himself to make sure she got the care she needed. The whole time he was locked in that tank, all he did was ask about the welfare of my daughter. He is not a monster."

"I should very much like to speak with your daughter, sir," Randall said.

"That's not possible."

"So, he didn't bring her back in time?"

"He did, and thanks to him, Doc Rhodes, and Aymee, my Macy lives."

Randall's gaze shifted from Breckett to Aymee. "Me and my men would love to talk with the two of you further over the coming days." He looked out over the rest of the crowd. "Anyone with information, we ask that you share it with us. Our job is to defend the humans of Halora. That means The Watch, and every other town on this planet. We can't make a decision that will potentially affect everyone on this world based on some anecdotes.

"Please, rest assured, we're not here to disrupt your lives. We're not here to stir up trouble. We're here to prevent any more of it. If this Jax is truly harmless, we'll move on."

The crowd burst into animated conversation as Randall stepped back. It took Walter several minutes to quiet them down enough to be heard. He thanked everyone for their time and wished them a good evening. The townsfolk trickled through the open doors and into the night.

Aymee finally released the fabric she'd held in her fist and stretched her stiff fingers before smoothing the wrinkles out of her skirt. Randall had a certain charm, a confidence and compassion that should have eased her fears.

But even if the men with him looked rougher, Randall had the hard features of someone who'd scraped out a living in the wilds.

She didn't want to think of Arkon becoming their target, but it seemed all too possible.

"Be careful, Aymee," Breckett said. "I know you're trying to protect them. I want to do the same, but we don't know these men. We don't know what they're willing to do."

"What were you thinking?" Jeanette demanded.

Aymee winced. "I know. I *know*. I shouldn't have spoken out like that, but I couldn't... They're not monsters!"

"We know that," her father said, placing a comforting hand on her shoulder, "but *they* don't."

"I'll talk to him," Breckett rumbled, glancing at the stage.

Aymee's brows lowered as she followed Breckett's gaze. Randall and his rangers were talking with a few of the councilmen; his eyes flicked to Aymee and held. He smiled.

Aymee looked away. She needed to warn Arkon, but it was another week before the next exchange.

"Just be careful, Aymee," Breckett said.

"I will. Thank you, Breckett."

They left the town hall together, saying their goodnights to Macy's father once they were in the square and the crowd had thinned. When they arrived home, Jeanette went to the kitchen to finish preparing dinner while Aymee excused herself, anxious to read Macy's letter.

She sat on her bed and reached for the letter, pausing as she lifted the jar of stones. Each of them had been selected and adorned just for her. Heart warm, she smiled. It was a small comfort, but every little bit mattered.

Sliding the paper from beneath the jar, she unfolded it. Macy's familiar handwriting was scrawled across the page, and though shorter than usual, the letter conveyed an abundance of happiness. Aymee wished they were together to share in that feeling.

One of the lines gave her pause. She read it again, and her lips spread into a grin. Aymee leapt from the bed and ran into the kitchen.

"It's a girl!" she shouted. "Macy had a girl, and she's *perfect!*"

CHAPTER 2

THE FACILITY WAS A CLUSTER OF HUGE, FAMILIAR PATCHES OF darkness set against deep blue as Arkon approached, its exterior lights insignificant in the vastness of the surrounding ocean. The humans who'd once dwelled within these buildings had called this world Halora, and the records they'd left behind claimed more than eighty percent of the planet's surface was covered with water. For all that he'd learned from those records, such a massive area was beyond Arkon's fathoming.

His people, the kraken, occupied a sliver of the ocean so tiny that it might as well have been a single drop of water.

He cast aside those thoughts as he neared the main building's entry door. In the past, such musings could have occupied him for hours or days at a time. But there was only one thing he longed to think about now, only one thing that held his attention — *Aymee*.

Tucking the supply canister under his arm, he entered the number sequence on the keypad. The red light over the door changed to green, and the entry slid open. Arkon swam into the pressurization chamber.

As the door closed behind him and the water drained, his mind's eye produced images of Aymee. He'd watched from the water as she walked along the beach, had marveled at her easy grace in the open air, had battled the urge to go ashore and speak with her. What would he have said? The single time they'd spoken, he'd been a stammering fool.

When he had gone onto land and retrieved the container, his hands tingled — Aymee had touched it. His tentacles detected a faint, familiar taste, sweet and light and alluring. *Her* taste. It was unlike anything in the sea.

"Pressurization normalized," the computer said from an unseen overhead speaker. The interior door opened after its light turned green, and Arkon moved into the corridor beyond.

The Facility had been his home for his entire life. He knew every hallway, every chamber, knew which lights worked and which tended to flicker. He'd always wondered at the mystery behind it all. Thanks to Macy figuring out how to access the computer's information, he'd learned much. The Facility was powered by an experimental reactor fueled by halorium — a rare, glowing stone often found on the seafloor. The computer's records could provide no estimate on how long the reactor would be sustained by its current halorium supply; the technology had been too new when the kraken took control of the place for definitive data to have been generated.

His eyes roamed over the lines and angles of the walls and doors as he made his way deeper inside. Though the dirt and wear of centuries was apparent everywhere, the precision with which The Facility had been constructed was just as noticeable. Everything was even, symmetrical, deliberate. Every overhead light, every doorway, every panel on the floors, walls, and ceilings were exact in size, shape, and placement. There was a certain artistry to it, but he found it somehow cold. Unfeeling.

What about that feeling put Arkon off after he'd spent countless hours seeking balance, symmetry, and precision in his own attempts at art? He'd never quite managed to satisfy himself in such pursuits, and yet, his works felt unerringly more alive than the Facility. Was it simply his inherent personal connection to his own creations?

He glanced down. A dried clump of seaweed had crusted onto the base of the wall and lay draped partly on the floor. Little clusters of sand were scattered on and around it. Though tiny in relation to the corridor — just as The Facility was tiny relative to the ocean — it served as a break in the otherwise perfect patterns made by the drainage grooves running along the edges of the walkway.

Was that the key? When he looked upon his creations, he held them against unattainable perfection and saw all the little flaws — the very flaws that drew the eye and instilled uniqueness in a piece.

What would Aymee see in these walls? What might she make them with some of her paint and adequate time?

Though he'd only spoken to her once, Arkon had no doubt she'd breathe life into this impersonal structure; Macy had managed as much by her mere presence in the Facility. What wonders might be wrought by Aymee's talent?

Arkon sought the *what-ifs* in the unadorned walls as he passed them, but he could not do her imagination justice; anything he might dream up was inadequate, unimportant, unworthy of her.

He crossed into the building marked *CABINS*, where the

Facility's human inhabitants had once dwelled, and his thoughts again shifted. The design here was softer — abundant curves muted the harshness present in the main building's perfect angles. It was an illusion, of sorts; everything in this living space was arranged with equal precision, and the repeating patterns were just as obvious.

Macy and Jax used one of these chambers as their den. No kraken had denned in this building before them, and few had reason or desire to do so even now — kraken could breathe and function adequately on land but were more comfortable in the water. The other buildings — either partially or fully flooded — suited Arkon's people better.

And yet, Arkon had chosen to claim a chamber of his own here, in the air, as Macy's pregnancy had advanced and his supply exchanges with Aymee continued.

Since the first such exchange, he'd taken to placing carved stones in the containers he left for Aymee. Macy had never mentioned whether Aymee asked after the stones in her letters, but none of them had been returned...and Aymee had begun including gifts for Arkon in her canisters.

He took the long way through the looping corridors to reach his den without passing Jax and Macy's. Once inside, he closed the door and took the supply canister in his tentacles. His hearts thumped, and his hands trembled as he removed the lid and placed it on the nearby bed.

Arkon peered into the canister. It was laden with the usual fare — soap, medicine, food, and clothing for Macy, along with the letters sent by her friends and family from The Watch. Tucked to one side was a large paper rolled into a neat tube.

He reached in and grasped the paper between forefinger and thumb, drawing it out of the container. It was secured around the middle by a bit of brown string, attached to which was a thick paper tag. *ARK,* it said in big, flowing writing; she demonstrated her artistry even in the mundane.

Arkon longed to hear his name from Aymee's lips again.

He gently worked the tip of a claw into the knot and loosened the string, sliding it off the paper. Then, mindful of his claws, he unrolled the tube.

The subject of the painting was immediately apparent — the jungle. Arkon had been in the jungle several times to help Jax gather plants for Macy to eat, but he'd never seen it as Aymee depicted it here. This was the jungle beneath the stars — deep, dark purples and blues contrasted by the shining silver and muted gold of the stars and moons, illuminated from within by strange, glowing plants.

Closer inspection revealed the strokes of paint that comprised the image; they were loose, almost haphazard, and meaningless on their own or in small clusters. But, somehow, they came together to form a vibrant, detailed whole.

He crossed the room and used a metal clip to hang the painting on the wall alongside the others she'd sent. The sea during a storm; sunlight shining through the window of a small room with a narrow bed cast in somehow sorrowful shadow; an unfamiliar, hair-covered beast in a grassy field; and his favorite, a painting that was nothing but a jumble of rich, expressive color, which belied an underlying method despite its chaos.

Backing away, he studied each painting. They were so varied in subject and approach, in colors, form, and emotion, and yet each bore a certain quality that marked them as *hers.*

And she'd given them to him.

Before he could get lost in thought again, he forced himself back to the bed. He replaced the lid on the canister and exited the room, making his way toward Jax and Macy's den.

The exchanges were for Macy, after all, and it wasn't right to make her wait any longer for news from her loved ones.

The door of their den was open, and the soft sounds of Macy's laughter drifted into the hall as Arkon approached. Stopping outside the doorway, he glanced inside.

Macy sat, leaning against the head of the bed, with Jax laid across it. One of his tentacles was raised, tip curled down to tickle the youngling between them.

Such simple, innocent joy had been a rarity before Macy came to stay at The Facility. Kraken had typically found satisfaction in solitude — Jax and Arkon's friendship was an oddity in its depth and sincerity, but each had still spent most of his time alone. What Macy and Jax had built here, their little family, had changed everything the kraken knew, and that sense of family, of community, was spreading to the others.

Macy and Jax had received visitors so frequently as of late that they'd taken to keeping their door closed more often than not to ensure their youngling, Sarina, received adequate rest. She was a wonder — the child of a human and a kraken. Potentially the future of their race when kraken females were so few and offspring so rare.

The connection between Macy and Jax was something Arkon couldn't have imagined possible, were it not before his eyes. That she considered Arkon a friend was humbling. He enjoyed his time with her; she appreciated his art, offered unique insights, and was even teaching him to read and write.

Arkon couldn't help feeling a hint of jealousy. He wanted a mate of his own, someone to share his den with. Someone he could talk to as often and openly as Jax to Macy. Someone who understood what drove him, even when he did not, who shared his interests and passions, and didn't view him as strange.

"Arkon?"

Jax's voice startled Arkon from his thoughts. Macy smiled at him from across the room, as welcoming and warm as she'd always been with him.

"Why are you just standing there? Come in, Uncle Arkon!" she said, motioning him closer.

Swallowing his embarrassment, he entered the chamber. Jax regarded him with a furrowed brow as he approached.

"Just drifting on the current of my thoughts," Arkon replied. He slid the supply canister into his hands and held it to Macy. "Fresh off the beach. Well, it was fresh a few hours ago. It depends on your personal criteria for freshness, I suppose."

Macy chuckled and took the canister from him. She set it beside her, removed the lid, and peered inside. "I can't thank you enough for doing this for us. You know Jax is more than willing to make the exchanges, so you don't have to leave so often."

"It is no trouble. Jax has spent years attempting to get me out of this place more regularly. He may count this as a small victory."

"I wanted you to explore *with* me," Jax said. "No matter the wonders I described to you, I could rarely draw your attention away from your work. Why are you so eager to leave now?"

Macy glanced at Arkon from the corner of her eye. "Maybe he's found inspiration elsewhere."

Though there was no malice in Macy's expression, Arkon found it unsettling. It was a knowing glance. "The more I can do to keep the three of you together during these early days, the better. I am curious to see the results of a youngling raised by mother and father simultaneously."

He moved closer to the bed and leaned forward, looking down at little Sarina — his *niece*, according to Macy. She was surrounded by a nest of blankets, tentacles drawn up tight to her body, green eyes open and alert. In most ways, she was a normal kraken, but she'd inherited a few traits from her mother — a delicate nose, soft features, and fine, dark hair on her head and at her brows.

She was the first baby he'd interacted with. Kraken younglings remained with their mothers — who largely kept to themselves — until the males were old enough to join the hunters.

"You make it sound like we're an experiment," Macy said.

Arkon slid the tip of a tentacle to Sarina's hand. She clamped her fingers around it, her tiny claws pricking his skin. "Every situation is an opportunity to learn."

"It is," she agreed, taking a letter out of the canister. Arkon glimpsed Aymee's handwriting upon it. She set it aside and proceeded to rummage through the other contents.

"The females will be gathering soon in the Mess," Jax said, sliding off the bed. "I will take Sarina this time if you'd like some quiet to read your letters."

"Are you sure?" Macy asked. "I don't mind going."

Jax brushed the backs of his fingers over Macy's blonde hair and leaned down to press a kiss on her lips before gathering their daughter. Sarina put up a brief struggle before relinquishing Arkon's tentacle.

"Rest, Macy. Read your letters. The females will most likely ignore me while they dote on Sarina."

"They'd better," Macy grumbled. "I've seen Leda eyeing you."

"I belong to you, Macy."

"You do, and she better remember that." She wore a hint of a smirk on her lips.

Not everyone approved of the changes since Macy's arrival. Leda was one of them. Most recently, she'd sought after Jax, Arkon, and Dracchus, and all three had turned her away. Many females clung to their ways, seeking males who would be the best providers for as long as they chose to keep that male as a mate. Arkon didn't doubt that Macy would fight for Jax, if it came down to it, though she was physically outmatched by any of the female kraken.

Jax kissed Macy again and looked at Arkon. "May the stones fall as you would have them lie."

Arkon smiled. "And the currents carry you where you would go."

After another peck on Macy's cheek, Jax left with Sarina.

Macy drew back the blanket and stretched her legs. "How was the swim?"

"The same as it usually is." At a casual pace, it was two hours of his heartbeats steadily quickening, of his mind racing over countless possibilities, of his imagination summoning images of Aymee. "The currents are strengthening. Storm season is building rapidly."

"And you haven't seen any more razorbacks?"

"No. Perhaps you finally taught them fear." Arkon smiled, but the expression soon faded. Macy had nearly died saving a kraken youngling from a razorback and still carried the scars from the battle. It had been a frightening time for everyone.

"Hey," she said, swinging her legs over the edge of the bed, "stop thinking about what might have happened. I made it. You saved my life, and we're all okay now." She grinned. "I single-handedly killed a razorback. Of course they're scared."

She was right, but it sent his thoughts along an unexpected path. Macy had faced her greatest fear — the open ocean — alone, just because there'd been a chance of her locating the missing youngling. Despite the terror and pain she must've experienced, she'd persevered.

And Arkon couldn't muster the courage to speak with Aymee a second time.

"Arkon, what is it?" She tilted her head, humor fleeing her expression. "You're fidgeting."

He exhaled through his siphons and forced his tentacles to still. He'd hunted countless times, had battled razorbacks and sandseekers, had faced the challenges of kraken larger and stronger, and had never known fear through any of it. But all of this was so new, so uncertain.

"I am in need of advice, Macy."

Her brows rose; usually, she sought advice from him. "Of course. What can I help with?"

"I... I have never approached a female. Some have come to me, but the interest has never been mutual. I have never given over to the notion of being used merely as a tool for the prosperity of another being without any reciprocation. It has always seemed so unfulfilling..."

Her features softened. "You want more."

"I do. You and Jax have shown me what could be, and it would be dishonest if I said I didn't want it, too."

"Is there a female who has caught your interest?" That knowing gleam had returned to her eyes.

"Yes." Arkon's chest tightened. "Very much so."

"And does this...female know of your interest?"

He'd sent Aymee gifts, and she'd sent gifts in return, but did that mean to her what it did to him? His knowledge of human culture had come from Macy, and it was limited. Male kraken gave gifts to females to display their ability to provide, but Jax hadn't won Macy in that fashion.

Did Aymee see their exchanges simply as two artists sharing in one another's works?

"I don't know."

"Arkon, why haven't you approached Aymee?"

He recoiled, mouth dropping open in shock. "I... How..." He moved closer to the bed. "Has she...has she mentioned me?"

"She told me about the pretty rocks you've been sending for her. At first, she thought they were from me, but I didn't know what she was talking about until she described them in her next letter. She even drew a picture of one of them to show me." Macy smiled. "They *are* very pretty, Arkon."

He looked down, his thoughts careening into an indecipherable mess. "She likes them, then?"

"She's told me so. She would have told you, too, had you spoken to her."

"I cannot simply... It's not that easy." The tips of his tentacles writhed on the floor, and he forced them to still once again. "When we spoke the day you left The Watch, I was not myself. I do not believe I left a good impression."

Do you not speak English as well as Jax does? Aymee had asked after Arkon's stammering.

He'd made a fool of himself in front of the only female who'd ever caught his interest.

Macy frowned and leaned forward, hands on her knees. "How so? Aymee isn't a judgmental person, and if that day was the only time you've spoken to her, then you have nothing to worry about. When she came back after meeting with you, she was excited. Even more than when she first met Jax."

His hearts pounded, and heat suffused his face. Fleetingly, he felt a strange sense of *lightness* he'd never experienced in the air. "She was? Was it... Was she excited about *me*?"

She laughed and touched his arm. "Arkon, *talk* to her. She's not like the female kraken."

"But what should I *say*? I do not know how to initiate that conversation."

"You both share something you're passionate about. Use that. You've already introduced yourself, you've been sending her gifts, and if I know Aymee — which I do — I'm sure she's been sending things back. Just be yourself." She paused and grinned widely. "And don't tell her that you'll *fit*."

He didn't fully understand her meaning until he met her gaze again. His color deepened to violet. The first time he met Macy, he'd been brimming with curiosity and fascination, especially when he'd learned that humans and kraken could mate. Jax had deemed Arkon's questions *inappropriate*. Still, he smiled at the memory. "I do not believe myself *that* inept at this. Close, perhaps, but not quite."

"I'm only joking with you, Arkon." She took his hand and gave it a gentle squeeze.

Kraken rarely touched one another, but he'd grown used to it in the months he'd known Macy. Humans used touch to layer emotion and meaning into their communication, and it was like a language unto itself. Early on, Jax hadn't liked Macy touching Arkon, and it had taken time for him to accept that the affection conveyed in such contact was innocent.

"I *knew* she was why you're so eager to make the exchanges." She released his hand.

"Is it that obvious?"

"To me it is, because I know you. Jax has his suspicions, but this is all still new to him, too. He hasn't decided if he thinks there's anything to it, yet."

"Does...Aymee know?" A chill flowed through Arkon, strengthened by its contrast to the heat that had coursed beneath his skin moments before.

"She only wrote about you when she realized I wasn't sending the rocks. Otherwise, she hasn't said anything more to me."

Arkon nodded and backed away.

"You'll talk to her next time, won't you?"

He inhaled deeply, filling his lungs with the Facility's clean, bland air. "Yes. I will."

"Good." She regarded him with that ever-present smile on her lips. "She'll love you, Arkon. I do."

Love was one of those words which — until recently — held little meaning to the kraken. Even Arkon hadn't known what it truly entailed. But Macy was showing them. It was as beautiful in its simplicity as it was overwhelming in its complexity and nuance.

To Macy, Arkon was a dear friend, a part of her family. He longed for a different sort of love from Aymee. How could that be achieved? What were the methods, the natural progression?

Shared passion.

His first opportunity, perhaps his *best* one, would be on that beach in a week. Would it be enough time to prepare? Would it be enough time to create something worthy of Aymee's attention?

He thought again of her dark eyes, curly hair, and lovely

smile, of the way his name had sounded from her lips, of the interest in her eyes as she'd gazed upon him.

Warmth blossomed inside him. Yes, it was time enough. *She* was reason enough.

"Thank you, Macy. You've been an immeasurable help."

"Of course. And as much as I love you—" she reached behind her and lifted the folded letter, holding it up for him to see, "— I'm going to ask you to leave so I can read my letter from *Aymee.*"

Arkon smiled. "I can read it to you. The practice wouldn't hurt."

"Uh-uh. If you want to know her secrets, you'll have to discover them yourself. From her."

"At least I can say that I tried. Rest well, Macy."

"Thank you, Arkon. I'll see you later."

He raised a hand to wave as he exited the room. Patterns swirled into being within his imagination, complex and colorful, and he pieced together what each would require. Gathering enough stones wouldn't be the issue; gathering the *right* stones would be, and he'd have only a brief window of time during which he could bring it all together.

For the chance to talk with Aymee, it would be well worth the challenge.

CHAPTER 3

JAMES EVERETT RELEASED A HISS OF PAIN AS AYMEE UNWOUND the bandage on his foot.

"Is papa's foot going to fall off?" asked Daniel, James and Maris's five-year-old son.

"Daniel!" Maris exclaimed.

"He's only curious." Aymee smiled at the boy. "Your papa had to give up his toes, but his foot's just fine. See?" She removed the remaining bandage, eliciting another hiss from James. The cloth was stained with ointment and rust-colored spots of blood that indicated his stitches might have seeped, a sign that he might have walked on it despite her orders.

"Excuse me," Maris said.

Color draining from her face, Maris put a hand over her mouth and turned away.

The healing process for such wounds could be a gruesome sight. Vorix venom caused necrosis around the bite that, when left untreated, could spread with surprising speed. Aymee had spent so much time here in the clinic with her father that she wasn't bothered by such things.

James was fortunate it had only been his toes.

Daniel stepped closer and stared at his father's foot, displaying none of his mother's squeamishness.

"Does it hurt?" he asked.

James laughed. "Like hell."

"Wouldn't hurt so bad if you stayed off it," Aymee said.

James dipped his head, grinning guiltily. "Guess I've been caught."

"Yes, you have." Aymee turned her attention back to his foot. It was healing well; despite James's stubbornness, he hadn't split open his stitches or picked up an infection. Yet. "Consider this a break. You'll be back up and moving before you know it if you rest and give it time to heal, but if you don't, you could lose the whole foot."

"You have to listen to Miss Aymee, papa," Daniel scolded.

Aymee laughed. "Right. *Always* listen to Miss Aymee."

She cleaned the wound, applied ointment, and wrapped it in a fresh bandage. Maris returned to her husband's side when Aymee finished, helping him onto his crutches.

"Thank you, Aymee," Maris said.

"Of course. Daniel, you're in charge of making sure your papa stays off that foot."

The boy's face brightened at the prospect of so important a task. "Yes, ma'am!"

"Have a great evening," Aymee said as Daniel rushed forward to open the door for his parents.

She stilled when Randall met her gaze from the hallway.

Her stomach sank.

She'd avoided speaking with him for an entire week; why

had he come *today*? Why, on the day she was to make the exchange with Arkon on the beach?

Randall took hold of the door for Daniel and bid the Everetts a pleasant evening. Once they were gone, he entered the room, boots thumping on the wooden floor.

"Miss Rhodes." His smile was warmer and more genuine than she'd seen in the town hall.

He was a handsome man, perhaps more so than any she'd seen, with a strong jaw, sculpted lips, and eyes the blue of a summer sky. Perhaps he might have caught her eye, *before*.

Now, her interests lay somewhere forbidden.

"Mr. Laster." She offered him a curt nod and turned away to clean up the supplies she'd used for James. "Is there something I can help you with?"

"I just have a few questions, if you'd oblige me."

"I'm currently working and have patients waiting—"

"The Everetts were the last, Miss Rhodes," he said, shutting the door.

She paused as she wiped the table, squeezing the cloth in her hand.

Damn.

"Then I suppose I can spare a few moments." She couldn't risk him following her. At least if she answered his questions, he'd likely leave her alone.

"Wonderful." He eased into the chair beside the door and leaned an elbow on the armrest. "I've heard it was a friend of yours who was taken by the creature. That correct?"

"*Jax.* His name is *Jax.* And yes." She washed her hands at the sink and turned toward Randall as she dried them, keeping the bed between herself and the ranger. "I take it you spoke to Breckett?"

"I have. He's a rough man, but he's honest. I admire that."

"I don't know anything more about all this than he does."

"You were Miss Sinclair's primary caregiver before she left town with Jax, weren't you? She was here, being treated for injuries sustained at sea?"

"Yes."

"Did she talk to you about anything while she was here? Any details about this creature, where it came from, what it's capable of?" He leaned back, never breaking his intense, piercing gaze.

"No. She only told me that *Jax* isn't dangerous. That his people were engineered by humans using human DNA. They think and act like us. Speak our language. In every way but appearance, they *are* human." She crossed her arms over her chest. "She didn't say anything else because it wasn't her right to do so."

"You said his *people*. How many are there, Miss Rhodes? How many have you seen?"

She could have kicked herself for the slip, and nearly bit through her tongue.

"I've only seen Jax. For him to exist, there have to be more somewhere."

Randall bent forward, resting his elbows atop his thighs, and sighed. "The glass on the tanks in that warehouse is thick. It's built to take a beating. A man could break it, yeah — a strong man like Breckett, with twenty minutes and a hammer. But by all accounts, he was walking his daughter down to the docks when all this happened. Someone led the guards away, and my guess is that more of those things came in to free *Jax*."

Aymee flattened her hands on the bed and leaned over it. She held his gaze. "Yes, someone led the guards away. It was all part of the plan to help him escape without anyone getting hurt.

Just like I'm sure Breckett explained to you. He gave Jax his blessing to take Macy, because that was *her* choice. And that tank was cracked on the inside before it was broken open. Jax could've broken free at any time."

"I understand, Miss Rhodes. You're very close to all of this, and I'm from out of town—"

"You're a Hunter."

"You have hunters here, too."

"They're not hunting Jax. That's what *you* are here for."

"I'm here to determine whether or not I *should* be hunting him. Anything that can break out of a tank like that and has humanlike intelligence is a potential threat, not just to this community, but to *all* of the settlements on Halora."

"Do you think we would've just stood by and done nothing if Macy was in danger? Me, her parents, even Camrin, the man she'd intended to join with? All of us helped her that night. There's never once been an incident with Jax's people in all the years I've lived here, and I've never heard of one in all the years before that. If they meant us harm, we'd have felt it already.

"Macy is *happy*. She's in love with Jax, and he loves her in return. If any of us had any doubt of that, we would've been hunting for him long before you heard about all this."

He ran a hand up his cheek and then over his short hair. "You had a few brief interactions with one of these things." He didn't waver at her glare. "Now it has an idea of how this town is laid out. Has an idea of your armament and defenses. And it knows that not everyone is going to be friendly. I've hunted a lot of dangerous prey, Miss Rhodes, and the more dangerous it is, the more we prepare. They could be planning an attack on this town right now. They could be watching this town right now.

41

"I'm not here to kill anything; I'm here to *protect* human life. And if it comes down to it, I will choose us over them, every time."

"Then leave them be," Aymee said. "Jax has no interest in this town or its people, apart from Macy, and he'd never do anything to place her in danger."

Clutching the arms of the chair, Randall pushed himself to his feet and stepped toward the bed. "Not everyone in town shares that opinion, Miss Rhodes. I *want* you to be right, but it's my duty to be *certain*, as much as it's your duty to tend to these folks when they're wounded or sick."

"And none of them were there. Like you, they want a monster to slay. But humans are usually more monstrous than the things they fear. His appearance means nothing. Would you hunt me, or any other person, like you hunt an animal?"

He frowned, and the iron in his eyes softened for a moment. "There's no such thing as monsters, Miss Rhodes, apart from humans. And like you said — Jax and his kind are human in all but appearance." He sighed and leaned over the bed, propping himself on his arms. "You and I didn't start out on the right foot, but I'm truly not here to hurt you or anyone you care about. I just want everyone to be safe. I want *you* to be safe."

Aymee frowned. He was close, *too* close, and his scent — leather, earth, a hint of sweat — drifted to her. It wasn't unpleasant.

What he said was true; when she'd seen the rangers in the town hall and heard their reason for coming to The Watch, she'd gone on the defensive. She'd do anything to protect Macy and Jax. To protect Arkon.

Not once had Randall responded with anger, despite her verbal attacks. He'd shown nothing but patience.

"I know," she said. "And thank you for that. I don't mean to be ungrateful or rude; I'm just—"

"Worried for your friend."

"Yes."

"It's all right, Aymee. I admire your loyalty, and if you're right about Jax and his kind, you don't need to worry about your friend anymore."

"They've left us alone for all these years, Randall. Even now that we know of their existence, they haven't come. We should follow their example and just leave it be. Leave *them* be. Stay here as long as you need to make sure the town is safe, but don't hunt them down. Don't give them a reason to think of us as a threat to their safety."

"If they're truly leaving us alone, I don't think we'll ever find them. It's a big ocean." He stood straight. "Thank you for your time, Miss Rhodes. I appreciate your being open with me."

Aymee nodded, eyes downcast. She felt...helpless. Her pleas wouldn't change Randall's course. He and his rangers were a threat, and because of their hunt, it was too dangerous for Arkon to continue the supply exchanges. She had to warn him.

She had to keep him away.

Her chest tightened; he was her only link to Macy, but the mere thought of never seeing or having the chance to speak with him again pained her.

"Have a pleasant evening." Randall lingered for a moment before he turned and walked out.

Aymee remained still until Randall's heavy steps were cut off by the sound of the clinic's front door closing, and then folded her arms atop the bed and buried her face in them.

Please don't let the Hunters locate them.

∼

It was later than usual by the time Aymee left the Clinic. She'd busied herself by organizing tools and medicines until she was sure Randall had moved on and then gathered a few supplies for Macy and her baby. Twice, she'd dropped items in her haste, and finally forced herself to take a breath and slow down.

Randall won't find him. He won't.

No matter how many times she repeated the words in her head, her anxiety persisted.

Aymee slung her packed bag over her shoulder and hurried out, jogging across the square. She slowed only when she was on the road leading to her home.

"Aymee!"

She turned to see Camrin loping toward her, his shaggy red hair flopping into his face.

"I thought for sure I missed you this time," he said as he neared.

"Lucky for you, I'm running late."

He swept hair back from his forehead. "Everything okay, Aymee?"

Frowning, she scanned their surroundings and shook her head. "I'm worried," she replied, lowering her voice.

Camrin's eyes followed her gaze. He moved closer. "Because of those men from Fort Culver?"

Aymee adjusted the strap of her bag. "Their leader came to talk with me."

"He talked to me and Breckett, too, right there on the dock. I heard he got the names of everyone who took a guard shift while Jax was in the warehouse, and spoke with all of them, too."

"He plans to hunt them down. He won't take anyone's word, and he won't sit around and wait."

Camrin frowned. "Guess I can't blame him. He probably didn't believe it when he first heard the stories about what happened here, but then he comes into town and finds out it was true? Stuff like that scares people."

"I know. I understand, I really do." She closed her eyes, sighed, and tilted her head back. "It's just...not right. As much as I want to believe they'd leave the kraken alone if they realized they're just people, I...can't. I just can't believe they'd leave them in peace."

"Well, for whatever it's worth, our people have been fishing these waters for generations and we've never found a kraken. If Jax and the others don't want to be found...I don't think they *will* be found."

"I hope you're right. I'm going to warn Arkon."

"If I can help at all, let me know." He extended his hand, holding a folded letter to her. *MACY* was scrawled on the front in his loud, clumsy writing. "Would you send this on for me?"

Aymee grinned, tucking the letter into her bag. "Are you telling her the good news?"

He smiled sheepishly and looked down. "It feels weird to, but yes. I just want her to know that I'm doing well."

"You're her friend, Cam. She'll be happy knowing *you* are finally happy." She pecked a kiss on his cheek. "I need to go. It's getting late."

Camrin gave her a quick hug. "Right. Be safe, okay, Aym? Those rangers act nice enough, but they're still strangers. Dangerous ones."

"I will. Tell Jenny I said hello."

"Will do." He released her and waved as she hurried away. "See you later, Aymee."

The house was empty when Aymee entered — her father was likely still making house calls, and her mother often worked the fields until sundown. She went to her room, set her bag on the bed, and lifted the canister into place beside it. Her mother had left a crate with fresh fruit, vegetables, and bread. She packed them into the canister along with the medical supplies from her bag before retrieving the letters from herself and Macy's parents from the dresser, piling them with Camrin's. Grabbing a pencil, she quickly added a warning to her letter about Randall and his rangers.

She placed the letters in the canister and turned back to the table to gather the last item — her gift to Arkon.

Aymee stared at the paper. It was the first drawing she'd done of him, one of her favorites. During the brief time they'd spoken, his eyes had emblazoned themselves in her memory; she'd used crushed capeweed petals to color them in this drawing, the closest she could come to their rich violet without mixing paints.

She rolled the paper carefully, secured it with a bit of string, and slipped it into the canister. The remaining space within became an abyss as she stared at it; she shifted her gaze to the table, where several jars of paint and a few brushes sat out.

Smiling, Aymee gathered the painting supplies, ensured the lids were secure, and added them to the canister.

It would be her parting gift to him.

The sky had taken on the hues of late evening, the indigo on one horizon bleeding into the golden orange on the other, when she reached the beach. Her heart raced, though her anticipation was clouded by sadness. This would be the last time. It had to be.

She glanced over her shoulder — not for the first time — as she descended toward the sand, searching the tree line for movement. Satisfied that she hadn't been followed, she brushed her hair out of her face and quickened her steps. Her arms burned with the strain of carrying the canister; she'd filled it more than usual, and the extra weight had only made the journey from town feel longer.

Her stride faltered as she neared the exchange spot.

Aymee stood, transfixed, and struggled to make sense of what she saw.

Hundreds, maybe *thousands*, of stones had been arranged near the drop-off spot, radiating out in a half circle from the edge of the rock face. They were stacked in piles of varying height, each spaced a precise distance from the ones nearby. As her eyes drifted over them, she realized there was a method to the stones' placement; together, they looked like the waves rolling on the ocean, dwindling gradually as they grew more distant from the cliff. Conveying motion, though they were unmoving.

The canister slipped from Aymee's hands and fell into the sand, forgotten.

She stepped forward, moving between the stones. It was like walking through a dream. And Arkon had created it...for her.

Bending down, she studied one of the taller piles. The rocks decreased in size from the bottom up, alternating in color from slate grays to pale blues. The delicacy with which they must have been placed just to remain upright was astounding.

"Most of it will be swept away when the tide rises."

Aymee gasped and quickly straightened.

47

"You're here," she said breathlessly. She turned to face him, and her heart leapt; she wasn't prepared for what stood before her.

Arkon's blue-gray skin glistened in the light of the setting sun. He was only a few feet away, standing tall on tightly-bunched tentacles. Her eyes swept over his lean, muscular torso, lingering on the dark stripes adorning his head, shoulders, and tentacles. His face was narrow, with high cheekbones and a strong chin. Despite his lack of a nose — he had only two slits where it should have been — and the tube-like siphons on either side of his head, his features were both strikingly alien and startlingly human.

Those violet eyes stared at her with undisguised interest and intensity.

"I had begun to think you wouldn't come," he said.

His words cast a shadow over her delight and reminded her why she'd been so late.

She took a single step toward Arkon, and when he didn't retreat, she closed the remaining distance between them. He was a couple heads taller than her, a towering presence, and she had to tilt her head back to look into his eyes. Slowly, she trailed her gaze from his face to his chest and shoulders, and then along his arms to pause at his hands. They were so human, despite the webbing between his fingers and the claws at his fingertips.

His skin darkened at his waist, urging her eyes farther down.

Unbidden, she reached out to touch him.

Aymee flattened her palm on the upper portion of his tentacle. Arkon inhaled sharply, muscles tensing, but otherwise remained still.

He was at once soft and solid, his skin damp but not slick or slimy.

"You really are magnificent," she said, unable to keep the awe from her voice.

Arkon lifted a hand slowly and brushed the back of a finger along her jaw, calling her eyes back to his. "You are even more beautiful than I remember."

Aymee smiled. The combination of his words and touch made her breath shallow. She couldn't believe he was here in front of her.

In full view.

She dropped her hand and stepped back, smile fading.

His brow furrowed, and he tilted his head. "I've said something wrong."

"No. It's just..." She shook her head and laughed humorlessly. "Of *course* you'd reveal yourself for our last exchange."

"I... Last? What do you mean, last exchange?"

"There are humans in The Watch who are looking for you. For the kraken."

"How does that differ from the last three months? We've seen the fishermen watching the water."

"These people are *Hunters*, Arkon. They're from a place farther inland called Fort Culver. Seven of them arrived the evening of our last exchange and called a meeting in town. Their leader approached me today, asking me questions about Jax and your people."

He moved closer, eliminating some of the distance she'd opened in her retreat. "My people are hunters, too, Aymee. And no one here knows anything about us that could endanger our wellbeing. Unless they have technology like Macy's suit, we are beyond their reach."

She placed her hand on his chest. His heart — hearts, for surely there were more than one — thumped beneath her palm. "But you're not. Every time you come here you put yourself at risk."

Arkon stared down at her hand before hesitantly covering it with his own. "I'm beginning to realize that life has little meaning without risks."

Determination and vulnerability filled his eyes.

"Why did you wait so long to show yourself to me?" She curled her fingers slightly beneath his hand.

"Because I didn't know what to say to you, or what you thought of me. I was...out of sorts when we first met."

"What I thought?" Aymee's brows furrowed. "I was fascinated by you. I thought that was clear."

"And I was stunned by you, so I stammered like a fool. I'm not... Interactions like this aren't something I am particularly skilled at. My experience with humans is understandably limited, so I couldn't be certain of how to interpret the way you acted toward me. I...I'm rambling now."

Aymee's grin widened with each word he spoke. "I find your rambling endearing." She rubbed her finger over his skin. "I watched you, you know."

His hand twitched, and his skin warmed under her palm. "You watched me?"

"After I leave the beach, I hide in the jungle along the clifftop and wait for you to retrieve the canister." She continued the motion of her finger, intrigued by the soft texture of his skin and the comforting strength of his hand.

"I've always watched you drop it off, but I never thought you'd wait to see me, afterward." Tentatively, he raised a tentacle and lightly brushed its tip over her wrist.

She watched, fascinated by the limb. It was long and thick, its lighter-colored underside lined with suction cups that lightly kissed her skin. Her heart pounded in her chest, and something powerful stirred low in her belly.

What did that say about her? This was only her second meeting with Arkon, and she was more aroused than she'd ever been with a human man. Was it the allure of the unknown? Had the details Macy relayed sparked a curiosity in Aymee that demanded to be sated?

Was there something wrong with her?

But how could she view this as shameful, unnatural, abhorrent? She didn't see it that way with Jax and Macy.

This didn't *feel* wrong. Not to Aymee.

"I wanted to see you." She slipped her hand from beneath his and brushed her palm over his suction cups.

Arkon's fingers trembled, and he released a shaky breath before shifting back, withdrawing his tentacle from her touch. "This is...I..."

Dropping her arm, Aymee regarded him with a smile. His eyes were wide, irises nearly consumed by his dilated pupils, which weren't quite round. His tentacles writhed in the sand, and his hands were at his sides, fingers tightly curled. His chest rose and fell with rapid breaths.

There was a hint of uncertainty in his heated gaze; he looked as though he held onto control by a thread and might break at any moment.

A rush of satisfaction coursed through Aymee; she'd done this, she'd instilled this want in Arkon. He was just as affected by her as she was by him.

Her smile didn't falter as she turned away and walked between the stacks of stones. The wind flowed through her hair, cooler now with night's approach, and the sound of the waves licking the shore enveloped her like a siren's song.

"This is beautiful." She gestured to his work with a sweeping wave of her arm. "I hate that it will be gone come morning."

"The person it was meant for has found joy in it. There's nothing lost, as long as you hold onto that emotion."

"Like a painting. A moment captured forever." She looked at him over her shoulder. "I've kept every rock you've gifted me. I wish I could keep this too."

He moved closer but didn't pass between the stones. "Keep this moment."

"I will."

She inhaled the briny air. The tide was rising as the day waned, and the light had taken on a magical quality that existed only during sunrise and sunset, when everything, for a short while, seemed new and incredible. It made Arkon's stone towers ethereal — they were a fleeting glimpse into another world, stolen while the foggy veil was drawn back for an instant.

This place hadn't felt like that to Aymee since she was a child, when she and Macy would splash colors on the rocks. Their *paintings* would last only until the next storm, and that had made them more precious.

Just like this.

She wanted to hold onto this feeling for as long as she could.

"Thank you, Arkon."

He dipped his head in a shallow bow. "It was my pleasure."

Aymee's eyes fell on the canister she'd dropped; it stood at an angle behind him, near the outer edge of the stones. Her joy faded. She weaved through the stacks, stopped before the container, and picked it up after a brief hesitation.

"I need to get back before it's dark," she said, walking to

Arkon and holding the canister out. "Don't want to raise anyone's suspicions."

I don't want to go. Not now that you are here.

Arkon placed his hands on the container, and they held it between them, staring into each other's eyes. "When can we meet again?"

Her grip tightened. "We can't. It's too dangerous for you to come back."

"So we will be cautious, and meet on a more sheltered part of the beach. One that isn't well visible from farther inland."

She meant to shake her head, to tell him *no*, but instead said, "There's a spot toward the other end of the beach where the cliff overhangs the sand. No one can see underneath unless they're standing on the beach nearby." She gestured toward it, though the place was difficult to make out from this angle.

"And...I will see you there tomorrow?" Arkon asked.

Aymee's eyes widened, and her mouth hung open. She hadn't planned to meet again at all, much less so soon, and her heart leapt at the prospect. "Tomorrow?"

After another moment, resolve strengthened his features. "Yes. Tomorrow. I will allow you to choose the time, as I've chosen the day."

"Will we need to exchange these again?" she asked, nodding toward the canister.

He glanced down and smiled. "No. Tomorrow will be just for us."

Her gaze fell on his mouth; his parted lips revealed his pointed teeth. Strangely, they didn't unnerve her. Arkon's smile took on a rakish tilt.

Something stirred in her again, a tingling heat at her core; familiar but unidentifiable.

"Tomorrow then. Same time as always," she said.

Arkon nodded and tucked the canister under his arm when she finally released it, though his eyes didn't leave hers. "May the stars smile upon you tonight, Aymee."

Clenching fistfuls of her skirt, she watched him go; his movements were graceful despite the alien nature of his gait. She didn't take her eyes off him until he disappeared into the sea, and only then walked between the stones to retrieve the container he'd left at their normal drop-off spot. Anticipation thrummed through her.

She'd see him again.

Tomorrow.

CHAPTER 4

THE OCEAN SANG WHILE ARKON WAITED; IT SOUNDED SO different from land, distant and otherworldly. This wasn't the dark, deep lullaby — felt more than heard — of his youth. It was music brimming with wonderment and possibility, with freedom and imagination.

A song for Aymee.

Arkon closed his eyes and filled his lungs with salt-kissed air. The sand beneath him was soft, the rock at his back had been warmed by the afternoon sun, and a light breeze tickled his skin. Though his senses were unchanged on land, the things he experienced with them were still largely new — as was what he'd felt when Aymee touched him.

He brushed his fingers over his chest, sparking a fleeting, ghostly memory of the thrill that had suffused his skin while he'd been in contact with her.

After imagining dozens of potential outcomes for their meeting, Arkon had been wholly unprepared for the effects of her proximity, her touch, her scent and taste. He'd barely maintained control of his body.

It had taken hours for him to calm after they'd parted, and his excitement had rekindled with startling intensity when he discovered the paints and brushes she'd left in the canister for him. And the art she'd given him! Being gifted a drawing of himself had been odd — he'd never considered that he would become the subject of anyone's art — but her work was exquisite, and the life she'd instilled in it with a bit of color in the eyes astounded him.

The implication of her offering had caught him off-guard when it dawned on him.

Aymee didn't see him as a monster.

He opened his eyes and stared out over the sea. The waves glittered in the late afternoon sun as though countless stars had plummeted to float upon the water. The ends of his fore-tentacles swept over the sand restlessly. He felt like his hearts hadn't slowed since their meeting the day before.

She'd been waiting for him to approach her all along.

However intelligent Arkon thought he was, he'd proven himself inept when it came to Aymee.

Something moved in his periphery vision. He turned his head to see Aymee rounding the wide bend. She carried a basket at her elbow, and the wind molded her clothing to her body, teasing at the curves hidden beneath the cloth.

Arkon rose slowly and allowed his skin to revert to its natural color and texture. The moment her dark eyes settled on him, her entire face brightened.

"You're here!" Aymee called over the wind and sea.

She closed the remaining distance between them at an easy run; Arkon watched, fascinated by the play of her lithe limbs and the brush of her curls over her cheeks. Her apparent joy validated his eagerness.

"Was there any doubt I would be?"

"No." She swept her hair out of her face. "Have you been waiting long?"

When Arkon's people hunted, they sometimes laid in wait to ambush unsuspecting prey from sunup to sundown. The few hours he'd waited on this beach had been almost unbearable due to his anticipation, but they were a small price, especially with Aymee as the payoff.

He smiled. "No, not long."

"Are you hungry?" Aymee set down her basket and lifted the folded brown blanket from its top. After spreading the blanket over the sand with one edge against the cliff, she sat down atop it.

"Yes, I am hungry. I would have brought food had I known you wanted to eat."

Though the kraken shared food, sharing *meals* was an unfamiliar concept to them. Arkon had only learned of the custom through Macy. It was a ritual with social and cultural significance, though he wasn't sure of its meanings beyond solidifying the bonds of family and community.

Pulling the basket closer, Aymee glanced up at him and smiled. "I wanted to spend as much time as I could with you, so I brought dinner with me. I made sure to pack extra, just in case." She patted the empty place beside her. "Join me?"

Arkon studied the way she was sitting before looking down at himself. He brushed as much sand as he could off his tentacles, folded them beneath himself, and settled down on the blanket. The soft-but-scratchy texture of the fabric was strange to him.

"What is this made from?" He brushed a tentacle over the blanket; its foreign scent was layered with Aymee's sweet smell.

"Sheep's wool. The original colonists brought many things from Earth when they landed — machines, plants, and animals. Sheep were among those things." She peeled back a smaller cloth that was draped over the basket, revealing a variety of food within. Arkon recognized much of it from the supplies Aymee sent Macy.

Plants.

As far as he'd been able to discern from the Facility's old lab reports, kraken could safely eat many of the same plants humans did without getting ill, but he hadn't dared to try any yet.

"We shear the wool from them when it gets long enough and use it to make clothing and blankets," Aymee continued.

Arkon pinched the fabric and rubbed it between his fingertips. "Is it like their hair?"

"Yes. We use dyes to change its color, like this." She lifted the hem of her blue skirt. "This isn't made from wool, though. It's made from whitesilk flower, which is native to Halora."

Arkon looked at the material between her fingers, but his attention soon drifted to the smooth curve of her calf. Did that skin feel different than the skin of her hand?

She released her skirt and rummaged through the basket.

Her movement tugged Arkon from his distraction. Her words hit him suddenly, tugging his mind in a new direction. Unthinking, he reached forward and touched her skirt. "This was made from flowers? What sort of process yields this result?"

Aymee chuckled. "When the flowers bloom, they leave behind these long silky strands. We gather those and spin them into thread." She removed a small, cloth-wrapped bundle from the basket and held it out to him. "I wasn't sure what you'd like."

Furrowing his brow, Arkon accepted the offering and unwrapped it. Though he couldn't guess its source, it was undoubtedly meat. The outside was browned and bore faint scorch marks — signs it had been cooked, like Macy did with all her meat.

If this had come from the sea, it was cut from a creature he'd never eaten before.

"What is it?"

"Krull."

"The long-necked beasts that live in the jungle?"

"Yes. You've seen them?"

Arkon nodded. "One of the times I went with Jax to forage for Macy. He voiced his curiosity regarding their taste."

"Now you can tell him what it tastes like."

"I think I'll tell him I know and leave it at that."

Aymee grinned. "He'll have to hunt his own."

Arkon grinned, too. "He just might. It's not often I can say I tried something before him, so I must relish these experiences as they come." Raising the meat to his mouth, he sank his teeth into it and tore off a bite.

Most of the kraken's prey yielded soft, sometimes chewy meat. This was tough, but the flavor quickly burst over his tongue and flooded his mouth. It was startlingly complex, and Arkon realized it wasn't solely the krull meat he tasted — the little flecks on the meat, which appeared to be finely-diced plants, added to the taste, altered it, enhanced it in ways he hadn't known possible.

"Do you like it?" she asked, chewing her own piece.

He shifted the meat to one side of his mouth. "I'm not sure. It's...a lot. Almost overwhelming. I've never had anything like it."

She swallowed. "You don't have to eat it if you don't want to."

"I *do* want to," he replied, and took another bite. "This is just very different from what I normally eat. It's even different from the cooked meat Macy's had me try."

"Does all of her food come from the sea?"

"The meat, yes."

They ate in companionable silence, enveloped by the sighing of the waves. Aymee turned her face toward the sea as she bit into a wedge of fruit. Arkon watched the wind lift locks of her hair, brushing them over her cheeks and shoulders.

"Is she beautiful?" she asked suddenly. "Sarina, I mean."

"Yes, she is." There was deep emotion hidden with Aymee's question. A hint of sorrow, perhaps?

The corner of her lips tilted up. "I knew she would be."

"I'm sure you'll be able to meet her yourself, before long."

She met his gaze. "Really?"

Arkon nodded. The hope in her eyes made his chest tighten. "Once she is a bit older, I do not doubt Macy and Jax will arrange for you to see her."

Aymee averted her gaze to the water. "It's not the same with the letters. I know she's the one writing them, but it's not *her*."

Frowning, Arkon looked at the sand. From hopeful to crushed in an instant. Her sadness was a weight on his heart; how would he feel if Jax, Macy, and Sarina were taken out of his life?

He'd feel the same emptiness if Aymee were taken, though this was only the third time they'd spoken.

He placed his hand on her leg; her thigh was warm through

the fabric of her skirt. "As soon as these hunters have moved on and Macy has recovered, I will make sure she starts to visit you."

"I'd love that. Thank you." Her smile returned, and after a few seconds, her eyes dropped to his hand. She tilted her head.

Arkon pulled his arm back. She hadn't invited the touch, hadn't given him permission, and he must have broken a rule of human interaction

Aymee caught his hand, hooking her fingers over his thumb, and drew it closer. Arm stretched toward her, Arkon leaned forward.

Her bronzed skin was dark against his pale blue-gray flesh, her hand tiny in comparison.

Aymee's heat seeped into him. She lifted her hand away and traced her fingertip along the webbing between his fingers and up to the tips of his claws.

Her delicate touch sent a tingling sensation along his arm. It gathered in his chest to halt his breath; he'd never experienced anything like it. His skin was sensitive enough to detect minute changes in water temperature and current — a gift from the humans who'd engineered the kraken, if he chose to look at it that way — and that sensitivity turned the contact with Aymee into something euphoric.

"Hands are one of the most difficult things to draw," she said, smoothing her palm over his. "But they are also one of the most beautiful."

His eyes fixated on her hand, and he drank in every detail from her delicate knuckles to her long, slender fingers and short, blunt nails. The slightly rougher spots on her skin enhanced the sensation of her touch. He attempted to agree with her, but he wasn't sure what sound, if any, came out.

She placed a finger under his chin and guided his head up

until his eyes met hers. Smiling, she slid her fingertips along his jaw until she reached his siphons. "Macy told me these are not ears."

Transfixed by her brown eyes, he shook his head. Her fingers moved with such grace, such gentleness, such confidence and precision, and his skin was ablaze beneath them.

"For breathing," he said distractedly.

She circled her finger over the end of his siphon. "What's it like? When you go from water to air and back again?"

Arkon swallowed and willed his mind to move past her feel, past her proximity and intoxicating scent. "It's...it is like being suspended between worlds for a fraction of a moment. A fleeting taste of mortality as lungs or gills give out and my body adapts to its new environment." He blew air through his siphons and Aymee yanked her hand back, laughing. Arkon shook his head again, unable to ignore the absence of her touch. "That sounds somewhat dramatic. I don't mean to exaggerate."

"I love the way you describe things." She canted her head to one side. "What you are is the embodiment of amazing. To live in two worlds..."

"I must admit to having not done much living in this world. Not until recently." He smiled, hearts thumping.

"Everyone has to start somewhere. I haven't done much living, either. I find enjoyment where I can, but I spend most of my days tending to the sick and wounded." She scooted back to lean against the stone wall and plucked a round, red fruit out of the basket. An apple. Macy had told Arkon that apples had been brought to Halora from the ancient human homeworld. "Our exchange days have been the brightest ones for me recently. It gives me something to look forward to."

Arkon glanced down and traced a circle in the sand with the

tip of a tentacle. "I spend my weeks anticipating the few minutes during which I'll see you on the beach."

"If only you hadn't been hiding from me."

He lifted his gaze to her; her smile had broadened into a grin. "As I recall, Aymee, you admitted to doing some hiding yourself."

"I didn't want to frighten you away."

His skin shifted to pale violet. It took him a moment to force it back to normal.

Aymee perused him with a peculiar look on her face. Finally, she met his gaze and held out the apple. "Would you like to try?"

Arkon set aside his questions about the way she'd just stared at him and shifted his attention to the fruit. Macy had described it as crisp, sweet, and juicy. "I...do not know that I am feeling quite that adventurous, this time."

She laughed and pulled the apple back. "Macy told me Jax still refuses to eat anything that didn't have a pulse. Do you *really* not eat plants, or is it just plants from topside that gross you out?" The crunch of her teeth sinking into the apple punctuated her question. She turned her mouth up teasingly as she chewed, juice glistening at its corners.

Though he was no more compelled to sample the apple than he'd been a moment before, he felt a strange urge to taste its juice from her lips. "We were designed to be hunters. Our senses, especially sight and smell, are far superior to humans'. I believe it was intended as a means to keep us somewhat self-sufficient. We hunted food while we were out, which meant less work for our human keepers. My understanding is that the creatures that were used as part of our basis were carnivorous, as well."

"Octi…" Her brows drew together as she struggled with the word.

"Octopus. It was a species of cephalopod from your people's homeworld."

"And the kraken were based on their myth?"

"No, not exactly. The kraken was supposed to be an octopus of immense size. A sea monster. Big enough to drag the huge ships the humans used to sail far below the surface. Our ancestors took the name from those legends."

"So, what is it like?" She took another bite of the apple and spoke around it. "When you hunt, I mean."

Arkon pushed himself off the blanket and onto the sand. "It's an exhilarating experience, much of the time, though there are often other tasks I'd rather attend. Kraken rarely socialize, but during a hunt, a group of us operates as a team, united by a common goal."

He leaned forward, bracing himself on his hands with his belly near the ground. "For most prey, we wait in ambush." To demonstrate, he altered his skin to match the color and texture of the sand beneath him. "When it comes close enough, we attack." He sprang up at an imaginary fish, kicking sand onto the blanket, and paused. "My apologies."

Aymee chuckled and brushed sand from her leg. "You're incredibly fast. What about hunting by scent and sound, without sight?"

"It's possible, but our eyes are our most powerful tools. There are…other creatures that excel in the dark, and the risk is rarely worth the reward."

She set her apple aside and pushed herself to her feet. "Would you like to try?"

He furrowed his brow. "Would I like to try what?"

"Hunting without sight."

"And what would I be hunting?"

She swept by him, trailing her enticing fragrance in her wake. "Me."

His hearts quickened. "That certainly sounds more than worth the risk…"

Aymee turned around and walked backward, toward the setting sun. "It's a game we played as children. The seeker keeps their eyes closed and listens for the hiders. We called it Blind Man's Bounty."

The notion of pursuing her by scent and sound stoked some primal instinct deep within Arkon. "Are there any other rules I should be aware of?"

"Only that I won't leave the shelter of the overhang, and that you must keep your eyes closed until I am caught." She stopped and lifted her skirt over her knees, tying the excess material into a knot at her hip. "Are you ready?"

Arkon's gaze dipped over her bare legs before he squeezed his eyes shut. "Yes."

The ocean hissed against the shore, and the breeze whisked over his skin. The sounds gained power as they reverberated off the cliffside and the overhang above. Sunlight warmed his skin, and the sand beneath his tentacles bore a myriad of tastes and scents — including the faintest hint of Aymee.

"Come find me, Arkon," she called in a sing-song tone.

He turned his head in the direction of her voice; it, too, echoed lightly off the nearby stone, obfuscating its point of origin. Slowly, he moved toward her and inhaled deeply, searching out anything beyond the smells of brine, sand, and stone on the wind.

"I'm over here." Her words drifted to him from an entirely different direction.

Adjusting his movement, he circled around the area he thought she'd spoken from, putting the wind at his back — if her aroma were blowing toward him instead of away, he had a better chance of locating her.

"You're getting cold, Arkon."

His hearts pounded in rapid succession. Both the sand beneath him and the surrounding air cooled; he'd moved into the shadows.

"I wonder what your reward will be?" she whispered from nearby.

Arkon extended an arm. He sensed a change in the breeze — its flow was rerouted by something nearby. When he moved forward a bit more, his palm touched stone. He extended his tentacles to all sides, running them over the ground.

His suction cups brushed over an imprint in the sand — one of her footprints — and detected her unmistakable smell. He followed the tracks, keeping his hand on the stone as he circled it. This was the pillar-like formation that extended down into the ground from the overhang.

Her scent hit him like an electric jolt.

"What would you like?" she asked, now from behind.

Having marked the pillar in his mind's eye, he had a better sense of the area. He turned toward her and hurried forward. "What are you offering?"

She released a squeak, and her feet whispered over the sand in retreat. He knew he was closing in on her by the strength of her smell and the sound of her movement.

He knew he'd won when her laughter filled the air.

Arkon opened his eyes as he lunged forward. Her eyes were

wide and bright, her smile radiant, and her scream brimmed with humor. Arkon threw his arms around her, and they fell together. He turned before they hit the ground, wrapping his tentacles around her and taking the brunt of the fall — which was softened by the sand — on his shoulders.

She shook with laughter, and her curls fell over his chest to tickle his skin.

"You've not told me my prize," he said.

Aymee placed her hands on his shoulders and pushed herself up, grinning down at him. "What would you like?"

As he paused to consider — she'd left open too many possibilities for his imagination to adequately examine — he realized their current position. Her pelvis and breasts pressed against him, and his tentacles were coiled around her thighs and waist, his hands on her back. The salty-sweetness of her skin — laced with something *more* — delighted him. Quite suddenly, his self-control was in jeopardy.

She lifted a finger to touch his bottom lip, lowering her head. Her hair fell to either side of his face, curtaining them from the outside world. "Perhaps a kiss?"

His breath shallowed, and his skin blazed. Everything but he and Aymee was unimportant, faraway, forgotten.

Kraken didn't kiss.

But Macy and Jax did. Often.

He could do little more than nod.

She smiled, holding his gaze as she eliminated the remaining space between them. Her warm breath danced on his skin, and his hearts raced. She touched her lips to his.

Arkon closed his eyes and tugged her closer. Her lips parted, and she applied more pressure, first at one corner of his mouth, then the other, and finally at the center.

Colors exploded behind his eyelids; he didn't even have a name for most of them, but they stole his breath. *She* stole his breath.

Holding perfectly still apart from the trembling of his hands, he inhaled, taking Aymee into him until she filled his entire being. She cupped his jaw, fingers spreading on either side of his siphons as the press of her lips grew firmer. Another scent clouded his senses — that mysterious, alluring hint he'd tasted before, stronger now than ever. It settled over his mind in a maddening fog, pouring fire into his veins.

He curled his tentacles up along her legs, reaching for the source of the alluring aroma.

Aymee gasped and stilled.

For the second time, his conscious mind noticed their position — noticed her pelvis was settled over his slit, and only her body weight kept his throbbing shaft hidden. The slightest easing of pressure, and he'd extrude immediately.

Arkon opened his eyes to see Aymee staring down at him.

"I hope your reward was worth the risk," she whispered. The dark pools of her eyes were filled with uncertainty and desire, mirroring his own emotions.

His nostrils flared as he released a slow, shaky breath; its speed was deliberate, but not its unsteadiness.

Calm. We were caught up in the moment, but the moment has passed, now... Regardless of how much I want it to continue.

"A thousand times over."

His hearts thundered, and Aymee's fingers were points of molten pleasure on his skin. Her entire body lay pressed against his, molded to him. How could he calm himself when she was touching him like this?

If she moved before he'd cooled off, how could he keep from extruding? How would she react if he did?

She smiled, but this smile was different. It was slower, almost self-satisfied, and it sparked a new light in her eyes. Her thumbs brushed along his cheekbones. "I'm glad." She raised her head, lifting away her dark hair, and evening light flooded in to drag Arkon back to reality. "It's getting late."

Calm. I don't need to embarrass myself any further or frighten her away.

"Is our time already coming to an end?"

She looked down at him, melancholy writ upon her features. "It is."

The thumping of his hearts faded, giving way to the gentler sounds of wind and sea. "Shall we meet again tomorrow?"

"No. It's too soon." Idly, she stroked her thumbs over his cheeks and jaw. "I don't want to draw suspicion. The leader of the rangers..." Her brows knit, creating a small crease between them that he wanted to soothe. "I think he's taken a liking to me."

There was a sinking, twisting sensation in Arkon's gut, and his breath stuck in his lungs for a few moments after he meant to exhale. His lingering arousal vanished that quickly, though his hearts didn't slow, and his blood had scarcely cooled. Instinct urged him to tighten his hold on her. Demanded he not let go. The mere thought of her with another male stoked a rage in him he'd never known.

"You're turning red," Aymee said, awe in her voice. She returned her hands to his shoulders, propped herself up, and let her gaze wander over his face and torso.

He forced himself to take another slow, deep breath, but

such feelings were not easily expelled. His skin reverted to normal, but not without effort. "When can we next meet, then?"

"In three days."

"Two."

She grinned. "Are you that eager, then?"

Eager enough that I'd consider coming tomorrow, just on the tiny chance you'll be here.

"I enjoy our time together."

"Me too. Two days it is."

Arkon stared up at her, committing every tiny detail of her face to memory. The sea crashed into the land and receded, crashed and receded, and the sun continued its slow, downward trek.

Aymee laughed. "You'll have to let me go sometime, Arkon."

"Let you go?"

She wiggled her hips and thighs.

Were it not for his embarrassment, her movement might have rekindled his desires. He unraveled his limbs from around her, relinquishing the possessive hold he'd taken. "Apologies," he muttered.

Aymee brushed her palm along his cheek, offered him a tender smile, and rose. She set about collecting her belongings. Arkon got up and helped shake out the blanket, fold it, and pack the basket.

"May the stars smile upon you tonight, Aymee," he said when they'd finished.

She stood on her toes and pecked a kiss on his cheek. "And may your dreams be filled with color, Arkon."

Cheek tingling, he watched her go. Each of her steps was a little more weight on his chest, but when she turned to look at him over her shoulder, a thrill coursed through him. Soon, she walked around the bend and out of sight.

Arkon pressed the pads of a finger to his lips and cheek, which still thrummed with the ghost of her kiss.

These were likely to be the longest two days of his life.

CHAPTER 5

THE CLINIC CREAKED IN THE HOWLING WIND, AND ITS WINDOWS rattled with each boom of thunder. The storm had come upon The Watch without warning in the middle of the night — not unusual during the wet season — and had raged throughout the day.

Aymee propped her chin on her hand, watching the rain batter the windowpanes. Enough water streamed down the glass that the building might as well have been standing in a riverbed.

Most people stayed indoors during such weather, which had made for a slow day at the clinic. It was just as well — Aymee was having a hard time focusing. Her father had departed an hour earlier to attend a bedridden mother-to-be and, left to her own devices as evening approached, she found herself uncharacteristically morose.

The change in her was astounding; a few days ago, she'd been content to wait patiently through an entire week just to chance a glimpse of Arkon. Now, every hour was a battle against her craving for his presence.

She smiled, brushing a fingertip over her lips. She'd kissed him.

What had Macy felt, what had she thought, the first time she kissed Jax? Surprise? Shock? Had she been confused to feel something so powerful for something — some*one* — so different, so *other*?

When Aymee looked upon Arkon, she saw something... familiar. A kindred spirit. His physical differences were nothing to instill fear and disgust; she'd been awed and inspired by him from the first moment she looked upon him.

Her finger paused on her lower lip, and for an instant, she felt his mouth upon hers again. He'd gone so still, his muscles tense, eyes wide with astonishment, and she'd known he'd never been kissed before. A thrill coursed through her at the knowledge — the thrill of being the one to give him that experience. She'd wondered, as she lay atop him, his limbs coiled around her legs and waist, if kissing wasn't the only thing he'd never done.

But how could that be? Arkon was powerful, agile, and intelligent — his people had to see that, too. Perhaps only kissing was new to him.

Aymee straightened in her chair and looked down at the desk. The papers spread over its surface were covered in sketches of Arkon's hands in varying poses. She traced her finger along one of the many lines — the webbing between forefinger and thumb — and recalled the feel of his hands. Heat sparked inside her.

She'd desired other men, but what Arkon made her feel with

a simple glance was beyond comparison — and beyond her understanding.

With a sigh, Aymee gathered the papers, slipped them into her leather satchel, and closed the flap. There was no point sitting in the clinic alone watching the rain fall. Though the night ahead seemed impossibly long, tomorrow *would* come.

She just hoped the storm would pass by then.

After ensuring everything was clean and the supplies were stored, she turned off the lights and made her way into the front room. She looped the satchel strap over her shoulder, pulled her coat on over it, and stepped out into the downpour.

Cold wind pelted her with stinging rain, soaking the bottom of her skirt before she'd managed ten steps. She paused in the middle of the square, shielded her eyes with a hand, and glanced toward the promontory, where the lighthouse's signal blazed in the gloom — *danger, danger, seek out shelter.*

Lightning streaked across the sky, illuminating the pale cylinder of the lighthouse. A deafening crack of thunder followed.

"It's really not safe to be out here in this storm," someone said behind her, their raised voice muted by the howling wind and torrential rain.

Aymee started and spun to see Randall Laster standing a few feet away, water streaming from his dark green poncho. "You should come into the town hall until the lightning lets up, at least."

Her gaze shifted to the warm glow spilling from the windows and open doorway behind him.

"The lightning could last all night," she said.

"Wouldn't hurt to give it a little more time, would it? Warm up and have a few drinks." Randall glanced over his shoulder.

He and his rangers were sleeping on cots in the town hall's back room while they were in town — not necessarily the sort of company she was eager to keep. She had no wish to find herself in another heated discussion with him.

"My home isn't far." Aymee glanced up as another bolt of lightning divided the sky, followed immediately by an earth-shaking boom.

"If it's not far, why not have a drink with me? Then I can escort you home and make sure you get in safely."

Aymee frowned. "I don't—"

"Please," he said, stepping closer. "Just as two people looking to unwind, not as a ranger and a doctor."

Blinking against the rain, she searched his face. It wouldn't kill her to be kind to him, to mend whatever discord existed between them. It could even curb her impatience. Sitting at home and staring at the walls wouldn't make tomorrow come any faster, so why not seek a brief distraction?

"Okay."

He smiled and stepped aside, gesturing her onward. "After you."

She hurried across the square and entered the building. Heat settled over her as she removed her coat and hung it on a peg near the door. When she walked into the common room, the townsfolk within greeted her with smiles and waves. She'd expected a few familiar faces, but at least a dozen locals were seated at the bar and tables, chatting and drinking.

"Hello Aiden," she said to one of the men at a table near the bar. The gray streaks at his temples seemed a little more pronounced every few days.

He twisted around in his chair and grinned when his eyes

met hers. "Aymee! What a pleasant surprise. What are you doing out in this storm?"

"I was just leaving the clinic."

"Closing early?"

"No one wants to brave this weather."

"Except Miss Rhodes, apparently," Randall said from beside her.

"Is that so?" Aiden chuckled. His gaze dipped to her skirt, which was dripping enough to have formed a small puddle on the floor beneath her.

"Sorry. Randall caught me while I was walking home." She seated herself on a stool at the bar.

Randall sat next to her, leaning forward with his forearms atop the bar. "How about a couple mugs of that mulled cider?"

"Sure, just a few minutes," Aiden said, giving them his back.

"It rains like this back in Fort Culver during the wet season, too. The river that runs nearby always floods and washes out the bridge," Randall said.

"Every time?"

"They've had to rebuild it almost every dry season for as long as I can remember. They make it a little higher each time. I think it'll get to a point where they build it so high, it'll just tips over on its own, without any flooding necessary."

Aymee laughed, and Randall smiled; the expression touched his eyes and lit up his face.

Why hadn't she reacted to him the same way she did Arkon? He was a physically attractive man and seemed to be a decent person, once she looked past his wanting to hunt her friends, but she felt only a flicker of interest that dissipated as quickly as the smoke from a freshly extinguished candle.

"Why don't they build a floating bridge?" she asked.

"There was a pre-fab bridge placed there during the colonization. Was supposed to be sturdy enough to last until production facilities were up and going and something permanent could be constructed." He shook his head. "That's most of the stuff on this world, right? It wasn't meant to last this long. So, when that original bridge collapsed into the river, the people built the best replacement they could. Didn't have the parts to make anything like the dock you have here."

"Here you go!" Aiden set two steaming mugs in front of them and moved off to speak with someone else.

Aymee wrapped her chilled hands around the cup and slid it closer. "Do you think it was always the plan to drop us off with this stuff and abandon us here?"

Randall lifted his mug and sipped at it, wincing. "Always burn my mouth on the first drink, but this stuff is so damned good."

Aymee chuckled.

He lowered his drink and stared into the steam. "I don't think that was the plan at all. Something happened here on Halora, and something happened out there — a war, I think — and it all just kind of fell apart. They forgot about us after that."

"I've always found it strange that we know so little about that history. Like this place. Why is it called The Watch? What were they watching for? I always assumed it was because of the lookouts at the lighthouse watching for storms, but that doesn't feel like the right answer."

"Your guess is as good as mine on that. All I really know is that Fort Culver was a military base, originally, and when everything went bad, my ancestors received a final order: defend the remaining humans against anything that comes, to the last man."

Aymee raised her mug and blew away the steam before taking a careful sip. The pairing of heat and sweetness was almost overwhelming. "So, you've been trained from birth to be a ranger?"

"Yeah. My father's in charge back home, and the tradition of it is considered a big deal." He shifted his voice to a deeper timbre. "For three hundred and sixty-one years, every member of our family has served the people of Halora in this capacity, and you will, too."

She arched a brow. "Must have been pretty intimidating to hear that growing up."

Randall chuckled and took another sip of cider. "It was. I resented him for it, you know? But I understand. Sometimes it seems like everything on this planet is designed to kill us, even the damned plants. So we're the ones who go out and kill it first. It's not glamourous work, but it's important."

So we're the ones who go out and kill it first.

Aymee dropped her gaze to her drink; it was cooling but retained a comforting warmth that she focused on to ground her thoughts. Their conversation didn't need to continue down that path.

"Do you have any other family, Randall?"

"Yeah, I have a sister. Larkin. Everyone calls her Elle."

"Is she a ranger, too?"

"She is. It was pretty hard on her, growing up. She had a soft spot for animals since she was little." The fondness in his voice was unmistakable.

Aymee smiled. "You two are close?"

"We are. Our father tends to keep her nearby when he sends me out, though. He thinks we soften each other up too much to be effective, or some krullshit like that." He frowned and glanced at Aymee. "Sorry. Rangers don't usually mind their language."

"It's all right. I've heard a lot worse treating injuries in town."

"How about you, Aymee? You have a brother, right?"

The leather strap of her satchel bit into her neck, rubbing uncomfortably against her skin. After adjusting it and finding little relief, she finally lifted the bag over her head and laid it on the bar. "Yes, Andrew. We're not close. My parents had difficulty after he was born, some complications, miscarriages. He was already nine by the time they had me."

"I'm surprised I haven't met him yet. I've been talking to as many people as I can since I got here."

"He hasn't been in The Watch for a few years." She smirked. "My family has its own trade that's been passed down through generations. My father started bringing us to the clinic with him when we were young and taught us the family trade while we grew up. When Andrew was old enough to strike out on his own, he started traveling to other towns to provide his services where needed. He ended up meeting a woman in one of those towns, and he's lived there with her ever since."

"I've been to a lot of places," Randall said, absently rotating his mug, "and met a lot of people. Everyone always talks about going somewhere else, about how much better it'll be, how much more exciting...but it all gets to be the same after a point. At least he found happiness. That's all anyone can hope for, right?"

Aymee's thoughts shifted to Macy. Macy, who'd been unhappy for years after losing her sister, who felt like she always had to do more, to *be* more, to atone for the pain she'd caused. It had taken her own near drowning and a rescue from

Jax to push Macy to take control of her life and choose happiness.

As Aymee opened her mouth to answer, a heavy arm fell over her shoulder. Cider — fortunately cooled enough not to burn — sloshed over her hand. The stench of alcohol and sweat hit her nose.

"Look at you, Randy, talking up the locals." The man peered at her. "Isn't this that fish-lover?" he asked, grinning broadly between Randall and Aymee.

Aymee recognized the cruelty in his smile. He was the man who'd laughed when she said the rangers had come to The Watch for themselves. She pushed her mug aside and frowned. "Please remove your arm."

"She's a pretty thing," the man said, turning his head toward her, his breath hot against her ear.

"Cyrus, get the hell off her," Randall warned.

"I'm just trying to be friendly, Randy. Isn't that what you told us to do?"

"Sir, if you do not get off me, I will make you," Aymee said patiently.

Randall pushed his stool away from the bar and stood up. Cyrus removed his arm from Aymee and stepped back, holding his hands up in surrender; he held a glass of beer in one. He looked to be in his late forties, his tanned skin weather-worn and his short beard flecked with gray, but he was tall and well-built.

"Relax, kid. We're on the same team, me and you, right?" Though his speech was slurred and his stance unsteady, there was a hardness in his eyes that belied a deeper meaning to his words.

"We are. Which is why you're going to apologize to Miss Rhodes and hit your bunk."

Randall and Cyrus stared at one another for several tense seconds.

"Pulling rank doesn't work the way you think, kid. Not out here," Cyrus said in a low voice before turning to Aymee. "Name's Cyrus Taylor, miss, and I'm awful sorry. Your town has some of the best booze I've ever had, and I seem to have partaken a bit heavily."

"That's all right. Just make sure you drink plenty of water before you hit that bunk." She slid off her stool and smoothed down her skirt.

Cyrus chuckled. "You're the doc's daughter, right?"

"Yes. Now if you'll excuse me, it's getting late." She smiled at Randall and picked up her satchel. "Thank you for the company."

"I'm sorry, Aymee. You don't have to go," Randall said.

"It's okay, ma—"

"Whatcha got here?" Cyrus snatched her bag and flipped it open before she could stop him.

Her eyes rounded as he pulled out several of her sketches. She lunged forward, grabbing for the papers. "Stop!"

Cyrus twisted away, holding the sketches out of her reach. "Well, what do we have here?"

Randall stepped forward and caught Cyrus's wrist. Their limbs trembled as Randall forced Cyrus's arm down. "Give them back to her, Cyrus."

"Just wanted to take a—"

"You have no right!" Aymee growled, wrenching her satchel from his grip and holding out a hand for her drawings.

Scowling at Randall, Cyrus opened his hand and let the

papers fall to the floor. Randall thrust the man back as he released his arm, and Cyrus stumbled into a nearby table, barely catching himself on the top.

"To your bunk, ranger," Randall commanded. "Now."

There were heavy steps approaching, but Aymee ignored them. She knelt on the floor and swept the papers into a pile. Her hands shook with fury and concern.

"Known the kid since he was shitting his pants, and now he's putting *me* to bed," Cyrus muttered as he walked away.

"Come on, Cyrus. You've had enough," another man said.

Randall crouched near Aymee and reached to gather some of the scattered papers, but his hand froze in midair. He tilted his head and slid one of the pages aside, revealing the sketch beneath.

One of the drawings of Arkon's hand.

He met Aymee's gaze. Her heart stopped.

Without a word, she collected the remaining sketches and stuffed them into her satchel, tying the lacings to secure the flap.

"Are those what I think they are?" Randall asked, voice flat.

"So what if they are?" she retorted, casting a brief glare at Cyrus.

"How many of those drawings do you have, Aymee?"

"It's none of your business." She rose and stalked toward the door, pausing to retrieve her coat and shove her arms into the sleeves.

Randall pushed himself up and followed. "Aymee! Don't just leave."

She rounded on him. "I will not stay here to be judged and treated this way!"

"If those drawings are accurate, they're important information. I need to—"

"They are *mine,* and I will *not* aid your hunt!" She flung the door open, wishing for some of Arkon's strength to tear it off the hinges and throw the whole damned thing at Cyrus. She plunged into the wind and rain without a backward glance.

"Aymee!" Randall called. His boots splashed in the water behind her as he hurried to catch up. "Stop, please!"

She marched into the wind without slowing, barely aware of the stinging raindrops hitting her face. Randall caught up and moved alongside her, but she didn't look at him.

"I've already made myself clear," she said over the storm. "That man had no right, and I will not give up my sketches for you to study."

"He didn't have any right, and I'm sorry that happened. But...any information I have on those creatures can save lives. Ours, and theirs."

"They are not a threat!" she shouted, stopping and spinning toward Randall. "No lives were at risk before you came, and I refuse to reveal secrets that aren't mine to give!"

Randall's clothes were soaked — he hadn't put on his parka — and rivulets of water streamed down his face. "I'm just trying to do right by everyone, Aymee. Some people say these creatures aren't a threat, but a lot more people think they are."

"Either way, I don't have to aid you, not when I know what is at stake."

"*Do* you know what's at stake? Do you really know what they are, *who* they are? We've survived this planet by taking nothing for granted and fighting every day for our survival, and if the kraken are anything like us, they've done the same, and they'll view us as just as much of a threat!"

"They are people! People who want to be left alone. It's you," she pointed at him, "who would disturb that peace and bring war to them."

"Aymee," he said, stepping toward her, "I'm not trying to bring—"

She took a step back. "I want to be left alone now, too."

Randall halted, clenching his jaw. His hands curled into fists at his sides. "I'm not your enemy, Aymee. I've never lied about that."

"Then don't make yourself one."

She left him, her heart pounding, body trembling, and hoped he wouldn't follow. There was too much on the line, far too much. Macy, Jax, Sarina.

Arkon.

As angry as she was, Aymee believed Randall. She believed he was doing what he thought right, that he only wanted to protect people from the unknown.

But at what cost? If the rangers found the kraken's home, what would they do?

The hard glint in Cyrus's eyes offered no comforting answer to that question.

So we are the ones who go out and kill it first.

Despite those words, she trusted Randall — at least his openness and honesty. But she didn't trust him with the kraken's lives. She couldn't.

Please let Arkon be right. Don't let the hunters find them.

CHAPTER 6

THE SURFACE OF THE POOL RIPPLED TO THE GENTLE HUM OF unseen filtration systems, like the surface of the ocean in miniature. Arkon studied the stones laid on the bottom. Their shapes were distorted by the reflection of the overhead lights on the water, but their patterns were clear — flowing, swirling lines and curves, like eddies in the water. There were thousands of stones, each placed with thought and purpose to contribute to the whole.

The display represented weeks of work. Weeks of locating suitable stones and transporting them to The Facility, laying them out and arranging them by color, shape, and size, and then placing them, one by one, on the floor of the pool; weeks before his vision had taken shape. Arkon hadn't been without his doubts throughout. Would it come out as he'd imagined? Would anyone care?

And now, after all that time and effort, after persevering through his doubts, he had to *force* himself to come and see it. Not because he didn't feel a sense of accomplishment — he was proud despite his self-criticisms — but because his mind had moved on.

The acrid chemical fumes — how he'd ever grown used to them, he couldn't understand — assaulted his nostrils. He moved around the edge of the pool and stopped near a metal ladder built directly into its wall, examining his work from a new angle. It felt like he'd made it a lifetime ago. So much had changed over the past few months.

What else could he do for Aymee? What else could he create for her? Countless possibilities tumbled through his mind, but how many were truly worthy of her attention?

Arkon frowned; several of the stones below were misaligned. Adjusting them would provide a temporary distraction from his thoughts of Aymee — *today, I will see her again later today!* — but he found himself strangely hesitant to do so.

Perhaps it was better as it was. If it wasn't worth looking at, flaws and all, how good could it really be?

The Pool Room door slid open. Arkon lifted his gaze to see Jax enter.

"Still staring at it?" Jax asked. "Do you see something different each time?"

Arkon smiled and glanced back at the water. "In a way...yes. I *make* myself see something new."

Jax stopped beside Arkon and stared down at the water. "You found your centerpiece."

At the heart of the circular pattern lay a shard of halorium, casting a gentle blue glow on the surrounding stones. Though rare, it was easily visible on the seafloor because of its inherent luminescence.

"The supply exchanges have granted me more time to search."

They remained silent for a time. Jax's unspoken questions thickened the surrounding air.

"You have spoken to her, then?" Jax finally asked.

Arkon's skin heated. Whether Jax had been told by Macy or finally discerned it himself, Arkon had kept his interest in Aymee a secret, and he took no pride in hiding it from his friend.

"I have," he replied, flaring his siphons. "I should not have delayed so long before doing so."

"No reason for regrets. You did it, even if it took time."

"How did you figure it all out with Macy, Jax?"

"I didn't, Arkon. None of this can be so simplified. It is all new, all a journey into the unknown."

Glancing at Jax, Arkon grinned. "That has ever been your area of expertise, Wanderer."

Jax smiled in return and shook his head. "I've never truly known what I was doing. You know far more about humans than I. The only difference with Macy and Sarina is that it *feels* right when I am with them, and I attempt to consider what would make them happy in all my actions."

"So, you're saying I am on my own in this?"

"You must find your own way, Arkon, as you always have. But you are never alone." Jax placed a hand on Arkon's shoulder.

The contact was unsettling, at first, and wholly outside typical kraken behavior. But Arkon recognized the gesture's meaning   reassurance. Jax was here, flesh and blood, and he would help however it was necessary short of endangering Macy and Sarina.

"Thank you, Jax."

Dropping his gaze, Jax nodded. It was some time before he spoke again. "A hunt has been called."

Arkon's stomach sank and twisted. Today was their meeting day. Seven or eight hours, and it would be time; time to go, time to see Aymee again.

A hunt could last for days.

"Kronus, this time. He wants to go for sandseekers, just off the reef," Jax continued. "They plan to leave within the hour."

"To the abyss with Kronus," Arkon muttered as he turned and moved away from the pool.

"This seems familiar." Jax's smirk was evident in his tone.

The two of them had been in this very room several months ago, when Jax had rescued Macy from the sea...only Jax had been cursing Dracchus then, and *Jax* had been the one who wanted to return to his secret human.

Jax had refused a hunt so he could spend more time with Macy. Why shouldn't Arkon do the same?

Perhaps because Jax's refusal set into motion a chain of events that left what meager semblance of society our people possess in a state of upheaval, and placed Macy in danger...

Arkon blew air through his siphons and slowed as he neared the lockers and machinery along the wall. He clenched his jaw and spun about, moving parallel to the pool. Aymee wasn't in a vulnerable position like Macy had been. As long as Aymee remained in The Watch, she was safe from the other kraken, many of whom were slowly warming to the notion of being in contact with humans.

Apart from Kronus and his pack. Despite being outmatched, they threw regular insults at Jax and Macy, and considered Jax, Arkon, and Dracchus traitors to their people.

But they didn't matter; *none* of them mattered. The kraken had always seen Arkon as too different, too strange, and he placed little value in their customs and the stunted social hierarchy they'd constructed despite their natural antisocial inclinations. If he refused this hunt, having never done so since he'd reached maturity, they would attribute it to his eccentricity and nothing more.

And to see Aymee, to look into her warm eyes and listen to her musical voice, would be more than worth admonishment from his people.

"Arkon."

Startled out of his thoughts, Arkon swung his gaze to Jax.

Frowning, Jax furrowed his brows. "You planned to see her today, didn't you?"

Was Arkon so addled that Jax was seeing through him? Usually, it was the other way around.

Jax moved in front of Arkon, and they met each other's eyes. "You have the choice, Arkon. But do not let your desires cloud your judgment. Our people cannot be forced into all of this."

Unbidden, red flashed over Arkon's skin. "After all of it — after I stood with you unwaveringly and trusted you blindly — you're going to tell *me* not to pursue what I want? Are you the only one of us allowed happiness?"

"Close your mouth, Arkon, and hear me." Jax's tone and stance might have been intimidating to other kraken, but Arkon did not fear Jax.

"You will not—"

"Arkon. Enough." Jax stared at him, and tension as had never existed between them crackled like arcing electricity.

They were on the edge of butting heads, of challenging one another. It was a sobering realization for Arkon. He snapped his mouth shut and forced his skin to normal.

"What I did has worked out only through luck," Jax said gently. "I would have done it so much differently if I had any sense. I endangered her through my actions. Do you understand? I might have lost her forever at many points along that journey, and I cannot forgive myself for what might have happened because of my poor decisions."

Arkon inhaled deeply, nostrils flaring. "You think I should go on this hunt."

"You have my support either way. But I *do* think you should come."

All the reasons for and against going ricocheted through Arkon's mind; each one seemed unimportant when he recalled the brilliance of Aymee's smile and the ecstasy of her touch.

She'd seemed just as excited for their next meeting as he was. Would she be disappointed if he didn't show up? Would it damage the relationship they were building?

Would she forgive him?

Aymee had wanted to exercise caution due to the presence of hunters in The Watch. Caution was the best course in dealing with the kraken, as well — they wouldn't likely suspect Aymee was the reason Arkon skipped a single hunt, but the tides of change had everyone on edge, and it was best to avoid anything that could exasperate their sense of unease.

At length, Arkon nodded.

Together, he and Jax exited the Pool Room and made their way through the long corridors. Arkon paid their geometry and construction little mind now. The tightness had returned to his insides and rode like a weight in his gut. There was a chance the hunt would end swiftly, and Arkon could make it to the beach in time. If not...the next exchange was in three days. He'd survive until then.

He wouldn't be happy, but he'd survive.

They entered the Mess a short time after; it was a large, open room, with folded tables and chairs pushed into the corner. It had served as the main gathering place for the kraken since before Arkon was born.

A small crowd had already gathered. Kronus and his supporters waited to one side, arms folded over their chests and scowls on their faces. Dracchus was opposite them, easily the biggest and strongest of all the kraken. Though he was alone, the others granted him a wide berth. A third group — at least a dozen kraken, including a few females — observed the standoff from a few body lengths away.

"I have called this hunt," Kronus growled, "and I will lead."

"I did not dispute your right to lead," Dracchus replied in his deep, rumbling voice.

His stance was nonchalant, his skin its usual black with dark gray stripes; he was the opposite of the agitated postures and angry colors of Kronus and his lackeys.

Jax and Arkon moved to either side of Dracchus and stared across the open space at Kronus.

Lowering his brow and flaring nostrils and siphons, Kronus glared back. "I will not allow *them* on this hunt."

Arkon was tempted to leave at that moment; he would have been more than happy to go meet Aymee, instead. But he knew now this was more than a hunt — it was a power struggle. Though the kraken were independent and preferred solitude, they looked to their most capable hunters for guidance and leadership. Unfortunately, that resulted in many males challenging one another to assert their prowess and claim places in the unspoken hierarchy.

"Arkon and the Wanderer are two of our best. We will find little success hunting sandseekers without them," Dracchus said.

Three months ago, Arkon wouldn't have believed it possible

for Dracchus to say anything positive about either of them, but the situation with Macy had created an unlikely alliance.

In the time since, that alliance had grown into friendship.

"We refuse to rely upon traitors to our people to obtain our food." Kronus's skin grew redder with each passing moment. "Those two are unwelcome, and you taint yourself by associating with them."

Dracchus straightened and rose up on his tentacles. Crimson pulsed across his dark skin. "Then I *must* challenge your leadership of this hunt."

Arkon flicked his gaze to the spectators; the males would join in the hunt regardless, but the females — at least those without mates — had likely come in search of prospective males to bring back to their dens. A challenge would be as much a display for female onlookers as it was a means of establishing leadership.

This challenge, however, could have serious ramifications. Kronus and his supporters were firmly against further contact with humans and would likely do Macy harm were it not for the inevitable, bloody vengeance Jax would visit upon them in retaliation. A show of dominance over Dracchus would help validate their stance.

"You might as well scurry off now, Kronus," Arkon said. "You will only prove your foolishness by accepting."

Kronus's skin became a mess of flashing, undulating reds and blacks. "Soon enough, your sort will have no place here," he snapped. His eyes shifted to Dracchus. "I will meet your challenge and defend my right. You and your treacherous friends will not call this place home for much longer."

A palpable, strangely eager energy filled the air as the kraken exited the Mess. Arkon had noticed it during other challenges, but he'd never understood it. Was it a desire for entertainment? Or had a thirst for conflict been ingrained at the core of their species?

Arkon, Dracchus, and Jax were the last to leave the room.

Dracchus's pace was easy. He stretched his powerful arms as they moved down the hall. "He aims to make this difficult."

"Change always is," Jax said.

Dracchus grunted. "Macy has proven herself. She is one of us, and our people owe her a great deal. Denying that is dishonorable and disrespectful."

"It is a natural reaction to cling to supposed traditions when faced with changes that may threaten one's power," Arkon said. "Kronus feels more threatened now than ever before because he is unsure of his place with humans coming into our lives."

"Kronus clings to the old hatred," Dracchus replied. "That is what he fears losing. He has already forsaken our traditions through his dishonor."

Arkon regarded Dracchus with new interest. "You mean to say that Kronus's identity is intertwined with the hatred for humans that has been instilled in us since we were younglings?"

"We are all taught humans are our enemies. It is a foundation of how we have survived and avoided contact with them all this time. Kronus and his ilk have not accepted that things must change for the sake of our people's future. Macy is not the threat."

"But she can be seen as a threat to our way of life, can she not?" Arkon offered. "She does things differently than we've known, and some kraken are adopting her methods. That's not to mention how some of our females feel about being replaced by human women."

"She is a danger to a way of life that would've had to change with or without her intervention, eventually. We must learn to adapt, for the good of our species." Dracchus looked at Jax, and the two exchanged a nod; the moment was surreal to Arkon.

How many years had they spent in conflict with Dracchus? How many years had they wasted, when they might have worked *together* toward a prosperous future throughout?

This power struggle was more important to the kraken than any in Arkon's memory; it was the difference between progress and stagnation, between a chance at peace and an inevitable war. Even knowing that, he could not shake his impatience — this needed to end, the hunt needed to end, so he could get to Aymee.

A crowd had already gathered by the time the trio emerged from the Facility — everyone who'd been in the Mess and a few newcomers. Kronus floated just over the seafloor, his skin its normal ochre and his intense yellow eyes locked on Dracchus, Jax, and Arkon.

As he followed Jax to take a place in the ring of onlookers directly opposite Kronus's supporters, Arkon relished the relative quiet in the water. The sea was never truly silent, but its ambience was typically gentle, a cocoon of serenity belying the savagery hidden in its depths.

It was preferable to listening to Kronus prattle on, at the very least.

Dracchus positioned himself in front of Kronus, and they flashed red at each other. It was a mutual acceptance of the challenge. A signal for the contest to begin.

Kronus was a male in his prime, an experienced hunter, and he'd been chosen by many females as a mate. He moved with confidence and speed as he commenced his dance. His tentacles were soon a blur of motion, spinning and undulating, and colorful patterns skittered across his skin. His performance would be the envy of many — the dance was about prowess, endurance, and control.

The nearby females watched, enrapt, and some of them shifted to maroon, openly signaling their interest.

Then, Dracchus offered his retort.

Though his heavy build suggested a lack of speed or grace, Dracchus's power leant him quickness, and his tentacles stretched and curled as he spun. The patterns pulsing across his skin created a hypnotic effect, altered by his spinning into ever-changing, scintillating shapes.

He matched Kronus's speed and then increased the pace. Their whirling bodies grew indistinct until Kronus's form faltered and his patterns broke.

Dracchus was a juggernaut; he showed no sign of slowing, no sign of tiring.

As Kronus flagged, his color solidified into the vibrant crimson of aggression and fury. Some kraken in the crowd signaled surprise or excitement. The result of the dance — which Arkon might have considered an art form under different circumstances — would be violence.

Kronus charged first, a fraction of a second before Dracchus, but his advantage yielded no favorable results. Their limbs thrashed in a chaotic tangle, but Dracchus's darker arms and tentacles enveloped his opponent. Within moments, Dracchus had an arm around Kronus's neck, and his tentacles coiled around Kronus's torso.

Four other kraken — Kronus's most steadfast supporters in his crusade to preserve the *old ways* — rushed forward.

Whatever informal rules had existed around the challenge were shattered in that instant. Arkon's hearts pounded, adrenaline poured into his veins, and he surged into the fray along-side Jax.

The water clouded with motion and dissipating blood. Arkon wove through flailing limbs, narrowly avoiding claws and tentacles, and lashed out at Kronus's lackeys.

His knuckles hammered into a jawbone. Tentacles wrapped around his arm before he could strike again, hauling him toward his foe. Bending and twisting, he slipped free and raked his claws over his opponent's ribs. More blood flowed into the water; they'd be lucky if the smell didn't attract a razorback.

Someone grabbed Arkon from behind, hooking an arm around his neck and slithering tentacles about his abdomen. The hold constricted.

Arkon tensed his entire body, battling the increasing pressure. He kept the flow through his siphons small; too much water expelled would allow his assailant to tighten their grip.

In front of him, the kraken he'd clawed had recovered himself and turned to charge at Arkon.

Gritting his teeth, Arkon bent at the middle. The crushing force around his stomach increased as he lashed out with his tentacles, twisting them to the right and closing all eight around the charging foe. The captured kraken struggled, and Arkon's vision dimmed. He had but one chance at this.

Focusing all his strength into the movement, he wrenched his lower half to the right, using the struggles of the kraken caught in his tentacles to increase the power. Arkon's body shifted, and for a moment, the enemy behind him held tight, fighting the motion. Claws bit into Arkon's tentacles.

Then Arkon twisted his body, breaking the hold.

He continued the spin, lashing out with both hands to open

new wounds on the chest and belly of the kraken who'd caught him while tightening his grip on the second foe.

As quickly as it had begun, the altercation ended. Kronus, still locked in Dracchus's hold, shifted his skin to pale, yellow-tinged gray — his admittance of defeat. The wounded kraken backed away warily. Arkon swung his tentacles, tossing the trapped foe into his companion so they could retreat together.

Dracchus released Kronus, and the two sides separated.

Several kraken sported fresh injuries which misted blood, including Arkon.

It was an *excellent* start to a hunt, especially considering Arkon hadn't wanted anything to do with it from the beginning. At least the wounds appeared superficial; all but the worst were shallow enough to close before the party reached its intended hunting grounds, so long as they were not agitated during the swim.

As he took position in the ring of onlookers, Arkon noticed one of the females — Leda — staring at him. She flashed maroon. Leda was an attractive female, and males often battled for her attention.

Leda smiled and waved a hand down to her waist. Her slit parted, revealing the petals of her open sex. An immediate invitation.

Arkon was aware of many other males she'd taken to her den, and they'd likely been many more beyond. Even if she had offered before he met Aymee, he'd have been hesitant; was he only worth her time because he'd spilled blood? Because he was capable of meeting violence with violence?

Only one female interested him. Only one female tempted him. And all of this was keeping him away from her.

He shook his head.

Leda scowled at his disinterest.

A tap on his shoulder called his attention away.

Jax signaled with a combination of limb movements and colors. *Can we trust them?*

Arkon looked at Kronus and his followers. Though Kronus had relinquished leadership to Dracchus for this hunt, his aggression hadn't diminished; he had shifted his color from the yellow-gray of submission to an angry red, and his features were drawn in fury. His companions wore similar expressions, though their anger was laced with pain, their wounds proof that their advantage in numbers had done them little good.

Kronus and his group would be complacent for a time, especially after suffering such a resounding, public defeat. But they'd eventually make another attempt.

For this hunt only, Arkon signed.

Dracchus hadn't moved from his place at the center of the crowd. All eyes rested on him. The sense of anticipation that had pervaded the onlookers had been replaced by recognition and respect. Dracchus, Jax, and Arkon had won despite being outnumbered and having been faced with an egregious violation of custom.

A pair of light posts stood on the seafloor nearby, detached from the Facility. Dracchus swam to them. The net hanging from one of the posts served as the signal that a hunt was being organized.

Staring at Kronus, Dracchus stretched the net and hooked it over the top of the other post.

The hunt had begun.

THE WATERS SURROUNDING the reef teemed with life. The variety of creatures was staggering; even Arkon didn't have names for all of them. Segmented, many-legged things scuttled along the bottom, fish in all shapes and sizes swam around and through the stone-like coral, and hundreds of different plants — and creatures that only looked like plants — swayed in place. Every shade of every color seemed to be on display here, constantly changing in the dancing rays of sunlight streaming through the surface.

How would Aymee depict this scene in a painting? What would her artistic eye latch onto and accentuate?

Arkon waited beside Jax, their bodies pressed to the rocks at the edge of an open patch of sand. More stones and tufts of plant growth were scattered about ahead, but the space was largely devoid of cover. Sea creatures only braved crossing it because it bridged two sides of the reef.

Prime hunting ground for sandseekers.

Tentacles writhing with impatience, Arkon looked up.

By the position of the sun and the quality of its light, it was late afternoon. He should've been on his way to the beach right now. Should've been on his way to see Aymee.

His eyes shifted to the colorful fish all around. Most of them were safe to eat. Between the twelve kraken in the hunting party, they could catch enough fish to equal the meat they'd obtain from a sandseeker, and they'd be done in less time.

Sandseekers provided ample bounty. They were larger than adult kraken when fully-grown, and despite their armored tops, they contained an abundance of tender meat, but they were patient predators. They buried themselves in the soft sand of relatively shallow waters, leaving only their top fins exposed.

The appendages looked like stone, down to the tiny plants that sometimes grew upon them.

Frustrated with the wait, Arkon signed to Jax.

Need to bait them out.

Jax shook his head, brow low. He flattened his hand, fingers extended, and flicked his wrist down. *Patience.*

Arkon clenched his jaw; he should have acted sooner, should have forced this hunt to its completion before he'd wasted hours of time in wait.

Features hardening, Jax signed again. *She will understand.*

Aymee likely *would* understand Arkon's reason for missing their meeting, but that wasn't good enough. It wasn't that he was afraid or unwilling to explain the situation to her; he simply didn't want to disappoint her to begin with.

His eyes flickered to the fish near the reef. Many had already crossed the open seafloor, but the sandseekers would only be roused by large enough prey. That meant either an entire school of fish or a single, sizeable creature. The possibility of using himself as bait flashed across his mind. It was the most direct method, the quickest, and he was confident that his reflexes were quick enough to avoid the initial lunge of any waiting sandseeker.

His reflexes were *probably* quick enough.

And what will Macy write to Aymee after I am killed by a sand-seeker? That I died in a sudden bout of impatience and stupidity?

Arkon returned his attention to the fish, focusing on those clustered in groups. Though he'd seen countless thousands of fish in his life, had he ever truly observed them, had he ever studied their habits and movements with care?

Most fish scattered when they saw or sensed a predator nearby, but the fish that swam in schools remained close to each other in their escapes. If they were spooked in a controlled fashion, by multiple predators…

Rising slightly, he signaled to Dracchus. Within a minute, Arkon, Jax, and Dracchus were drifting on the surface, their heads above water.

"What?" Dracchus asked with a frown.

"Arkon…" There was warning in Jax's tone.

"We need to force some fish to swim across the sand," Arkon said. "If we work in unison, we can funnel them exactly where we want them to go, and their passage should lure out the sandseekers."

"That is not our way." Pupils slitted, Dracchus lowered his brows. "This is unlike you."

Arkon blew water out of his siphons. "I have ever questioned our ways."

"Not with this impatience."

"We have no reason to lay in wait when we could lure our prey out. Weren't you the one ready to charge into The Watch blindly when Jax was imprisoned just because you thought we'd waited too long?"

"Neither of you charged in blindly," Jax said. "You were sensible about it. This is a different situation, but requires equal caution and planning."

"We do not know how many sandseekers are hidden there," Dracchus said. "If we scare fish across the open ground, we may disturb all the sandseekers at once, and they will go into a frenzy."

"So, we can pick one off the edges." Arkon thrummed with a strange energy; anticipation and dread pulsed through his limbs. Despite his impatience to get to Aymee, the allure of a new hunting method excited him.

"The chance for danger—"

Arkon cut Jax off. "Is little greater than at any other time. We are hunters. Sometimes, that means we must make our own opportunities."

He and Jax stared at one another, and he saw Dracchus's concerned gaze shift between them at the edge of his vision.

"This is important enough to you to warrant the risk?" Jax asked.

After inhaling deeply, Arkon nodded. "Life requires risks to have meaning, doesn't it? And our people must continue our advancement and refine our methods as much as possible if we want to overcome the limitations designed into us."

"Sounds like the same sort of justification I made when I found Macy." Jax ran a hand over the stripes on his head. "Perhaps it is worth an attempt. It may benefit future hunts."

"I do not understand what secrets the two of you keep," Dracchus said, "or why you are set on doing this differently. Do you *know* it will work?"

A lie would have been easy — the *easiest* response, perhaps, and the most likely to result in the outcome Arkon wanted. But even now he couldn't bring himself to do it. He was adept at half-truths and withholding information, but an outright lie felt wrong.

"No. I believe it will work, but I cannot say for sure."

Nothing is certain.

Somehow, Dracchus's frown deepened. Once, that would have given Arkon a smug sense of satisfaction, but now it only compounded his guilt.

I have always done my duty, regardless of how the others viewed me. I should feel no guilt for seeking out my own contentment, not after all this time.

"We will try your way. I will have the two of you wait on the bottom while the rest of us guide the fish into the area."

"You do not want to participate in the kill?" Jax asked.

"It would bring me joy," Dracchus admitted, "but you are both faster. You are more likely to make the kill and drag it clear before chaos erupts. I will not be far, in any case, and can lead the others to take down outlying targets beyond the first."

They submerged and returned to the hunting ground. Arkon lowered himself to the rocks beside Jax, and they both took up the long, metal spears they'd brought from the facility. Changing his skin to match the stone, he watched Dracchus direct the others with a series of quick, concise signs.

The hunters rose from their waiting places, spread out in a wide formation, and swam slowly toward the reef, keeping close to the bottom. Their confusion was apparent — and Kronus's rage undiminished — but they had accepted Dracchus's leadership by following him after the challenge. Inquiries would be saved until they were home again.

The kraken moved like a closing net, slowly drawing their formation tighter. Startled by the approach of predators, many of the fish panicked and fled; the kraken served as a funnel, guiding the fish toward the open patch of sand.

Adjusting his hold on his weapon, Arkon thrust aside all other thought; it proved more difficult than ever before, but he could focus only on the hunt now, only on the kill. He and Jax crept closer to the edge of the rock.

The shadow of the approaching fish darted across the bottom a moment before the creatures passed overhead. The kraken kept on the fish's flanks, holding their formation. Their weapons gleamed in the sunlight. They were too high, though, to make a killing blow — sandseekers had to be attacked from beneath.

The sound of rushing water produced by the fleeing creatures was suddenly overpowered by something deeper, something felt more than heard — the sudden displacement of a large amount of water.

A few body lengths ahead, a sandseeker leapt from the bottom. A cloud of sand rose with it, particles streaming from the crevices on its armored back. Its broad, flat belly fins paddled frantically, pushing it toward the approaching fish.

Arkon darted forward, trusting Jax was directly alongside him. He came into the shadow of the sandseeker, his vision obscured by the sand, and twisted. He was just able to see the underside of its jaw in the murk.

He thrust his spear upward.

The sandseeker thrashed as Arkon's spear connected at the same instant Jax's weapon plunged into its soft underside. The creature's upward momentum shifted. It bent its broad body, angling its mouth down — mandibles spread to the sides to reveal its jagged teeth — and directed itself straight at Jax and Arkon.

Barely keeping hold of his spear, Arkon shoved himself away as the sandseeker's mouth hit the sand, sending up another cloud in its thrashing. Arkon wrapped two tentacles around the haft of his weapon and pushed it forward, twisting the head inside the creature. Jax entered his peripheral vision, took a firmer grip on his own spear, and the two of them used the leverage of the weapons to force the sandseeker onto its back.

Its struggles were short-lived; the other kraken swarmed the beast, hitting it with more spears.

Arkon felt the thrumming movement of water again as another sandseeker emerged nearby.

Dracchus and three other kraken — Kronus among them — rushed forward as the beast leapt high, parting its mandibles to sweep a cluster of fish into its toothy maw. Before it sank, the kraken hit it from below with spears and harpoons fired from guns. Its blood mingled with the sand in a miasma of crimson and gold.

As more sandseekers erupted from the seafloor, the kraken hurriedly dragged their kills to the rocks, away from the agitated predators. They pulled their weapons free of the carcasses and bundled them with ropes to be hauled home, working quickly and without instruction.

Dracchus signaled his approval to Arkon, who nodded in acknowledgment.

Now that the hunt was successful, he wanted nothing more than to go to Aymee. There was still time.

But at this point, his sudden departure would only rouse suspicion. He wasn't ready to have the sort of confrontations Jax had gone through with the other kraken. Impatience was no reason to cause potential future trouble for Aymee; he wanted one day to bring her among his people to tell them all with pride: *She is my mate.*

He'd have to wait until the kill had been returned to the Facility.

It was the longest journey of his life.

CHAPTER 7

THE SUN HAD SET BY THE TIME ARKON MOVED ONTO THE BEACH, and the reflection of the first rising moon shimmered on the surface of the ocean. He hurried through the surf, hearts thundering and muscles tense.

There was a chance she'd waited, wasn't there? A chance that, despite him being hours late, she had lingered, held in place by her desire to see him?

The sound of the waves was amplified more than usual by the overhang in their meeting spot; the tide was rising with the moons. He slowed his pace. The water had nearly reached the base of the cliff, and there was no sign of Aymee on the shrinking swath of dry sand.

Exhaustion jabbed at the edges of his consciousness. It had been a day of soaring hope and anticipation, and those hopes had been smashed. The rational part of his mind, usually the dominant portion, insisted this was no reason for disappointment. He'd missed an hour or two in her company. That was insignificant, viewed against the larger picture.

But the rest of him — the side that had been gaining strength over the last few months — deemed every moment precious, and any moment spent with Aymee invaluable. Time had no finite weight to it. The seconds of his day, though each equal in length to the next and the previous, were not equal in their importance.

He craved the sound of her voice and laughter, her unique scent, her soft, bold touches. After a lifetime spent searching for deeper meaning in things others considered trivial or foolish, he could not help but feel Aymee was the key to something greater. She'd lead him to experiences beyond his imagining.

He wanted her. Wanted to make her his.

Frustrated, he moved out from beneath the overhang and followed the beach, the surf flowing around his tentacles.

Despite his constant questioning of kraken traditions, he knew his people had one aspect of relationships correct: *she* had to choose *him*.

Arkon didn't want a mate for some fickle span of time. He wanted a life mate; he wanted what Jax and Macy had. Security, dependability, companionship. Even before he'd known that was a possibility, no female before Aymee had caught his attention — and *caught* was too mild a term. He was ensnared, enthralled, wrapped up so completely that his infatuation was likely to crush him.

But he couldn't make the choice for her any more than he could force her decision. All he could do was present himself as appealingly as possible and hope she found him worthy.

No easy feat, considering the limited time they had together. When their visits amounted to only a few hours over the course of a week, every minute counted. And he'd missed her today.

Missed out on the opportunity to know her a little better and show himself — his *true* self.

He swept a pair of tentacles aside in frustration, splashing water, and released a growl.

"Arkon?"

Though the ocean did its best to drown out that voice, he'd heard it.

He turned his head to see Aymee sitting upon the rocks just beyond the beach, past the high tide line.

His chest swelled, and his elation and relief were so powerful it seemed he'd burst.

She had waited for him. Though he'd hoped she would, it had been a hollow hope, meant only to assuage the anger he harbored for himself. Yet here she was.

This exhilaration surpassed both the thrill of the hunt and the fulfillment of completing one of his works.

She gingerly stood up. The wind pulled at her clothing and tousled her hair.

Arkon made his way toward her, sped forward by the tide. When the water retreated, he dug his tentacles into the sand, anchoring himself against the pull, before continuing. She smiled and extended her arms as he neared.

"It's about time," she said.

He helped Aymee down from her perch, a tingle running across his skin when she grasped his shoulders to steady herself. "You waited."

"Against my better judgment." She held onto his arm as they moved along the beach, her grip tightening when the water splashed around her legs. "It wasn't very smart of me."

"With everything that is going on, it's not likely smart for either of us to be here to begin with."

She frowned. "It's not. Is that why you're late? Do you want to end the exchanges? Our visits?"

"No. No!" He stopped and faced Aymee, keeping himself positioned between her and the sea. "I do not want to stop. I would see you every day were it not so dangerous." Reaching forward — hesitantly, as he wasn't sure of the rules for such contact — he brushed hair out of her face with the backs of his fingers, careful to keep the tips of his claws from raking her skin. "A hunt was called, and I could not refuse."

She turned her face toward his touch. Her smile returned, and his hearts thumped at the sight. "Was it fruitful?"

"Yes. Though I would much rather have arrived here on time than contributed to it."

"You have duties, Arkon. I won't hold that against you. I knew you'd ha—" She let out a shriek as water swept past them, pulling her feet out from beneath her.

Aymee clutched his arms, and Arkon slipped a pair of tentacles around her to keep her upright. She laughed. Once the water receded, he released her, and she stepped back.

"One moment." She jogged up the beach, toward the larger, higher rocks well away from the water.

Tilting his head, Arkon moved closer to her, leaving the surf behind. He froze when she took hold of the fabric of her skirt, bent, and slid it down her long legs. She straightened and lay the skirt over the rocks, placing a heavy stone on top it. The hem of her long-sleeved shirt hung past her bottom; it flipped up in the wind, granting him a view of the small, triangular scrap of cloth between her legs.

Desire pulsed through him.

Arkon trailed his eyes from her feet to her ankles, over her shapely calves and past her knees, along her supple thighs and the curve of her backside. He swallowed. His shaft throbbed against the inside of his slit, threatening to extrude. The reactions Aymee stirred in him were uniquely powerful.

Was this a test of his restraint, or a testament to her trust in him?

She removed her footwear and placed it upon the rock. Looking at him, she smiled. "Take me swimming."

A hundred arguments against taking her out surfaced in his mind — she was human, without one of the diving suits Macy wore when she swam; the tide and currents were especially intense this time of year; he had no idea how strong a swimmer she was.

He cast them aside.

"Only if you agree to one condition."

She tilted her head as she stepped toward him, and Arkon couldn't keep his eyes from dipping to the juncture between her legs. It was no mystery to him — he'd studied human anatomy through the computer in the Facility, and he'd seen Macy when he helped seal the wounds on her leg — but Aymee's cloth covering added an allure he hadn't thought possible. Even if he was familiar with the basic form of a female, he'd never seen *hers*.

"What condition?" she asked, stopping in front of him.

"You must hold onto me the entire time." He feared, in that moment, that she'd somehow hear the rapid beating of his hearts even over the ocean's restless murmuring.

"I can agree to that." Grinning, she moved behind him. Her hands settled on his back and slid upwards slowly until they rested on his shoulders. "I was thinking the same thing."

Arkon closed his eyes and drew in a deep breath; it was followed by a shaky exhalation. He welcomed the thrilling slide of her palms over his skin, though such contact was still unfamiliar to him.

"Wrap your arms around my neck." He spread his tentacles over the sand, sinking down so she could reach.

She did as he said, pressing her chest against his back. "Like this?" Her warm breath and dangling curls tickled his neck.

"Yes." A tremor ran through Arkon as he reached behind himself and cupped the backs of Aymee's thighs; her skin was even softer and smoother than he'd imagined. He glided his palms toward her knees, lifting her off the ground.

Aymee wrapped her legs around his waist, locking her ankles at his stomach. The position placed her hot core against his back. His hands continued their slow movement until they settled over her calves; she shivered and squeezed her thighs tighter.

His shaft pulsed. Aymee's heat flowed directly into him, gathering in his pelvis. Her heels were less than a hand's length from his slit.

He needed to get into the water.

Arkon rose on his tentacles and slithered into the surf, trying to ignore the aching throb in his loins. Water sloshed around him, freezing cold compared to the fire raging through his body.

She loosed a peal of laughter as the incoming tide splashed her.

When the water reached his waist, Arkon leaned forward, reluctantly releasing her legs to paddle with his hands, and swam — first pulled along by the retreating current, and then battling against its landward flow. Despite the recent storm and rising tide, the sea was relatively calm.

Aymee held tight as his tentacles left the bottom.

The entirety of the sea stretched before them, the waves strips of black rolling through shimmering moonlight. Both moons had risen now, two huge orbs of light hanging in a surprisingly clear sky that was only a few shades lighter than the dark water on the horizon.

He kept his pace easy and soon had broken beyond the cresting waves and the inexorable pull of the tide. They floated in open water, a pair of tiny creatures drifting in the unfathomable expanse of the ocean.

Aymee stretched an arm and ran her fingers through the silvery reflection of a moon. "What do you see when you're below?" She rested her cheek against his. "What's it like down there?"

Suddenly, Arkon regretted having declined Jax's many invitations to explore over the years. For someone who considered himself observant, he'd paid relatively little attention to the ocean as a whole, to the interesting locations scattered throughout. Too often, he'd kept his eyes downcast, looking for rocks and other small objects that might be of use in his works.

"It...it is open, endless, and liberating, and stifling and lonely all at once. It is deceptively quiet despite its constant sound, and you can never see too far in any direction. It lulls you into a sense of isolation. Reminds you how small you are, and how the possibilities stretching before you are as vast as its entirety."

"That sounds...dismal." Aymee pulled her hand back, flattening it over his chest, and was silent for a time. "Are you lonely, Arkon?"

He glanced down; her hand was hidden underwater. "That depends on how I choose to define the word."

"How would you define it?"

"If I have friends, a home, people I interact with and hunt with, can I truly consider myself lonely?"

Of course I can.

"Do you feel like you belong? Even when you're with the people you care about, does it feel like something's missing?"

They rose and fell with the easy rhythm of the surface, and Arkon searched within himself for the words. He already knew the answer, even if he'd never admitted it. Her questions reminded him of a conversation he'd had with Jax.

It is missing something, Arkon had said.

It needs...heart, Jax replied. *Something in the center to give it life.*

They'd been discussing the arrangement of stones in the pool at the time, but Jax's words were oddly fitting now. Arkon had always been missing *something*. He'd spent most of his life trying to determine what it was, trying to locate the piece to fill in the hole. The thing that would make him truly content.

"Is that how you feel amongst your people?" he asked.

"Sometimes. It's strange how you can be surrounded by people who love you, and yet, still feel like no one *sees* you. Like no one really understands you." She rubbed her nose against his cheek and nuzzled his siphon.

His breath caught in his throat. There was something so gentle, so intimate, about the way she'd touched him; it was beyond his comprehension, too far outside his experience. "I... They try. That means something, doesn't it?"

"It does, but it's not the same," she said softly into his ear.

Arkon closed his eyes and *felt* her; the press of her body, warm even in the water, the smoothness of her skin, the tickle of her damp hair and the caress of her breath. The hidden strength in her lithe legs and the heat of her core.

Was that what he and Aymee had shared thus far? A mutual

understanding so deep and natural that it hadn't required voicing, that it had existed without his conscious acknowledgment?

"Arkon?"

"Hmm?"

Aymee hooked a finger beneath his chin and guided his face toward her. He opened his eyes the moment her lips brushed his; they closed again as a heady thrill spread through him. She cupped his jaw and deepened the kiss, parting her lips. His entire body tensed when her tongue flicked across the seam of his mouth.

Caught by surprise, he jerked his head away; he'd seen Macy and Jax kissing but didn't know they used their tongues.

Aymee followed him, taking advantage of his shock by flicking her tongue between his open lips.

Arkon dropped his hands to her legs, squeezing gently. Her taste was sweet. He tentatively sought her tongue with his. She stroked his mouth, explored it, and with every caress, he sank deeper into the kiss. Her sighs emboldened him.

This was seduction, sensuality, a mating of mouths; Arkon's tenuous control slipped.

She stiffened and pulled mouth away. "Arkon!"

He recognized her alarm slowly, as though emerging from a daze, and opened his eyes just as his head — and Aymee's immediately after — dipped underwater.

Her hold became desperate, arms and legs squeezing him with crushing force. He fanned out his tentacles and thrust them down, propelling himself back to the surface.

SHE SPUTTERED, spraying water to either side as she shook her head, and raised a hand to sweep hair out of her eyes.

"Aymee! Are you all right?"

He turned his head to look back at her, eyes wide and shining with reflected moonlight. If he twisted any further, he'd spin them in circles.

Aymee burst into laughter at the mental image conjured by that thought — Arkon turning endlessly, trying to locate her as she spun along with him, perched in his blind spot. It reminded her of games she and Macy played when they were kids, giggling as they hid behind an adult who'd turn slowly and pretend not to see them.

His brow furrowed, and his mouth opened as though to speak. It was a moment before any words came out. "You're... laughing? I don't... What is amusing? You could have drowned."

Arkon's confusion only made her laugh harder. She shook her head and burrowed her face into his neck. "I'm fine. Really. I just...just need a minute."

"Aymee?" he asked when her shoulders finally ceased their shaking.

"I'm fine," she repeated, and took a few steadying breaths. When she lifted her head, her lips were curved into a wide grin. "Guess I kissed you senseless."

His skin darkened, though the moonlight neutralized his color. "In the interest of honesty, I must admit to being...unfamiliar with such attentions."

"I assumed as much." She ran her thumb along his jaw.

He gently covered her hand with his own as his lips parted, allowing her a glimpse of his pointed teeth. They should have been disconcerting — Jax's had been, when she'd first seen his — but they were simply another part of what made Arkon himself.

"Have you ever been with another?" she asked.

"Have I ever been with another? I am not sure that—" His eyes rounded. "You mean…?"

Aymee chuckled. "Yes."

He flared his siphons, releasing a light spray of water. "Have you?"

"Hmm." She leaned close and pressed her cheek against his again.

Aymee was bolder than most. Perhaps it was a result of working in the clinic for so many years? Sex was a fact of life to her, and it was easy to forget that not everyone shared so open a view. Her attitude was too forward for some people.

She lowered her hand and absently flicked the water with her fingers, watching the droplets disturb the shimmering surface.

"I wonder what you think of me," she said softly, draping her arm around his neck in an easy embrace. "We barely know each other, you're a kraken and I'm human, and yet…"

"Any discomfort I've expressed has been solely the result of my inexperience, Aymee. I have greatly enjoyed our time together."

"I have, too." Smiling, she sighed and closed her eyes, letting the serenity of the ocean's song and gentle motion wash over her. "You're the only one I would have trusted to bring me out here. I'm not like Macy. The sea has never called to me like it does her. Even after her sister drowned, I think part of her still wanted to come out here and feel all this.

"In a way, I fear it. I know what it's capable of. But with you…" She opened her eyes and turned her head, taking in his profile. "I'm not afraid."

"Even after I nearly drowned you?"

"Even after," she said with a chuckle. "We should get back."

He nodded and swam back toward the beach in silence. The rhythm of his movement was even more soothing than the rise and fall of the water. Soon, the waves swept them forward, carrying them effortlessly toward land.

As soon as the water was shallow enough, she unlocked her legs from his waist and lowered her feet to the sand. She kept her arms around his neck, steadying herself, as they emerged from the sea.

Sand squished between Aymee's toes as she walked to the spot where she'd left her skirt. Arkon moved alongside her, his tentacles spread wider than usual; his stance reduced his height to something a bit more human.

"I know you asked me first," he said, eyes downcast, "but... have you? Been with anyone?"

Aymee's steps slowed. The faces of other men came to mind — all of them different now than they'd been, if only a little. Despite the way rumors typically spread through The Watch, her trysts had remained secret, even from Macy. Aymee wasn't sure if shame or disappointment had kept her from telling her best friend. "Three."

"Three," he repeated, voice low and flat.

Aymee tensed and looked at him. What should she make of his response?

He halted and turned toward her, frowning deeply as he studied her face. "I have upset you."

"Do you think poorly of me?" she asked.

His jaw muscles bulged, nostrils and siphons opening wide for a moment. "There is a sinking feeling in my stomach at the thought of you with another male, and I am envious of those men, even though I do not know them."

Her eyes widened.

Jealous? He was *jealous.*

"But no, I do not think poorly of you." He shook his head and tipped it back, looking up at the sky. "I have no right to feel the way I do. For a kraken female, three is…nothing. It was your choice, besides, and I cannot hold such decisions against you. My desire to tear the males you have been with to shreds is irrational, and quite unlike my usual self. I simply thought…Macy said humans choose *once.* Is that untrue?"

Warmth blossomed in her chest, spreading farther each word he spoke. She stepped closer, took his cheeks in her hands, and tilted his head down to meet his eyes. Silver moonlight bathed half his face, while shadow shrouded the other side save for the faint point of reflected light in his eye. The contrast strengthened his expression — jealousy, vulnerability, passion, and longing were writ upon his features.

She tucked this moment away in her memory; it would make a powerful painting.

Aymee stood on her toes, placed a light kiss on his lips, and moved back to sit on a rock near her skirt and sandals.

Arkon lifted his hand to touch his lips as though in disbelief. His chest swelled with a deep inhalation before he approached and sank into a squat in front of her.

"Macy's not wrong," she said. "Humans choose when they are ready to join with another. There's more to it than sex, though, and once you make that choice, it's *meant* to be forever."

"*Meant* to be forever?"

"That's the intention. But people just… I guess we just don't always work that way. It's great in concept. One person to share your life with, to share everything of yourself with…" The wind blew her drying hair into her face; she dragged her fingers through the curls, tugging them aside.

"You do not sound very excited by the prospect."

The corner of her mouth quirked up. "I wasn't."

"But…you are, now?"

The hopeful note in his voice went straight to Aymee's heart. She wanted to move closer, to touch him, to hold him, but she remained in place, staring silently at him until she forced herself to look away.

Take what you want. Take it all. Do not hesitate, because it could all be gone faster than you can blink.

Maris's words echoed in Aymee's mind.

Hadn't she done that already? Hadn't she jumped headlong into taking what she wanted with those other men? It had never brought her fulfillment. Why would it be different with Arkon?

She couldn't answer that question, but she knew she'd regret it for the rest of her life if she didn't try.

"I was sixteen when I had sex for the first time. I'd heard whispers from other kids my age, and I'd learned some things from working in the clinic. I was curious." She dropped her hands into her lap; the bare flesh of her thighs reminded her only then that she'd not yet pulled on her skirt.

"I didn't think too hard about the decision. I just told one of the boys who was interested in me that I wanted to, and…we did. It was horrible. There were a few moments when it felt nice, but mostly it was painful." She wrinkled her nose. "I knew there'd be pain the first time, but I guess I wasn't prepared for how much. I just laid there, waiting for him to finish, and when it was over I felt…hollow. Afterwards, I got angry."

"I…" Arkon sighed. "I understand the pursuit of curiosity, at least. What were you angry about when it was done?"

"I felt like I'd been lied to. That I shared my body and was left bereft. The experience was nothing like what I'd heard." She rubbed a finger against her leg. "It wasn't until a year later that I decided to try again, with a different guy. It felt a lot better, but there was always something missing. We got together a few times, but eventually, we both moved on.

"Then I started a fling with another guy a few years ago, until I found out he was seeing other women. And I didn't feel anything. I wasn't jealous, I wasn't hurt. I just...didn't care." She frowned and stared down at her feet as she dug her toes into the sand. "I don't regret any of it. I just wanted to know what it's *really* supposed to be like. I just wanted to find that missing piece."

Aymee smiled, kicking the sand. "Macy found it with Jax."

"Perhaps you were simply...starting from the wrong place."

"Or maybe I was looking too soon." She lifted her gaze to him. Shadow obscured his features, his entire body silhouetted against the moons. "Do you believe in fate, Arkon?"

He was silent for a long while. "Sometimes, I do. It implies that the universe works in ways I cannot possibly understand — which is unsettling, if I pause to think about it — but none of us can understand everything."

"I didn't believe in it. But what were the chances of Macy meeting Jax? For her to have gone out on the water after avoiding it for so long, to get caught in that storm and swept out to sea at the exact moment he happened to be there?"

"Near impossible," he replied. "And yet it happened."

"It did." She wished she could make out his darkness-clouded expression.

He moved closer. "And their meeting, whether fate or not, was the first link in the chain of events that brought you and me together."

That increasingly familiar warmth sparked in her chest

again. "It did." Aymee would never have met Arkon if not for Macy and Jax. She glanced up at the sky. "It's late. Is it safe for you to travel home, after dark?"

"There is no need to worry about me. Is it safe for you?" He turned his head and looked at the jungle, which was lit from within by countless glowing plants. The crease between his brows was visible now that the moonlight touched his face.

"I told you waiting wasn't very smart of me."

"But you didn't say why."

"It's not very safe to go out at night. Especially in the jungle."

He frowned before turning back to her. "Then I will accompany you, or you will wait here with me."

Aymee pressed her thighs together and curled her hands into loose fists. "You'll stay the night here with me?"

He reached forward and took one of her hands. "Without hesitation, Aymee."

Her heart skipped, and she forgot to breathe for a few moments. The depth and meaning behind those simple words was too much to decipher. Once again, she thought of what Maris said that day in the square.

Squeezing his hand, she leapt up and pecked a kiss on his cheek before pulling away to gather her skirt. "Do you think this spot is safe enough from the tide?"

He seemed briefly dazed by the kiss; he visibly shook himself before tilting his head to study the ground. "The tide line is here," he said, moving his hand horizontally to indicate a strip of ground about two meters away. "We're above it, but it'll get close."

"Will we be okay through the night?" she asked, stepping into her skirt and pulling it on.

"Putting the near-drowning behind us…you'll be safe with me."

Aymee chuckled. "I didn't doubt you for a second." She sat on the sand and patted the ground beside her. "After hunting, I imagine you're tired, too."

Arkon slithered over and eased himself down. "I am accustomed to sometimes going days without sleep. It is often necessary for the hunt."

"How long do they usually last?"

He lay back, putting one hand behind his head and the other over his abdomen. "A few hours; a few days. It varies greatly, depending on what we are hunting and where we go to find it."

Aymee scooted closer and lay on her side next to him, resting her head on his shoulder. Arkon tensed; he'd said he wasn't used to touching like this. Still, she wrapped her arm around his chest and held him. She couldn't resist snuggling closer. "Today's hunt was a quick one, then?"

Though he hesitated a few times in the process, he eventually slipped his arm around her shoulders. "Yes, relatively. I… must confess to some degree of impatience that fortunately sped it along."

"Really? I thought you had great patience."

Heat radiated from him, branding her arm where his hand rested. His claws lightly pressed against her through her blouse, fingers occasionally twitching as though he wanted to run them over her body.

"Apparently not when it comes to waiting to see you."

She mockingly gasped. "Are you blaming me for your impatience?"

His skin darkened. "No, not at all. It is my fault, but I had been looking forward to our meeting so eagerly since the last time and—"

Aymee laughed and slid her palm over his chest. "It's fine, Arkon."

Her hand rose and fell as he inhaled and released a shaky breath. "I just want very much *not* to disappoint you, Aymee."

She rubbed her cheek against him. "Perhaps it was fate at work again. If you'd been on time, we might not have shared this night together."

"How do you always find the positive aspect of any situation? You waited here, alone, for hours."

Aymee yawned. "I knew the time with you would be worth it." She found his hand and laced their fingers together as much as his webbing allowed. "And I was right."

He held their intertwined hands up, turned them slowly, and lowered them again. She was on the verge of drifting to sleep when he spoke, his voice low. "I have never mated with anyone."

She smiled and kissed his shoulder. "I know."

CHAPTER 8

AYMEE'S BROW TWITCHED. A COOL BREEZE WAFTED OVER HER, tousling her hair and fluttering her clothes, and she shivered as it made its way up her skirt. The sound of waves was louder than usual, as though the entire ocean were in her bedroom. Inhaling deeply, she stretched. The weight on her lower body gave her pause.

A slow smile spread across her lips — the tentacles wrapped around her waist and legs, keeping her in place, belonged to Arkon. He held her in one arm, hand at the small of her back. Despite some stiffness after a night on the ground, there was nowhere else she wanted to be in that moment.

She opened her eyes. A faint, early morning glow tinged the sky, granting her vision of him outside the night shadows. His chest rose and fell with his gentle breaths, and minuscule movements flickered through his tentacles and suction cups. The intimacy of their position sent a rush of heat spiraling through Aymee, creating a sudden, needy ache between her legs.

One of his tentacles shifted. Moving hesitantly, it slowly slid up along her inner thigh.

Her breath hitched. Arkon tensed.

"It's okay," she whispered.

His tentacle resumed its upward path, suction cups trailing whisper-kisses over her skin. Aymee fisted her hand against his chest and parted her thighs when the tip of his limb brushed her mound through her underwear.

Arkon shuddered. The tremor ran from his chest, through his arms, and along his tentacles, turning his light caress into a needful press. She caught her lower lip between her teeth and squeezed her eyes shut. She lifted her pelvis toward him, seeking the ecstasy of his touch.

His trembling hand gripped a fistful of her shirt as he brushed the tip of his tentacle over her again and again, each stroke sending a thrill of pleasure through her.

It wasn't enough.

She trailed her hand down, between their intertwined bodies, and slid it beneath her skirt. Her fingers moved over the smooth, soft skin of his tentacle before finally settling on her thigh.

Aymee paused, her tension and desire reaching new peaks with each passing second.

This is what I want.

Hooking her finger in the fabric, she tugged her underwear aside.

Arkon's tentacle froze against her parted sex. The single, simple touch made her moan.

"Aymee."

She'd never heard Arkon's voice like that — a low, husky, desperate growl clawing up from his chest.

He withdrew his tentacle abruptly. Before she realized his intention, he released his hold on her and rolled away.

Aymee gasped as she tumbled onto the sand. Pushing herself up on her hands, she raised her head.

Arkon was upright, his back toward her, shoulders heaving with ragged breaths. The tension in his body exaggerated the definition of his muscles.

He'd put at least two meters of distance between them.

She moved onto her knees and fisted her hands in her lap, squeezing her thighs together in hopes of easing her arousal; it felt somehow tainted, now.

What have I done?

She'd pushed too far, too soon.

"Arkon?"

"I...I just... A moment, please." His head dipped briefly and then tipped back. "I'm not...not accustomed to..."

"I understand."

He looked down again. "I don't know that you do..."

Aymee lowered her gaze. Perhaps she didn't. She'd been the one pushing her affections onto Arkon during their few, too-brief meetings. What if he didn't want her the way she wanted him? What if he couldn't see past their differences like Jax had with Macy?

Clutching the fabric of her skirt in both hands, she climbed to her feet and collected her sandals from the nearby rocks.

"It's all right. You don't need to explain anything." She closed her eyes and struggled to regain some semblance of calm. "We'll meet again in two days for the exchange."

"Aymee, I..." Arkon released an unsteady breath. His head and shoulders sagged, contrasting the tension in his balled fists. "Two days, then."

She opened her mouth to say goodbye, but it felt too final. Instead, she slipped on her sandals and left without another word. Without looking back. The widening distance between them hurt more with each step.

She walked along the dirt footpath through the jungle, back to the main road, and returned to The Watch without allowing her emotions to get the better of her. It didn't matter how much her eyes burned, or her heart stung.

"Early morning trip to the beach, Miss Rhodes?"

Aymee stopped and lifted her head, meeting Randall's eyes. Leaning against a wall a few meters away, he wore his usual green-and-purple attire. The knives on his belt were accompanied by a holstered pistol today. Though his arms were folded across his chest, relatively far from the weapon, it added menace to his visage.

"I needed some fresh air," she said, resuming her walk.

"A good hunter has an eye for patterns," he said as she passed. "We have to learn the habits of the creatures we hunt to become more effective. People have habits, too. Routines they don't often break."

"Are you insinuating something?"

"Just observing. I couldn't help but notice the change in your routine today, and I wanted to make sure everything was okay. There anything you want to talk to me about?"

"You've been here all of twelve days. What do you know of my habits?" She narrowed her eyes at him as he fell into step beside her. "I don't find it very comforting to know you're stalking me."

He laughed and shook his head. "I'm not stalking you. Like I said, people just have their habits. Not hard to pick up on them, once you know what you're looking for."

His scrutiny was unnerving, and for once she was grateful that she'd have to wait until the next exchange. It gave her time to take precautions.

"I go to the beach when I want to think. It's calming. Macy and I used to go when we were kids."

"You have to walk through a stretch of jungle to get to that beach. Wouldn't it be safer just to go to the one by the dock?"

"Like I said, we went there as *children*. And the beach by the docks is too distracting."

He lifted his hands in surrender. "Fair enough. I've told you already, I'm not your enemy, Aymee. I just want everyone to be safe."

Aymee closed her mouth. She didn't want to get into the same argument with him, she didn't want him to be her enemy, she didn't want to deal with any of *this* — not now or ever. Under different circumstances, she and Randall might've been good friends.

But the *what-ifs* didn't change the current situation.

Randall stepped in front of her, palms displayed in a supplicating gesture. "Just stop and listen to me for one minute, please?"

Frowning, she halted. "Randall—"

"I'm not starting an argument, I promise. I just wanted to say again that I'm sorry for the other night. That was not how I intended for it to go, and it was my fault. I should've known better with them so deep into their cups. Cyrus is my father's friend and… Look, it may not mean much to you, but I'm pretty sure my father sent him along to keep an eye on me. I would like nothing more than to leave this place without ever seeing a kraken."

Aymee's brows furrowed. She searched his eyes and saw no deceit in them. "Why?"

"Because I don't know how that encounter would turn out, and I don't want to cause you grief."

Though he'd made no secret of his interest in her, Aymee hadn't believed it strong enough for him to forgo what he viewed as his duty — unless it was all a ploy. "Why? I'm one person. Isn't your responsibility to all the people of Halora?"

"I want to believe what you say about them. I want it to be enough for me, but it's not. It can't be. Because men like Cyrus and my father won't accept it."

She stared at him; the hardness she'd noticed in his features that first night had returned. Understanding dawned on Aymee at that moment.

"It won't be enough until one side is dead," she said.

He nodded. "I'm not going to ask you why you really went to the beach. But I am going to tell you: *be careful.* If this all escalates...I don't think I can stop it."

Her heartbeat accelerated. Randall knew. He knew she'd gone to the beach the night before, that she hadn't returned until now. He knew she was up to something and had inferred it was related to the kraken.

But he hadn't *seen* Arkon, or else he wouldn't be here talking to her. The dread in her gut eased, if only slightly.

She took in a deep breath and slowly exhaled. "Like I said, Randall, I went to the beach for some time alone."

There was scrutiny in his gaze, but it was somehow gentle. "Have a good day, Miss Rhodes." Randall turned and walked away, adding over his shoulder, "And be careful on that jungle road. Could be dangerous creatures around."

Aymee watched until he was out of sight. By the time she got home, her nerves had only further frayed, and she thrummed with anxiety.

She stepped through the door and stopped short, nearly colliding with her father.

"Aymee!" He pulled her into a tight hug. "Where were you? You didn't come home last night."

She embraced him, meeting her mother's worried eyes over his shoulder. "I was with Arkon."

"All night?" Jeanette's eyes widened. Unspoken words lingered in her expression; while Aymee's parents held no prejudice against the kraken, it didn't mean they were without reservations.

Aymee pulled back and smiled. "We were perfectly safe."

"Aymee..." Kent ran a hand through his gray-streaked blonde hair. "It's not safe for either of you."

"I know." Aymee sighed and rubbed her eyes with the heels of her hands. "I know! Everything was fine until *they* showed up. Now..."

Kent took hold of her shoulder and gave it a gentle squeeze. "Just be careful."

But I am going to tell you: be careful. If this all escalates...I don't think I can stop it.

"I am. I'm trying."

Jeanette stepped closer. "Maybe it's time to stop. Macy has moved on, and I know it will hurt to let her go—"

"No!" She stared at her mother, chest constricting, but it wasn't Macy on Aymee's mind.

"Just for now," Jeanette amended. "Until the rangers leave."

"They might *never* leave!"

"If they go long enough without finding anything, they will," Kent said. "They're not going to stay if there's nothing to hunt."

"And every time you meet with Arkon, you're putting him in danger," Jeanette added gently, rubbing her palm along Aymee's arm. "I'm sorry it has to be this way, but we don't want anyone hurt, especially you."

Aymee blinked, tears dripping down her cheeks.

She never cried, but God, this hurt. She felt like her entire world was shattering, the pieces falling around her feet. Worst of all...her parents were right. Aymee knew they were. She'd known from the moment she first saw Randall on that stage, and she'd still foolishly, selfishly continued to meet Arkon.

"Aymee..." Kent wiped tears from her cheek.

"I know. You're right." She drew in a shaky breath. "We meet in two days. I'll tell him that it'll be the last. I'll tell Macy."

"I'm sorry," Jeanette said.

"Do you want to stay home today?" Kent asked.

Aymee shook her head. "No. I... The distraction will help."

Kent nodded. "I'll see you at the clinic soon, then. Take all the time you need." He leaned forward and kissed her forehead before stepping outside.

"I need to wash up," Aymee said.

"Are you hungry?"

"Not right now."

"Okay. I'll make something for you to take with you."

"Thanks, mom."

Aymee retreated to the bathroom, where she removed her clothes. Her skin felt gritty with sand and dried salt. For a moment, she stood in silence, a hand settled over her stomach, and recalled the way she'd felt pressed against Arkon and coiled in his embrace. He'd held her like she was the most precious thing in the world. Her skin tingled with the memory of his hesitant, curious, intimate touch.

And she'd ruined it.

She hurriedly washed, scrubbing her skin and hair, and dried off.

Stepping into her room, she dressed in a loose skirt and a short-sleeved blouse. As she buttoned her shirt, she glanced at her nightstand and froze.

Her jar of rocks lay broken on the floor, the precious stones scattered amongst shards of glass.

Numb, Aymee stepped forward, narrowly avoiding the pieces of glass. The nightstand's bottom drawer was open. She removed the books from it one by one, hardly breathing. It wasn't until she found the small stack of folded letters that she released a relieved sigh and sagged onto the bed.

She lifted her head and scanned the room. The dresser drawers were partially opened, their contents disturbed, and the objects on her table had been moved. Her attention caught on her satchel.

It had been laid atop the table, flap thrown open, papers spilling out.

"No," she rasped and quickly crossed the room, somehow missing the glass shards. She stood the satchel and pulled out the papers with shaking hands. "No. No!"

Every drawing she'd made of Arkon — *every single one!* — was gone.

Icy fear flooded her, thawed by rage close on its heels.

How dare he?

He'd come to her this morning in peace, but it had all been a lie. His kindness and friendship were false fronts meant to lull her into lowering her guard.

Aymee left her room, striding toward the front door.

"Aymee?" Jeanette frowned as Aymee passed her. "Aymee!"

She ignored her mother as she threw on her shoes and stormed out, stalking down the street toward the town center. She paid no mind to the people milling about the square.

Shoving the double doors open, she strode into the town hall.

Aymee swept her gaze over the room and spotted Randall standing at one of the tables, bent forward with his hands on the tabletop. He turned his head, eyes widening when they fell on Aymee. The other two men — Cyrus and one she hadn't met — shifted their attention to her, as well.

"Where are they?" she demanded, closing the distance between them.

Randall quirked a brow. "Where are what, Aymee?"

"My sketches," she bit out. "You took my sketches!"

He frowned, but the mild confusion on his face didn't fade. "I gave them all back to you after they fell. I handed them directly to you."

"But you came for them. You searched my damn room for them!"

"Hell, Randy, this one's a firecracker." Cyrus wore an amused smirk beneath his hard-eyed gaze.

Aymee turned her glare to him, meeting his gaze unwaveringly. "I want my sketches back. Now."

"I don't have them, Aymee. I'm not a damned thief," Randall said.

"That's right, *Aymee*," Cyrus drawled. "He doesn't have them."

"*You* do," she said.

Cyrus stepped around the other ranger and approached her. He towered over her. "Prove it, fish-lover."

Aymee balled a fist and, without thought, she punched Cyrus in the face.

140

His head snapped to the side. He slowly turned it back to her, running his tongue along the inside of his cheek. "Gonna have to do a lot better than th—"

A choking noise cut off his words as Aymee rammed her knee into his crotch. He doubled over, face red, hands dropping to his groin. She placed her palms on his shoulders and pushed him to the floor.

"Do *not* speak to me that way again," she said through clenched teeth.

Cyrus grunted and reached up. His face darkened as he took hold of the table's edge and dragged himself to his feet. "You little fish-loving—"

Randall and the other ranger imposed themselves between the two at that moment. Items rattled on the table as they restrained Cyrus. Before Aymee could get another shot in, Randall caught her wrist.

"Enough, Aymee. It's probably best you go," he said.

She yanked her wrist out of his grasp and stepped away from him. "I want them back, Randall. Someone was in my room. Someone took them, and I don't care if it was you or him. I want them back." She turned and stomped toward the door.

"That's not what we do, Aymee," Randall called, raising his voice over Cyrus's swearing.

Aiden blocked her. "Are you okay, Aymee?"

"I'm fine. Sorry for the disturbance."

He looked over her shoulder, toward the rangers, for an instant. "I'd kick them out if I could, but..." he whispered.

"I know. Thank you."

He nodded and moved aside, letting her leave.

CHAPTER 9

THE EVENING SUN CREPT TOWARD THE WATERY HORIZON, ITS angle casting illumination on most of the sand beneath the overhang. The scents on the wind teased a coming storm, but only sparse white clouds drifted across the sky.

Arkon clenched his jaw as he stared at the tiny stones and shells scattered in the sand. He'd intended to create something new for Aymee, another surprise, but his plans had met only frustration. He was too preoccupied. Whenever he sought a potential pattern in his mind's eye, his thoughts returned to that morning two days before.

To the hurt in her voice.

He raked his claws over the design he'd etched into the sand. For all his curiosity, all his excitement, all his interest in Aymee, he'd fled the situation. He'd allowed his lack of experience to become a lack of self-control, and *she* had paid the price.

The tip of his tentacle still tingled with the remembrance of her taste, scent, and feel. It had been so potent he'd nearly tasted her on his tongue. In that moment — when he'd touched her, flesh to flesh — he'd wanted her so much it hurt. He'd extruded almost instantly. The immense, aching pressure in his shaft would've burst at her slightest touch.

He stared down at the backs of his hands and the tiny grains of sand sticking to them. Creativity had never been difficult for him; he saw intricate patterns everywhere, and his visions for his work were always clear from their inception.

That had all seemed to flee him after hurting Aymee.

Lifting his head, he glanced down the beach. His hearts stilled when Aymee rounded the bend in the cliffside and entered his view. Her brows were drawn, and she wore a troubled frown. Turning away, she walked backward, seeming to search the beach behind her.

Arkon pushed himself upright. He'd never seen her in such a state, and he'd only himself to blame. Perhaps he valued knowledge and learning more than any of his kind, but he'd been a fool.

She faced him again and approached, the canister swinging in her hold. She wore a bandage on one hand.

"What happened, Aymee?" He moved close and gently took her wrist, raising her arm to study the cloth wrapped around her knuckles.

"I lost my temper with one of the hunters."

His muscles tensed, but he was careful not to strengthen his grip. "Did he harm you?"

"No. The others caught him before he could." She tugged free of his hold. "I can't stay. And this...needs to end."

Arkon's arms fell to his sides. His chest tightened and his brow furrowed as he processed her words, and his initial response — *What?* — caught in his throat. A strange sort of anger followed; it wasn't directed at her, but at the situation, at the hunters, at the world.

"No."

Her eyes shot up to meet his. "Yes, Arkon. It isn't safe."

"Life isn't safe. Fear and intolerance separated our people long ago, and I refuse to allow the same keep us apart."

Aymee squeezed her eyes shut, and a pained expression flitted across her face. The container dropped from her hand and hit the sand with a soft *plop*. When she looked up at him again, she pressed her fingers to his chest.

"We're asking for trouble," she said quietly. "They took my sketches, Arkon. They know what you look like now, and at least one of them knows about my trips to this beach. I won't be coming here again until they leave town."

The finality in her tone sapped the strength of his resolve. He didn't want this to be the end, couldn't bear it to be, but the choice, ultimately, belonged to her. Just as it had from the beginning.

And she was right.

"Holy shit," said a deep voice from behind her.

Arkon lifted his gaze. A human male had just rounded the bend, a long gun in his hands. He was large enough to rival Macy's father, Breckett, but there was something harder about this human — an emptiness behind the gleam in his eyes.

Aymee spun toward them. "No!"

Arkon swept her behind him as two more humans came into view, both with similar clothing and weapons.

"They're real," the first man said, mouth spreading into a wide grin. The expression drew attention to the cut on his lower lip and the purple, swollen flesh around it. "The damn fish men are real."

"Just turn around and walk away," Arkon said, fire flowing into his veins. "No one needs to come to harm today. Our people are not enemies."

"And they *do* talk!" The man turned to one of his companions, a younger human with a strained look on his face. "You were right, Randy."

Randy's eyes were on Aymee. The emotions in his features were jumbled; Arkon guessed they bore a deeper meaning but had no idea what.

Aymee ducked beneath Arkon's arm and inserted herself between him and the humans. "Arkon, go. Now."

"I am not going to leave you alone with these men, Aymee."

"They won't hurt me, but they *will* hurt you. Go."

"Nobody needs to get hurt," Randy said. "He just needs to come with us willingly."

"Krullshit," the first man spat. "I *owe* her, and I'm not giving this thing a chance to get away." He shifted his gaze to the third human. "Joel, you bring that rope?"

Joel shifted his long gun into one hand and reached behind him, removing a coil of rope from his belt. He was tall and broad-shouldered, his skin nearly as dark as Dracchus's, head shaved bare. "I did. It gonna hold him though, Cyrus?"

"He's not going with you," Aymee said.

Cyrus casually moved a hand to the bolt of his long gun and slid it back, checking the chambered round. "He is. One way or another. This bullet's big enough to go through you on its way to him, so think real hard about how much you want to argue with me."

"Stand down, ranger," Randy said through clenched teeth.

Cyrus's grin faltered; he pressed his lips into a tight line. "Excuse me, Randy?"

146

"Stand. Down."

"Arkon, go," Aymee hissed over her shoulder.

"I am *not* leaving you with that man." Arkon didn't take his eyes off Cyrus. This was the human Aymee had stricken, the one she'd lost her temper with, and he was threatening her. "Come with me."

"Neither of you are going," Randy said.

Aymee backed up into Arkon.

"Just one bullet, and we've got our prize and her mouth is shut for good. Worth a round of ammo," Cyrus said, "maybe two."

"No. We're here to protect people, damn it." Randy met Arkon's gaze. "Just give yourself up. You were right; no one needs to get hurt today. Cyrus, Joel — guns down."

Joel grimaced, but leaned over and stood his long gun against the cliffside, its butt in the sand.

"Fuck that." Cyrus raised his gun, barrel pointed at Aymee.

As Arkon grabbed hold of her and spun to shield her with his body, Randy caught the barrel in his hand and halted its upward motion.

"Taking one alive was the plan from the beginning, wasn't it?" Randy demanded. "He hasn't threatened us in any way. Weapon down, *now*."

"I can't tell if your daddy would be proud right now, or if he'd be beating the snot out of you."

Arkon watched over his shoulder as Cyrus tugged his gun out of Randy's grip and tossed it into the sand. They all wore knives and smaller guns on their belts, but hadn't drawn them yet.

"We need to go," Aymee whispered, clutching his arm.

"If we try to flee, they will shoot us," Arkon replied. His

options were limited in this situation; he wanted to believe the Randy, who appeared to be their leader, but — apart from Aymee and Macy — could humans be trusted? "I need to go with them."

"You can't! They'll hurt you."

"It will be all right, Aymee."

"Arkon, don't. This is *not* like what happened with Jax."

"I know." He reached up and cupped her cheek with his palm, brushing the pad of his thumb over her soft skin. "But the stakes are just as high. If we resist or run, you're likely to get hurt."

"If this doesn't move along, I'm just going to shoot him," Cyrus said.

Arkon smiled down at Aymee, turned toward the hunters, and raised his hands. He kept his breathing steady and willed his hearts to slow. He realized, as the humans cautiously advanced, that he'd lied to Aymee for the first time.

There was little chance things would be all right.

The three males stopped a short distance from Arkon and stared up at him.

"Are all of you this big?" Cyrus asked.

Arkon made no reply; instead, he met Randy's eyes.

"Joel is going to restrain you," Randy said.

Joel stepped forward — without hesitation, though it must have been strange for him to be so close to a kraken for the first time — with the rope in his hands.

Aymee approached them. "Randall, don't do this." She motioned toward Arkon. "You see him with your own eyes, now, and he's complying. He isn't a threat to anyone."

"He's a predator." Cyrus scowled at Aymee. "That makes him a threat."

"So are you," she shot back with a glare.

"None of this is necessary," Arkon said calmly. "I will go with you, but I will not be restrained. If I am expected to trust you, then you must extend similar trust to me. I would like us to be friends. My understanding is that humans do not make captives of would-be friends."

Randall hesitated, seeming conflicted.

"Shut your mouth and put your hands behind your back," Cyrus growled. "I've had enough of her running her mouth. I'm not in the mood to hear you, too."

Cyrus tugged the rope out of Joel's hands.

"Take it easy, Cyrus," Joel said. He hadn't removed his eyes from Arkon. "We don't know what this thing's capable of."

"We don't, but I guarantee you my gun can put a hole in him as big as it would in anything else." Cyrus grasped Arkon's wrist.

Aymee leapt forward and grabbed hold of the rope. "You're not taking him."

Releasing his hold on Arkon, Cyrus backhanded Aymee across the face. The force of it sent her to the ground.

Something within Arkon broke. Though it happened in a fraction of an instant, he was acutely aware of the process — it was as though a wall had collapsed, and rage like he'd never felt poured in through the opening. His skin shifted to crimson.

Randall took a fistful of Cyrus's shirt and hauled the man backward, shock and anger on his features.

Cyrus scowled. "Stupid little—"

Arkon wasn't interested in hearing anymore. He swung his left arm, the back of his hand connecting with Cyrus's mouth. Twisting, the human tumbled to the sand.

The other hunters were quick to overcome their surprise. Joel stepped forward and hooked Arkon's arm with his own and extended a leg behind Arkon's tentacles, pulling back as though to drag the kraken off-balance. It was little surprise that a land-dwelling being would resort to such tactics — someone with legs would have fallen.

Arkon shifted his weight, spreading his limbs wider to remain upright, and wrapped a tentacle around each of Joel's legs.

"Stop!" Randall shouted.

Arkon pulled Joel's feet out from beneath him, and the man hit the sand hard, the back of his head striking the cliffside as he fell. Ignoring Randall, who hadn't moved to attack, Arkon returned his focus to Cyrus.

The man had regained his feet. Blood trickled from the corner of his mouth, and he wore a ghastly grin. He pulled a long knife from his belt. The blade glinted in the evening sunlight.

"Come on, then. Nothing wrong with a little sport." He spat crimson onto the beach.

"God damn it, that's enough!" A desperate tone had entered Randall's voice; the situation had spiraled out of control. Arkon knew well how that felt.

"I accept your challenge, Cyrus," Arkon said.

"This has gone far enough! Both of you, stand down!"

"Quiet now, Randy. Let the adult settle this." Cyrus advanced toward Arkon.

Randall drew the gun from his hip, raised it, and fired into the sand in front of Cyrus. The boom was deafening, amplified by the rock walls.

Cyrus halted, turning a furious, wide-eyed gaze to Randall.

"I *said* stand down, ranger. That is an order," Randall said.

"This pulling rank shit doesn't work in the field, kid. Only thing that matters out here is respect, and you don't—"

"Don't what? Have yours? You think I care, Cyrus? I gave you an order. We're doing this my way, so back up and put your knife away."

"Arkon isn't going with you," Aymee said, voice hard.

All eyes turned to her; Cyrus's blossoming smirk quickly faded. She stood beside the prone Joel, clutching the man's sidearm in both hands. Her arms were steady, keeping the barrel pointed toward Cyrus and Randall. Arkon recognized the fire in her eyes. It was more intense now, but it stemmed from the same passion she displayed for art, for joy, for life.

Randall neither raised nor lowered his gun; his face was contorted with conflicting emotion again. "Aymee—"

"No! I'm done hearing about your *good intentions*. From what I've seen and heard, there was *no* intention of letting him live."

"At this point, I don't have any intention of letting either of you live," Cyrus said.

"You kill me, and the entire town will turn on you."

The man's grin might as well have been filled with razor-sharp teeth — they would have accompanied its malice rather well.

"Most of the townsfolk think these things are dangerous. We tried to save you, but the monster was too quick...so we took it down to avenge your death."

"Is that so, Randall?" Aymee asked.

Randall dropped his gaze. "It doesn't need to be. We just...we just need to put the weapons down, and we can still talk this through."

Something flickered in Aymee's eyes as she looked at Randall

— a hint of sorrow in her anger. "You're just as monstrous as him."

Arkon eased himself toward Aymee, moving slowly. Randall's brows lowered over the bridge of his nose, falling over pained eyes.

Aymee looked at Arkon. "We're going now."

"You're not going anywhere," Cyrus growled. He lunged forward and thrust his hand out.

Something glinted in the air. Arkon's hearts skipped — it was the knife. He twisted his torso aside to avoid the flying blade. It skimmed across his chest, leaving a line of fire in its wake, and clattered against the cliffside.

"Arkon!" Aymee screamed.

Cyrus was already in motion when Arkon turned back.

The human had closed the distance between himself and Aymee. Before Arkon could react, Cyrus grabbed her wrists. She struggled, and he slammed his knee into her stomach.

The gun in her hand went off with a boom. Its recoil kicked the weapon from her grip as she doubled over with a wheeze.

Arkon surged toward them. Cyrus released Aymee and met Arkon's charge, and they tumbled into the sand.

Skin a deep crimson, Arkon rolled atop Cyrus. The human swung his arms, fists balled. Arkon shrugged off the blows and coiled tentacles around Cyrus's arms and legs, wrenching them apart; the man was strong, but not strong enough. Arkon slammed the edge of his fist down into Cyrus's face. Again, and again, each time seeing Cyrus hit Aymee in his mind's eye.

Warm blood splattered Arkon. The human's struggles weakened.

Cyrus's head lolled to the side, and his breath rattled. Arkon drew back for another blow.

He hesitated. These men had come to hunt monsters. Arkon refused to be one.

He cast aside his rage, and concern flooded into its place. Pushing up off Cyrus, he turned to Aymee.

She'd crawled to Randall — who lay on his back in the sand — and knelt over him, sobbing. Arkon moved to her.

Randall's face was a mask of pain, teeth clenched and bared. Aymee had torn fabric from her skirt and held it to his shoulder. Blood covered her hands and seeped from Randall's wound.

"I'm so sorry," Aymee cried.

Arkon frowned and lowered himself beside her.

"I shot him, Arkon," she said, turning her watery eyes toward him. "I could have killed him. He could still..."

After glancing at the unconscious forms of Joel and Cyrus, Arkon returned his attention to Randall. Though he'd spent countless hours learning everything he could from the Computer back in the Facility, studying human anatomy with particular curiosity, he possessed no practical experience; he'd been lucky to succeed in sealing Macy's wounds from the razor-back, nothing more. He knew only that humans were more fragile than kraken.

"I need to get the bullet out," she said.

"We need to leave, Aymee."

"But he—"

"How likely is it that people in town heard those shots, Aymee?"

"They would have heard," she said quietly.

"How many more of these men are there?"

She was silent for several moments as she stared at Randall's wound. "Go."

"I will not leave you with these men," Arkon said, hooking a finger under her chin and guiding her face toward him. "It very well might have been *us* sprawled out in the sand bleeding, Aymee. Only we wouldn't have had a chance to get back up. Do what you can for him, quickly, and your father will see to the rest."

Aymee searched his eyes and, finally, nodded. "Keep this in place and lift him."

Arkon pressed his hand over the blood-soaked cloth on Randall's shoulder when she pulled away, and slowly raised Randall's torso off the sand.

Randall groaned. "Don't go," he said. "It won't... How will it look? You have to stay. Explain."

"You can tell them the truth," Aymee said as she tore another long strip from her skirt. She wrapped it around Randall's back and chest, tying a knot over the wadded cloth Arkon held in place.

Shouts carried to them from inland. Arkon didn't want to drag Aymee away from all she knew, but after this experience, how could he entrust her safety to other humans? How could he believe that she'd be all right while Cyrus and the hunters were near?

"Come, Aymee. The others may not hesitate to use their long guns when they come upon this scene."

She nodded and stood up, but Randall caught her wrist.

Fire burst through Arkon's chest. He clenched his teeth, barely keeping himself from attacking.

"Aymee..." Randall rasped.

"Arkon is right," she said, gently prying his hand off. "I'm sorry. I tried to tell you." She stepped back. "It didn't have to be this way. It still *doesn't* have to be this way. Tell them the truth."

"My people do not want another fight," Arkon said, moving

beside Aymee. "Please, do not bring one to us. The past does not need to be repeated."

He held out his hand to Aymee and met her gaze. She took it, and together they picked up the canisters they'd planned to exchange and moved toward the sea.

This was not the Aymee he'd known; the light of life had dimmed in her eyes, and there was no trace of joy on her face. He only hoped the change was temporary, and that he wasn't the one responsible for breaking her spirit.

Arkon wouldn't be able to live with that.

CHAPTER 10

It was a long while before Arkon's hearts eased and the frantic energy in his limbs dissipated. All he focused on, at first, was getting Aymee well away from the beach. He'd moved quickly, and though the choppy water splashed her face numerous times, she voiced no complaint.

He'd expected to hear the boom of a gunshot at any moment, to feel the jolt of impact.

He slowed only after they were well beyond the landward current and the voices from the beach had long since faded. The cut on his chest stung, but the pain was tolerable; once they found a place to shelter for the night, it would have plenty of time to heal.

Aymee clung to him as he swam — arms around his neck, legs encircling his torso, chest pressed against his back. Apart from her occasional coughing or sputtering after being splashed, she was quiet. Tremors pulsed through her limbs; each time she trembled, she squeezed him a little tighter.

The sun sank rapidly, unconcerned with their plight. The

ocean's surface rippled like liquid gold. Part of him recognized the beauty on display all around, but he rejected it. Only Aymee's safety mattered, and all the beauty in the world wouldn't help that.

Where should we go?

He'd acted in the heat of the moment, had operated on instinct, having known only that they needed to depart before more humans arrived. But Arkon was unaccustomed to life on land, and Aymee didn't have a diving suit to survive under water. She'd need one of the suits Macy used if he wanted to take her to the Facility.

Not that he *could* take her there. Even after the trials she and Jax had faced, Macy still wasn't accepted by all. Introducing another human — unproven and unknown — could push the tensions past the point of sensibility and control, leaving Aymee and Macy both in unnecessary danger.

That left only one place; the location was oddly fitting.

He continued along the coastline toward the Broken Cavern.

When Jax had first convinced Arkon to visit the place, they'd been younger — kraken hunters who'd only just reached their majority and begun truly contributing to their people's wellbeing. It was amongst the first places Jax discovered in his early wanderings, and his excitement, coupled with the promise of seeing some amazing human creations, had coaxed Arkon into going.

By the time Aymee and Arkon reached the Broken Cavern, the daylight had dwindled to a soft glow. The entrance was a rectangular opening carved into the rocky shoreline.

"What is that place?" Aymee asked, weariness and curiosity evident in her voice. It was the first time she'd spoken since leaving the beach.

Midnight blue water flowed into the Cavern, where it met solid, impenetrable blackness.

"It is a place your people built long ago, intended to house large, underwater boats."

She fell silent. Arkon imagined her brow furrowing as she studied what little of the structure was visible.

Arkon activated his lights — points of bioluminescence within his stripes that cast a soft blue glow, not unlike that of halorium — as they passed into the tunnel.

Aymee's gasp echoed off the walls. "You *glow?*"

"Just another part of our design." His light was bright enough to touch the concrete walls on either side, but only barely. "It was likely meant to allow us to work at night or in undersea caves."

She unraveled an arm from around his neck and ran her fingertips over the stripes on his head. "Macy didn't mention *this*. And she didn't say much about what happened."

His skin tingled under her touch, and he felt some degree of guilt at his body's reaction, after everything that had transpired.

"About what happened? Do you mean between our people?"

"Yes." Her arm slipped back around his neck. "You said something about it on the beach."

He frowned. Their voices, though hushed, reverberated off the walls and ceiling, and the sound of the ocean was muted, leaving only the steady splash of water against concrete. This dark, abandoned place seemed the wrong location to speak of such things, but that sentiment was irrational.

"The kraken were engineered by humans to collect a rare element from the seafloor called halorium. Our first generations were essentially slave laborers, but they learned much faster than the humans realized. After years of poor treatment and experimentation, my people revolted against the humans in the underwater facility that served as the operation's head-quarters."

"Where Macy is now."

"Exactly where she is now. There was fighting, but it seems to have been largely one-sided. The humans were comfortable in their dominance. They never saw it coming."

The tunnel opened into the huge main chamber; a gaping hole in the ceiling granted a glimpse of the sky, which was now filled with dark clouds. The dim light from outside reflected on the surface of the water and glinted on the mangled remnants of one of the bridges that had spanned the water.

"How did we never know?"

Her question was likely rhetorical, but Arkon couldn't help but answer. "I know there were attempts made to contact the mainland, but I do not know if any of those communications were transmitted. The kraken had grown knowledgeable enough to damage the communications array of the Facility and isolate it completely."

"How do you know they tried to contact mainland?"

"Because the Computer in the Facility has records of those attempts."

Macy had discovered one such message after she figured out how to access the Computer's data, and Arkon had found several more in the months since. Regardless of what had brought about the situation, despite the mistreatment that had preceded the kraken uprising, the emotion in some of those messages was overwhelming. They had been desperate people looking death in the eye.

"What did they say?" she asked.

Arkon swam them to one of the ladders inset in the

concrete wall and helped Aymee onto it. "They...begged for aid, mostly. For rescue. And the last one told anyone listening to stay away. That there wasn't anything — or anyone — left to save."

Aymee climbed to the top rung. Water streamed off her, and her tattered clothing molded to her body. She stepped off and moved aside.

"I wonder if that's why we know nothing of that place — of you. That the humans in charge wanted it secret to keep people safe."

He shifted the canisters to his tentacles and pulled himself up the ladder. His bioluminescence did little to light this area; most of the chamber was utterly lost in darkness, save for the edges highlighted by the night sky overhead.

When he turned to her, he paused. His light caught in the moisture on her skin, giving her a glow of her own — a thousand tiny points of reflected light, more beautiful than the star-filled sky. Though she wore the suffering of the day's events in her expression and the bruise on her cheek, she was breathtaking. An ethereal vision he might not have believed was real had he not touched her, held her, kissed her.

"I..." It took no small degree of concentration for Arkon to recall what she'd said a moment earlier. "I think...yes. That's plausible. There was some connection between the Facility, this place, and The Watch, but I have been unable to find solid information in that regard."

He moved away from her, tucking the containers under his arms again, and scanned their surroundings. Though most of it was lost in darkness, the cavern was huge, with two tiers — their current level and another above it, with several wide sets of steps linking the two. The set-up was mirrored on both sides of the water. Everything was built of the same manmade stone, its planes too perfect to be natural.

Arkon shifted his attention to the ceiling. The damage there was likely the result of time and weather. The massive chunks of broken concrete had destroyed one of the two bridges that linked the sides of the bay, and Arkon little trusted the area around the damage; even a small piece could prove deadly.

Aymee's gaze dropped. She inhaled sharply and stepped toward him. "You're hurt! Why didn't you say something?" She lifted her hands to his chest, her touch light as she inspected his cut.

Despite her gentleness, the wound burned. Fresh blood oozed from it.

"I... I have nothing to stitch this with," she reached down and grasped her skirt with both hands, "but we can bandage it for now." There was a helpless note in her voice.

He coiled a tentacle around each of her wrists, halting her hands. She looked up at him with a desperate gleam in her eyes.

"It is fine, Aymee. I am fine."

"You're bleeding."

"Once we settle down and rest, the wound will have ample time to heal. It will nearly be gone by morning."

Her gaze dipped to his chest again, dropped to her wrists, and she burst into tears.

Arkon frowned and set the canisters on the floor. He'd seen Macy cry before, but nothing like this. It writhed through his insides, tugged on something in his chest, and made his hearts thump.

Aymee is a healer, not a hunter. What she went through today was probably unlike anything she's experienced in her life.

Releasing her wrists, he drew her into a close embrace,

smoothing her hair down with his palm. Aymee embraced him, clinging tight. Her sobs were ragged and painful, and shudders tore through her body.

She buried her face against his shoulder. "This is my fault."

"No, Aymee," he said softly. "You and I are not blameless, but we did not push it to this point. I should have listened to you from the start. You were the one thinking logically, the one trying to be safe."

"But I d-didn't fight you. I wanted to see you. I wasn't careful. They found you because of me, because I couldn't k-keep quiet, because of my sketches."

He carefully combed the tips of his claws through her wet hair. "You did nothing wrong, Aymee. Nothing. I knew the danger. You warned me many times. But...I couldn't stay away from you either. You were worth the risk. You *are* worth the risk."

For a time, the only sounds she produced were the occasional whimper or sniffle. Her hold on him didn't loosen. When she'd finally calmed, she rested her cheek, still damp with tears, against the uninjured side of his chest.

"I shot someone," she said softly.

"It was an accident."

"I know. I know it was, but I can't stop thinking about it. If it had hit him a few inches to his right, it would have killed him."

"But it didn't." He settled his chin atop her head. "Those men are hunters, Aymee. They made their choices and accepted the risks. Every time they go out, each of them must know in his heart that he may not return. And one of those men would have killed you if he'd had a little more time."

She released a shaky sigh. "Despite the circumstances, I'm glad you're here with me."

Relief flowed through Arkon; though the day's events had pushed his worries from his mind, he hadn't let go of the notion that he'd wronged her, that he'd turned her away, that she'd lost whatever interest she might have held for him.

He cupped his hand behind her head and pressed his face to her hair. "Me too."

After a few moments, his gaze drifted to the break in the ceiling. "Let's find a spot to rest. We can talk more in the morning."

"Okay." She stepped back; he released her reluctantly.

Arkon collected the canisters and led her to the steps farthest away from the structural damage. Placing the containers at the base of the steps, he eased himself down against the wall beside them. When Aymee sat next to him, he pulled her close, and she slipped her arms around him.

He settled his arm over her shoulders, and Aymee — warm, soft, and vulnerable — leaned into him. Had things gone differently, he might have brought her here one day, if only to show her the massive painting on the lower level's rear wall. Perhaps they'd have come by boat or fetched one of the diving suits for Aymee to use. Either way, sharing in their mutual appreciation of such works would've been worth the journey.

In the relative quiet — the sound of the water lapping the walls was almost gentle here, and wind whispered across the gap overhead — his mind turned to the events on the beach. Had he chosen correctly? Had he handled it as he should have?

What would the hunters tell their comrades, what would they tell the townsfolk?

Arkon thought of the hologram recordings of the last humans in the Facility, of their fast, brutal battles against the kraken. Of the slaughter and the blood.

He could only hope he hadn't set a similar conflict into motion.

He looked down at Aymee. Her eyes were closed, her breathing deep, and her body relaxed against him in sleep. Arkon hadn't lied; she *was* worth all the risks. Jax had defied two peoples because he thought Macy was worth it, and Arkon would do the same without hesitation for Aymee.

There was little value in tormenting himself with questions of what might have happened. The past was finished; they could only move forward from where they were. They were alive and together, and for now, that was enough. That was reason to be thankful.

*T*HE GUN FIRES *with a deafening boom.*

Aymee's body jerked, and her eyes snapped open. Her vision cleared; Randall wasn't dropping into the sand with a shocked expression on his face, she wasn't on the beach, she wasn't anywhere familiar. There was no telling how large this place was — most of it was masked by gloom, cast in a palette of drab grays and blacks that made the air feel oppressive and thick. Seawater splashed restlessly against the walls below, and torrents of rainwater poured in from above.

She shivered, and Arkon tightened his arm around her.

"Is it normal for humans to sleep through such noise?" he asked. "The storm began during the night, but you didn't stir through most of it."

Tilting her head back, she looked up at him. His face was shadowed, but she caught a hint of the violet in his eyes nonetheless. "When we sleep deep enough." She winced at the pain speaking caused her and touched her tongue to the inside of her cheek. Her face throbbed — she likely had a nasty bruise — and her entire body ached as she shifted in Arkon's hold. The air was chilly, and she didn't want to leave his warmth. "Did you sleep at all?"

"Yes, a bit. Before the thunder began." He stretched a few of his tentacles over the floor in front of him. "How do you feel?"

"Sore, though I imagine you feel worse sitting on this concrete."

He smiled gently. "After a while, I couldn't feel much of anything at all. A small price to pay for your comfort."

"Oh!" Remembering his wound, she pushed away, but he didn't let her move far.

"I am fine, truly. When you are ready to get up, we will get up, but I doubt you're eager to face the chill."

"No, I'm not." She carefully settled against his chest, tucked her arms between their bodies, and drew her knees up. Arkon draped his tentacles over her exposed calves and feet. "Thank you."

"How do you feel...emotionally?" he asked. "I'd guess you don't experience situations like the one yesterday very often."

A flash lit the cavern for an instant, granting her a fleeting glimpse of Arkon's face. It was followed by a crack of thunder that rattled the stone around them. Bits of debris tumbled from the break in the ceiling and splashed into the water.

"Drained," she replied, gazing toward the hole. "I've dealt with emergencies in the clinic, but this... No, nothing like this." She frowned and looked back at Arkon. "Are *you* okay?"

"I am still angry that you came to harm. Still sorrowful that it ended in violence. But more than any of that, I'm grateful you are safe, and we're together." He lifted a hand and brushed her

JEWEL OF THE SEA

hair back from her cheek. "As much as I have locked myself away within the Facility, I've still shared in the struggles of my people. Our lives are dangerous. The sea is dangerous. It does not surprise me that land is, as well."

She reached up and took his hand, guiding it down to kiss his knuckles. "I hate that you're being hunted, and it'll only be worse now. They've seen you."

Arkon frowned and brushed the pad of his thumb over her skin. "You are the one who has been forced away from your home."

"I don't think Cyrus would have done anything. Not with Randall there."

"He would have."

"Not if you had left before—" She shook her head; Arkon was right. How could she look back on those events and believe Cyrus wouldn't have killed her? "It doesn't matter. What's done is done. How is your..." Eyes wide, she stared at Arkon's chest and tentatively traced her finger over the thin, raised scar that had been an open wound only hours before. "How?"

"I told you I just needed time. It only stayed open for so long yesterday because my movement while swimming wouldn't allow it to seal."

"But it's fully healed! It would take a few weeks for a cut like that to reach this point for a human."

"I am not a human, Aymee. And it was a relatively minor wound."

"This...this is fascinating!" She looked up and met his eyes, bubbling with excitement. "You heal this quickly with any injury?"

"It depends upon the nature and severity. We are not invincible, by any means. Cuts such as this are quickly healed, but more serious wounds take days, if they are not mortal to begin with. Jax once lost a tentacle during a hunt. It regenerated over the course of many weeks."

"Did they know this? The people who engineered your race?"

"They did." He smiled down at her, and her excitement was reflected in his eyes. "It was one of the traits inherent to the cephalopods they used as a basis for our design. As I mentioned, I believe they wanted us to be as self-sufficient as possible. Eliminating the necessity for regular medical attention would've gone a long way in that regard."

Lightning flashed again, dragging thunder in its wake. The sound vibrated through Aymee as she ran her fingertips over his scar. Arkon's hearts thumped against her other palm, which rested flat on his chest.

"It's amazing," she whispered.

What would Halora be like now if those long-dead humans had treated the kraken differently? Might humans and kraken have lived and worked together to build a mutual society on land and sea alike?

What wonders might have been accomplished with tools that could alter life, that could create it? How many lives had been lost in the years since the first landing because so much of that technology, so many of those techniques, had been swallowed up by time?

One of Arkon's tentacles cradled her bottom. Aymee started; she'd been so shocked and excited upon discovering his wound had healed that she'd straddled him without realizing.

He settled his hands on her hips.

She stared into his eyes, and awareness crackled across her skin — awareness of his touch, of his heat, of *him*.

Of her desire to have him.

Aymee hurriedly climbed off and sat on the step beside him. The fabric of her skirt offered no protection from the cold radiating from the concrete. She didn't want to force a repeat of the situation three days before, when he'd fled her attention; she couldn't handle the rejection right now.

"Are we going to the Facility?" she asked.

He shifted upright and faced her, frowning. "No, we will not be going. But I should."

"You're leaving me here?"

"I wish that I didn't have to, but there's no other choice, Aymee. I have to inform my people of what's happened, have to warn them, and there are supplies I can retrieve that will benefit you."

Relief flooded Aymee, easing her tense limbs and pounding heart. "Then you're coming back?"

"Of *course* I'm coming back. After everything, do you think I would truly abandon you?"

Now that he'd said it aloud, the ridiculousness of her fear dawned upon her. If her emotions hadn't already been so frayed, she might've felt shame, but she had to cut herself some slack — the last twelve hours or so had been some of the hardest of her life. "I'm sorry."

"No need for apologies."

"You can't take me with you?"

He shook his head. "You would not survive the journey, Aymee."

"Why?" But she already knew. She stared down at the concrete beneath her feet. With Arkon here, this place was dark but tolerable, and all the sounds — most of them produced by wind and water — were almost soothing once they faded to the recesses of her consciousness. But alone?

Every little noise could easily become a monster creeping toward her through the murk — Cyrus with his battered face dragging himself up the ladder, or Randall with a neat little bullet hole in his head.

It was irrational, but this place was foreign to her, and Aymee would have only her thoughts to keep her company until Arkon returned.

Aymee's imagination had always been active, especially when no one was around to distract her. Normally, that was a good thing — it allowed her immense surges of inspired creativity — but given her current mental state, the prospect frightened her.

"Even if you could hold your breath for long enough, the pressure at that depth could cause you harm. I will bring a PDS back with me. Those are the suits Macy wears to travel underwater. But...even with the suit, Aymee," he hooked a finger beneath her chin and turned her face back toward him, "I do not think it wise for me to take you to the Facility."

Her brows lowered. "Why not? Macy is there."

"As are kraken who only tolerate her presence because they fear repercussions from Jax, Dracchus, and myself."

"Is she in danger there?"

"No. The ones who disagree with her presence avoid her, but they will not dare do her harm unless things change drastically. If it was unsafe, Jax would take Macy and Sarina away immediately."

"And my being there?"

He sighed, blowing air from his siphons. "Macy has earned the respect of the kraken through much hardship. For some, that is encouragement to extend tentative trust to humans. For others, she is but the exception to the rule. You are an unknown entity."

Aymee nodded. "I understand." The possibility of seeing Macy again and finally meeting baby Sarina had been a beacon of hope in a dark landscape. That hope was now snuffed out. It was for the best, she knew — she didn't want to cause trouble for Arkon or Macy, especially if the stakes were so high. "We're staying here, then?"

"At least for a little while. We will have to decide on a way forward together." Arkon straightened and dragged the two canisters closer, opening their lids. He took the letters and the little carved stone out of the one he'd brought to the beach and placed them on the step beside her. "Macy has plenty to eat down there, so I would like you to eat some of the food you packed for her."

Aymee stared down at the items. She picked up the stone, clutched it in her fist, and held it to her chest.

Arkon removed a piece of cloth from the supplies — a hand-kerchief Macy's mother had embroidered — lifted the other empty canister, and carried it closer to the opening in the ceiling. Coiling his tentacles around one of the large mooring posts along the edge of the platform, he leaned out over the seawater.

Extending four of his front tentacles — two grasping the container, and two stretching the handkerchief over its top — he held the canister beneath a stream of water pouring in from above. After a minute or so, he pulled himself back onto the platform and returned to Aymee.

"How did you know to do that?" she asked.

"I've had many conversations with Macy," he said, standing the canister on the floor against the wall. "I was fascinated when

I saw her drinking water, so I naturally asked her questions until she eventually shooed me out into the hallway and closed the door behind me." Aymee chuckled, and Arkon smiled. "There was a waterfall in the cave where Jax originally brought her that provided for her needs. Because she was unable to boil the water initially, she used some cloth to filter some of the impurities. Our waterfall is only temporary, but if I can, I will bring water from the Facility. Macy says it is the cleanest she's ever had."

"Thank you."

Arkon crouched in front of her. His eyes dipped to her cheek and an angry glint sparked in them as he raised his hand and gently stroked her bruise. "I will be back before dark. Rest, if you can."

Her fingers tightened over the stone; he was leaving already? "Okay."

Arkon removed an apple from Aymee's supply canister and held it toward her. "Eat."

She took it in numb fingers. "I will."

He leaned forward and lightly pressed his forehead to hers. "I will return soon, Aymee. I will allow nothing to delay me this time."

She smiled at him, forcing the expression to remain in place as he pulled back and turned away. His shoulders rose with a slow, deep inhalation, and then he dropped off the edge of the platform, hitting the water with a large splash.

Thunder punctuated his sudden absence with a finality that made her stomach clench.

CHAPTER 11

THOUGH HIS MUSCLES BURNED WITH EXERTION, ARKON COULD not still his tentacles as the water drained from the Facility's entry chamber. His nervous energy had been of benefit during the journey, but now it fluttered inside him with no outlet, shifting into a sense of dread that churned his gut. He didn't intend to spend a single moment longer than necessary here. Aymee was alone, and the weight of her trauma from the prior day was but one of the problems she faced.

"Pressurization complete," the Computer finally announced.

Arkon hurried through the interior door, and his mind raced down several of the corridors at once, seeking out a disorganized list of supplies from a confused set of locations. He hesitated, dripping water onto the hallway floor.

What did humans *need* to survive?

Food and water. Seawater was no good, and there was no permanent supply of fresh water at the Broken Cavern, as far as he knew. And here at the Facility, Macy was the only one who had food fit for a human.

Using every handhold within reach to pull himself along, he hurried toward the cabins.

He halted abruptly after turning a corner.

"Can't transport anything without a container."

Shaking his head at himself, he turned around and wound through the corridors to the Pool Room, which held the largest airtight containers he knew of in the Facility.

The door slid open, and Arkon entered. He was mentally mapping what he could fit into the various container shapes and sizes when he looked up and stopped again.

Dracchus was beside the pool, powerful arms folded across his broad chest. He glanced at Arkon, creased his brow, and looked back down at the water.

"I do not understand this, Arkon. What is it meant to be?"

Jaw agape, Arkon could do nothing but stare for several seconds. Dracchus was the last person he might have expected to find here, studying the patterns Arkon had created on the bottom of the pool.

"It is...well... I think that... It is meant to be whatever you *feel* it is, Dracchus."

"But what is it to *you*?"

Arkon moved beside Dracchus and turned his attention to the design. Its creation seemed so long ago, now, it may as well have been the work of a stranger.

"To me, it is...motion."

Dracchus grunted.

After many seconds of increasingly awkward silence, Arkon backed away and went to the empty containers stacked along the wall.

"There is a strange scent upon you, Arkon."

Arkon paused in the middle of reaching for one of the large chests. "I...have been to a few new locations recently."

"Overnight?"

"I was caught up. Searching. For stones. I've only come for a container to bring some back here."

When Arkon glanced over his shoulder, Dracchus was facing him fully. The confusion that had been on the big kraken's face a moment before was gone, replaced by open suspicion.

"You are distracted," Dracchus said, moving closer, "but not as you normally are. What are you hiding, Arkon?"

Arkon looked back at the chest, grasped the handles on its sides, and lifted it from the stack. "Nothing."

He turned and carried the container toward the door.

Dracchus imposed himself in Arkon's path, tipped his chin down, and flared his nostrils. "That is the scent of a human."

"I visited Macy when—"

"You are still wet, Arkon. You just entered the Facility. And that is not Macy's scent."

Arkon envisioned one of the clocks that were in all the cabins — seconds ticking by, tumbling into the past one after another, each representing a bit longer that Aymee spent alone with her guilt in an unfamiliar place.

"And I am just leaving. If you would—"

"Arkon."

The potential paths the situation could take flowed through Arkon's mind in rapid succession over the course of an instant. He was faster and more agile than Dracchus, but he wasn't likely to outmaneuver the larger kraken in such close quarters. Even if he did, what would it accomplish? There was always the possibility of a challenge, but that would attract the attention of more kraken, and Arkon wanted only to obtain what he needed and leave. Besides, Dracchus had given up challenging Arkon long ago. Would he even be interested now?

Yes, of course he would be. When Dracchus had suspected Jax of treachery, he'd questioned Arkon tirelessly and had even followed him into unfamiliar waters to determine whether his suspicions were justified.

"I am gathering supplies for Aymee. I am sheltering her in the place Jax calls the Broken Cavern — the place you followed me to when you attacked Macy."

"Aymee? The woman you spoke to on the beach?"

"Yes."

Dracchus's brows fell, and his frown — which seemed to be his default expression — deepened. "You have her in your keeping?"

"Do you really require me to repeat everything I just told you?"

"Have you learned nothing from Jax?" Dracchus demanded. "This is foolish, Arkon. You told us the humans have hunters seeking our kind, and now you have taken one of their females?"

"I didn't *take* her, Dracchus," Arkon said, squeezing the container's handles. "The situation with the hunters has...escalated, and she was no longer safe there."

Dracchus straightened, lips parting and eyes widening. "They saw you."

Arkon clenched his jaw. Perhaps later, he'd find amusement in how he'd not cared for Dracchus's opinions, one way or another, a few months ago.

The air around Dracchus crackled; his frustration was palpable. "You put our people at risk, Arkon, over a human."

The guilt that had been building within Arkon flared and twisted into anger in a flash.

"Have *you* learned nothing from Jax?" Arkon growled. "My connection to that human is stronger than I have to any of our people, and I have done no wrong in spending time with her."

"She is your mate, then?"

Arkon hesitated; his instinct was to reply *yes*, but that wasn't true no matter how much he yearned for it. "It's...complicated. And what difference does it make? She helped Jax escape, so has she not proven herself a friend of our kind?"

A hint of crimson pulsed over Dracchus's skin. "The risk to our people was great enough during the situation with Macy. The danger has only increased, and you pushed on even though you were directly aware of the greater danger. We do not know the capabilities of these human hunters. What if they are able to reach our home?"

"They are but a single, small group of humans! They do not represent the entirety of their race."

"That Macy, Jax, and Sarina are here, safe and content, should tell you I know that, Arkon." Dracchus spoke through clenched teeth, his jaw muscles bulging. "Whether there is one of them or one hundred, they are an open threat to us. Yours is not the only blood that might cloud the water."

Arkon snapped his mouth shut. He'd been the one who endangered their people this time. The kraken had avoided detection by humans for hundreds of years; a few more months should have been simple. All Arkon had to do was stay away until the hunters decided The Watch was a waste of their time.

But he couldn't stay away from Aymee. Arkon refused to abandon her; even if she'd not chosen him yet, he'd chosen her.

"This needs to stop, Arkon."

"So...you will help me transport the necessary supplies to Aymee?"

Dracchus furrowed his brow and leaned back. "What?"

"I'll have many things to carry. The journey would be quicker with your help."

"Did you listen to anything I said?"

Arkon held out the container to Dracchus. "Yes. And you're correct. But that doesn't change my decision."

"Arkon, you—"

"I have chosen. You have a choice, as well. You can forget you saw me, and I will return to the Broken Cavern, laden with supplies for Aymee. You can tell the others that I am keeping a human and give Kronus another supposed betrayal to rail against. Or you can help me, and know that I would be immensely grateful, as little as my gratitude must be worth. However *you* choose, I am returning to her.

"What's done is done. She did not want to leave her people behind, but for now, she has. I do not wish to leave my people behind, but I will if I am forced to make a choice."

Dracchus was silent for a long while as he scrutinized Arkon, his expression surprisingly difficult to read.

"If you consider it a matter of honor or duty, Dracchus, I will accept your challenge."

Those words seemed to strike Dracchus deeper than anything else Arkon had said. The big kraken's eyes flared for a moment in surprise, and he shook his head. "You have declined my challenges for years."

"I am aware."

"Abyss take you, Arkon," Dracchus grumbled. He accepted the container.

Arkon turned away and released a shaky breath. He'd taken a

gamble in pushing Dracchus; their exchange had been more likely to end with the two of them out in the water, facing one another down in front of a crowd. There was no time for such displays.

He collected another container from the wall. Before he moved away, the lockers caught his attention.

Encountering Dracchus in here had disrupted what little clarity of purpose Arkon possessed when he'd entered — he might've left without taking a diving suit for Aymee.

Placing the container on a nearby bench, he retrieved a PDS and the accompanying mask from one of the lockers. The system's outward simplicity belied its sophistication; the relatively small piece of black material stretched to fit the wearer's body almost perfectly, and, when paired with the mask — itself looking like a plain, curved piece of glass or plastic — protected the user from variations in pressure and temperature, in addition to filtering oxygen out of the surrounding water.

He placed the items in the container, closed it, and carried the chest to Dracchus.

"What else?" the big kraken asked.

"Fresh water. I believe there are suitable containers for that in the room attached to the Mess. And food. We'll need to see if Macy has any she can spare for the time being."

"Is there truly going to be this much food?" Dracchus dipped his chin toward the chest he was holding.

"Not likely," Arkon replied, moving through the doorway and into the hall, with Dracchus just behind, "but I am certain there are other things I will need to bring."

"She has shelter, and you are bringing food. What more could she require?"

"I don't know. Human things."

Dracchus grunted.

They stopped in the Mess. In the connected room — Macy called it a kitchen and used it to cook her meals — Arkon located two large plastic jugs. He rinsed them out, filled them with water from the sink, fastened their lids, and placed them in Dracchus's container. Dracchus frowned but said nothing.

Arkon led the way to the Cabins at a rapid pace, his sense of urgency restored now that he'd obtained assistance.

Jax and Macy's door was open when Arkon reached it. He peered around the doorframe to see Jax — the mighty hunter and explorer — near the bed, making strange, exaggerated expressions to entertain the youngling in his arms.

Arkon tapped the edge of the chest on the doorframe.

Jax looked up and smiled. "We expected to see you yesterday. Come inside, Arkon."

Despite the invitation and the countless hours he'd spent in this room with Jax, Macy, and Sarina, Arkon always felt as though he were intruding upon a private space when he entered. He supposed it was a simple matter of his people's ways having been ingrained in him since childhood — kraken kept to their own dens. Entering another kraken's den was enough to spark a fight.

Arkon crossed the threshold.

Jax furrowed his brow when he looked at the chest in Arkon's hand, and his eyes widened when Dracchus entered behind Arkon.

"My instinct says I should not ask," Jax said.

"Is Macy in?" Arkon knew Jax wouldn't allow her to wander far without one of the three kraken present alongside her and at least two weapons on her person, but he couldn't stand there in silence.

JEWEL OF THE SEA

"She just stepped out of the shower." Frowning, Jax's eyes shifted from Arkon to Dracchus and back again. Sarina wrapped her tentacles around his forearm and made little cooing sounds. She turned her large eyes to Arkon.

"Oh. Well, I suppose we will wait until she is all done." Arkon turned and placed the container on the floor. When he rose, he moved to Jax and held the tip of a tentacle to Sarina. She latched onto it with her little fist and shook it before bringing it to her mouth "She's getting strong."

"Arkon…" Jax said.

There was a thump as Dracchus put down his chest, and he came up immediately behind Arkon, looking over his shoulder. Sarina turned her attention to the big kraken and smiled. She released her hold on both Arkon and her father and stretched her chubby arms toward Dracchus.

Arching a brow, Arkon moved aside. His surprise and confusion were mirrored in Jax's face as Dracchus gently lifted Sarina and brought her close. Her tentacles wrapped around his wrists and her hands cupped his cheeks. She made more of her baby sounds and blew out of her siphons.

Dracchus mimicked her, and she smiled so broadly that she nearly tipped backward.

Jax and Arkon exchanged a perplexed look.

The bathroom door opened and Arkon's gaze shifted to Macy as she stepped out. She paused, one foot over the threshold, before a smile brightened on her face. "Arkon!"

She approached them, casting a warm look at Dracchus and Sarina as though it wasn't a strange sight. "It never stops surprising me how fast she's advancing compared to a human newborn." Her smile faded slightly. "She's only four weeks old but she's so alert, and she's more responsive and mobile than a six-month-old. I feel like she's growing too fast."

"As I told you, Macy, kraken younglings develop quickly after birth," Jax said gently, putting an arm around her shoulder and drawing her against his side. "Her growth will slow when she gets older."

"But she won't be a baby for long." Macy sighed wistfully. She pecked a kiss on Jax's cheek, turned her gaze to Arkon, and stepped out of her mate's embrace, eagerness gleaming in her eyes. "Did Aymee have more letters for me?"

"Yes, she did," Arkon said. "But...I do not have them."

Macy glanced at the container and frowned. "What do you mean?"

"There is a situation," Dracchus said. He had Sarina up high, moving her around as though she were flying. She waved her arms and tentacles in a pantomime of swimming.

"What situation?" Macy demanded.

"Aymee is safe. Her injury was only a minor one," Arkon replied.

"*What?*"

"A bruise! She's only bruised. She was struck in the face by one of the hunters yesterday, but it should heal normally."

Macy stared at him, jaw agape, eyes wide, but there was a moment's delay before true anger tinted her expression. Fury etched itself into every line of her features. "Tell me what happened."

Arkon nodded. He spoke rapidly, telling them about the exchange from beginning and end, leaving out his regrets — even if different choices might've resulted in a different outcome, it was no longer important. The past was done.

"Bring her here," Macy said as soon as he finished. It wasn't a request.

"I do not believe that to be a wise choice, currently," Arkon replied.

"What do you mean? She's out there alone and hurt. I know how that feels. She should be here, where we can keep her safe."

Jax winced at her words but shook his head. "Macy, this place is not even fully safe for you, and you nearly died to protect a kraken. It would be an even greater risk for her."

"She could have died protecting Arkon! How is that any different? She's been trying to turn the hunters away from kraken, surely she's proven herself enough."

"No one outside this room has witnessed any of the things she's done. For some, our word will not be enough," Jax said. "Another human brought here without the approval of our people as a whole might well be enough for Kronus to throw everything into chaos."

"He does not need everyone's support," Dracchus said. "He only needs them to doubt, and it will further his goals."

Macy visibly deflated. "Then what can we do? I hate that she's out there by herself."

Seeing her so suddenly resigned hurt Arkon; his spirits sank. In all his life, Macy had been only the second person he'd considered a friend, and he did not enjoy feeling as though he were the cause of her distress.

"She won't be," he said. "Help me gather whatever will be useful to her. We have fresh water, and if you have food to spare, it would be of benefit. I do not know what else, though I am certain there is more."

"I'll gather things for her." She closed the distance between them and wrapped her arms around him, hugging him tightly. Arkon returned her embrace. "Thank you. If it were anyone else, I'd probably still be arguing to have her brought here...but I trust you."

Once she released Arkon, Jax hooked a tentacle around Macy's waist and drew her back against his chest, enfolding her in his arms. Arkon exchanged a look with him; there was no threat from Jax, but he wasn't likely to ever be comfortable with another male touching her, with another male's *scent* on her.

And wouldn't Arkon himself feel the same regarding Aymee?

"I will keep her safe, Macy."

CHAPTER 12

TIME HAD NEVER HELD MUCH MEANING TO AYMEE IN THE
Watch; she woke with the sunrise most days, worked in the
clinic, painted, sketched, visited her friends, and readied for bed
around sunset. On her few free days, she often helped with
other duties — mostly tending crops, before Macy had left.

But the passage of time had altered after she met Arkon.
Days spent in longing and anticipation dragged on through
eternity, while moments with him fluttered by much too
quickly, falling away into the past with startling finality.

Worst of all was time passed alone and scared in a cold, dark,
unfamiliar place.

The rain continued long after Arkon had left, but the
thunder and lightning diminished as the storm swept inland.
Despite their lessened intensity, each bone-rattling boom quickened her heart and shortened her breath, leaving her on edge.

She glanced toward the entry tunnel frequently, seeking
signs of Arkon's light in the dark water. Eventually, the hunger
gnawing at her stomach grew unbearable, and she finally drew

the canister closer. She relinquished her white-knuckled grip on the carved stone and placed it in the container for safe keeping. After eating the apple Arkon had handed her, she devoured one of the muffins her mother had baked for Macy — after everything, she *still* felt a pang of guilt at doing so — and drank from the water he'd collected.

Aymee wasn't keen on wandering this dank, dangerous place; with little to do but wait, she read her letter from Macy, angling the paper toward the grayish light spilling in with the rain.

Aside from her concern about the rangers, Macy's words were happy. She'd written about Sarina's rapid development — she could already swim on her own! — and life in the Facility. Though she hadn't fully recovered from giving birth, Macy was up and moving without trouble.

Smiling to herself, Aymee read through the letter again and again; she wasn't so desperate as to open the letters sent along by Macy's parents. After a time, she returned the letter to the canister, replaced the lid, and lay on the cold, hard floor with an arm curled beneath her head. She watched the run-off pouring through the ceiling gap and listened to the seawater thrashing against the concrete below.

Her eyelids soon grew heavy, and she lapsed into a fitful sleep.

A loud splash woke her. The sound echoed through the dark chamber. Her eyes went immediately to the hole; the sky had dimmed, and night was fast approaching.

Another splash.

Gasping, Aymee jerked upright. Something thumped against the metal ladder leading down into the water.

A figure squatted at the edge of the platform, leaning over it.

Arkon.

"Just pass them up," he whispered. "That's why I handed you mine to begin with."

"I can manage," replied a deeper voice from below him.

"But you do not *need* to."

"Who is that, Arkon?" Aymee asked, easing closer.

Arkon lifted his torso and glanced at her, offering a smile. "My goal was to not wake you, Aymee. Dracchus is helping." He turned toward the water. "*Helping*," he repeated.

A grunt of assent came from below. Arkon swayed back as he caught the large chest Dracchus tossed up. He hurriedly set it aside to catch the second chest just before it struck him.

"That was juvenile, Dracchus."

Arkon moved toward Aymee.

Her lips twitched with amusement before Dracchus hauled himself up the ladder, drawing her attention. Only his head had been above the surface of the water the one time she'd seen him — the night Macy left The Watch. Between the sea's motion, the poor lighting, and his dark coloring, she hadn't been able to make out much detail.

When he reached the platform and stood on his tentacles, Aymee's eyes widened. Jax and Arkon were both big — at least two meters tall without stretching — but Dracchus was *huge*. His shoulders were at least half again as wide as Arkon's, and his body was thick with muscle. Even in the relative gloom, his eyes were stunning amber that stood in stark contrast to his black skin and gray stripes.

"Thank you for helping," Aymee said.

Dracchus studied her in silence for a time before finally nodding. "You have helped my people. It is only right that I help you."

Aymee frowned and folded her hands in her lap. "I feel like I've made a mess of things."

As Arkon moved the containers closer to Aymee, Dracchus shook his head. "Not you. Him. But he was persuasive enough to convince me to help, anyway."

Aymee glanced between Arkon and Dracchus. "What did he say?"

"He said you were—"

"I was simply honest and forthright about the situation." Arkon pushed the first chest before Aymee and opened the lid. "Macy helped us gather what would be useful for you."

Her heart warmed when she saw the items within — clothes, bedding, a hairbrush, soaps, and more. A letter rested atop it all, Aymee's name scrawled on the paper in familiar handwriting. She picked it up and opened it.

AYMEE,

I wish more than anything you could be here with me. Know that we will do whatever we can to make it happen, but for now, it's not safe. I trust Arkon, and I know you do, too. We'll figure something out soon. Until then, I hope all of this helps.

Macy

"OH, I could hug her right now," Aymee said. It hurt to smile, but that didn't stop her.

"There's food and more fresh water in the other container. I know this is not an ideal place to stay, but I want it to be as comfortable for you as possible while we're here."

"Thank you, Arkon."

He slithered closer to her and extended his arm, lightly pressing his hand over hers. "How do you feel?"

She brushed her thumb against his, tracing the claw to its tip. "I'm okay."

Arkon lifted her hand and leaned down, pressing his lips to her knuckles. "I am sorry I was away for so long."

"I know you would've returned sooner if you could have. And all of this," she gestured toward the large containers, "is amazing."

Dracchus approached, stopping a couple of meters away, and sank down to her eye level. "I will not ask you to betray your people, but we need to know whatever you can tell us about these hunters to protect ourselves."

Aymee slowly withdrew her hand from Arkon's grasp as she faced Dracchus; she immediately missed its warmth and comfort. "What do you want to know?"

Arkon slid into place beside her and slipped a tentacle around her waist, draping its tip over her thigh.

"Anything you are willing to tell me. Arkon told us what happened on the beach. These humans do not seem to be your friends, but you know more about them than we."

"It's...complicated. I think one of them, Cyrus, is only inter- ested in the thrill of the hunt, but the others... Their leader, Randall, wants to protect people, but he's confused." She cringed as the memory of him getting shot replayed in her mind. "He knows what I told him about the kraken is true, but all the same, he's been trained to view your existence as a threat, and he's dedicated to eliminating such threats."

"Will they be able to hunt for us underwater?" Dracchus asked.

"I don't know. I haven't seen them with anything that would

allow that, but that doesn't mean they don't have it. They walk around with guns, but they haven't exactly opened up their equipment and tactics for us to study. The one diving suit I know of in The Watch hasn't worked in decades."

Dracchus nodded, brows lowering, and looked at the floor. "How many hunters have come?"

Aymee glanced down, recalling their faces, and only then realized her fingers were absently petting Arkon's tentacle. He curled the limb's tip around her hand. She stilled and peered up at him.

His pupils dilated, his alien eyes bright with intensity.

She cleared her throat and looked at Dracchus. "Seven, I think."

"We must remain alert." Dracchus swept his gaze over their surroundings. "Do you require aid with anything else?"

"No. I think you've brought plenty, thank you." She tucked her hair behind her ears and frowned. "For what it's worth, I'm sorry. I didn't want this to happen. Never meant for it to. I tried to turn them away from this, but..." She spread her hands, palms up.

Dracchus shook his head. "I do not hold you responsible. What Arkon says about us being part human must be true. Both our peoples are prone to stupidity."

She smiled. "They are."

"I will tell the others of the situation with the hunters." Turning, Dracchus made his way to the edge of the platform, where he hesitated. "The last time I was here, I pushed the matter with Macy and Jax into violence. I do not wish for any more of it between our people. But if they attack us, we will fight."

Just as she'd told Randall. She didn't want more bloodshed,

but the kraken were well within their rights to defend themselves.

How many rangers were on Halora? Would it be a single, brutal battle, or the beginning of a prolonged war?

Aymee looked at Arkon; her heart ached at the thought of him caught in the middle of all this, and the pain only increased when she thought of Macy, Jax, and Sarina. What would Macy do if something happened to her mate, to her child? The guilt would eat her alive.

What would the *humans* do if they discovered Sarina?

"I understand," she said. "I just hope it doesn't come to that."

Dracchus nodded. He lingered for a few more seconds before dropping into the water with a huge splash.

"The outcome of all this is not predetermined. We will find a way, Aymee," Arkon said.

"Is the Facility really hard to find?"

"It is located some distance away from shore, in a relatively remote area on the seafloor. However, the diving suits have integrated computers that seem to be able to access its systems and may even be able to pinpoint its location from afar."

She scowled. "Then let's hope they *don't* have any of those suits."

He smoothed the crease between her brows with the pad of his thumb. "For now, let us not worry about things we have no immediate control over. Are you hungry or thirsty? We brought warmer clothes, and Macy included some handheld lights if you are tired of the gloom."

That simple, considerate touch was enough to make her smile. "Will you eat with me?"

"Of course. Macy gave us some spinefish she cooked earlier. She said we were to eat it today, to ensure it would not spoil."

Remaining low, he moved to the second chest and opened it. The jugs of water were immediately apparent, and they were accompanied by a variety of food — most of it forage from the jungle. Arkon removed a wrapped bundle and held it out to Aymee.

She took it and peeled back the cloth to reveal large fillets of white, flaky meat. Their mouthwatering aroma wafted to her and made her stomach growl.

"Come sit beside me, Arkon."

After rummaging through the chest for a moment, he produced a plastic cup. He removed the cap from one of the water containers, lifted the jug with one hand, and filled the cup. The ease with which he did so was a testament to his strength — the container looked to hold at least fifteen liters. Her eyes flowed over the play of muscles in his arm, shoulder, and chest, and then fell to the darker skin beginning at his waist.

She'd felt the hard press of his now-hidden shaft once when she lay atop him after their game on the beach. She wanted to *see* it.

While Macy was recovering in the clinic, she'd revealed that she'd been intimate with Jax, and Aymee's curiosity had made it impossible to hold back her questions. She'd wanted to know *everything*. Macy had described the anatomy of male kraken in detail despite her obvious embarrassment.

Once the jug was down and the cap replaced, Arkon returned to his spot beside her, trading the cup of water for a fish fillet.

"Thank you," she said, dragging her gaze away from him. The sudden discomfort between her legs had her shifting on the hard floor.

"Are you all right, Aymee? You appear flushed."

"I'm fine," she replied quickly, taking a drink from the cup and setting it aside. "Macy said you normally eat the fish alive." Anything to steer the conversation away from her body, from its reaction to him, anything to distract her. She couldn't stand another rejection, but *God*, she wanted to touch him. Wanted *him* to touch *her*.

"Raw, yes. Most fish don't tend to survive after you take a few bites out of them."

He scooped bite-sized pieces of meat into his mouth with his claws, offering her a fleeting glimpse of his pointed teeth.

"Do you have a preference?" she asked.

He stared down at the meat on his palm. "Perhaps it is simply because it is different from everything I've known before, but I prefer most of it cooked. The changes it causes in the flavor and texture of different meats is fascinating."

Aymee smiled. "I love how you find pleasure in the smallest things."

"There's always something new to be excited about, even if it seems insignificant at a glance. I suppose, though our particular interests are different, Jax and I are more similar in our curiosity than I once thought." He lifted his gaze to Aymee. "Is it not also similar to the way you seem to find the beauty in everything you see?"

She stared into his strange eyes, which were vibrant even in the dim light. When she'd first met him, she'd only seen his eyes amidst the sand and water, and they alone had captivated, had drawn her into their uniqueness and depth.

Beautiful.

That's what Arkon was to her.

∼

AYMEE PICKED UP A FLASHLIGHT; it was a long, thin, plastic device that didn't look like it could light up her little bedroom, much less this place. The moment she clicked on the switch, it cast a broad, powerful cone of bright white light from its end, annihilating the shadows in its path.

She nodded appreciatively, turning the light off and on several times. "Have you ever explored this place, Arkon?"

"No." Arkon looked around the massive chamber, most of which was cloaked in darkness. "I've only been here a few times before I brought you here. Jax has tried, but he said the doors would not open."

Shining her light into one of the chests, Aymee searched through its contents. She was thankful for everything Macy and Arkon had thought to pack. "And they can't be broken into?"

"I do not know. I assume Jax must have tried, but I do not believe he found any success."

Aymee removed a stack of folded clothing from the chest and set it aside, reaching back into the container. Near the bottom, her fingers brushed over an unfamiliar fabric, thicker and heavier than the rest. The flashlight's beam revealed a hexagonal pattern on the dark material. She lifted the garment out of the chest.

It was a PDS — Personal Diving System. Though it appeared small, she knew it would fit almost anyone, regardless of size or body shape. Until Jax had brought the injured Macy to town, the only other such suit Aymee had seen was the one on display in The Watch's small history museum.

The suit Macy wore had no apparent seams or seals, and none of the tools in the clinic had been able to cut the material. Only through sheer luck had Aymee's fingers brushed over the small plastic piece on the suit's wrist, activating the holographic display that introduced her to Sam, the suit's computer.

He'd been frustratingly cheerful as he opened the suit's seal, allowing Aymee to peel it off Macy's feverish body.

Folding the suit over one arm, Aymee glanced into the bottom of the chest, where a clear mask lay.

"Arkon, didn't you say the computers in these suits can connect to the computer in the Facility?"

"They can. It allows Macy to bypass the entry codes."

"Do you think it could work on the doors here?" She looked up at him as he approached.

Arkon tilted his head and smiled. Excitement gleamed in his eyes. "I think it is well worth an attempt."

"Then let's do it." She rose to her feet with the suit in one hand and the flashlight in the other.

Bending down, Arkon plucked up another flashlight and turned it on. He ran its beam over the faded painting on the nearby wall and hesitated. "I was hoping to show you this when there was sunlight to see it by."

Aymee stepped closer and studied the painting. Time had faded its colors, and the paint had peeled, chipped, and flaked away in many places, but she could still make out the people it depicted.

"Even though I know more about how it must have been created than ever before, I find it no less amazing. I puzzled over it for days after Jax first showed it to me. And when I finally met a human and asked how it had been made, she told me she knew someone who could do this." He turned his head and looked at her. "But this, despite its scale, is nothing compared to what you can do. Even when it was fresh and undamaged, I doubt it would have compared."

A spark of pleasure lit inside her, and Aymee's cheeks heated. She tucked the suit beneath her arm and rubbed a finger over the paint. "What were you trying to puzzle out?"

He lifted a hand and gently touched the painting, as well. "I don't know. How the colors were brought together. How it could look so disjointed up close, but so coherent from farther back. How it could appear alive, despite so many years of damage."

She glanced at him. "Think of it as...a moment in time. A single moment of motion, of feeling and expression, frozen and forever captured." Leaning closer to the wall, she traced a fingertip over the colors; they were only blobs and smears so close, but she knew each brushstroke had been deliberate. "Everything in that moment has a shape to it, and those shapes are so familiar that sometimes you only need to imply their presence. Our minds take all those little shapes and fill in the blanks to make something whole."

Stepping back, she looked at Arkon fully. "It's just like how the stones you set up on the beach for me implied motion, even though they were still."

His hand lingered on the wall, but he dipped his head. "So, then...it is a matter of understanding the component pieces and how they relate to each other to create something greater?"

"Yes, and how to use them to communicate what you want to express."

Arkon dropped his hand and met her gaze. "What do you seek to express when you paint?"

"Life. Beauty. Emotion."

He smiled. "Then you are truly successful at your craft."

Aymee chuckled. "We'll paint together someday."

"I brought the paints and brushes you gave me. They are in one of the chests."

"You did?" Anticipation swept through her; she couldn't wait to create art not just for him, but *with* him, and it would provide an enjoyable distraction from her worries. "Then we'll be painting together soon. We're likely to be stuck here for a while, right?"

"Though I cannot deny I am eager to spend the time with you, I am sorry, Aymee." He reached forward and took her hand in his. "These are not the circumstances under which I had wanted to share this painting with you."

She turned her hand to fit it over his palm, curling her fingers around his. "Don't apologize, Arkon. I'm happy you're here with me, whatever the circumstances."

He gave her hand a soft squeeze. For a moment, she thought he'd pull away, but he hesitated, maintaining his gentle grip. "We had best get to it before the hour grows much later. I imagine the chance at a relatively warm and dry spot to sleep is too good to forgo."

Aymee grinned. "This suit better work."

CHAPTER 13

ARKON HELD AYMEE'S HAND AS HE LED HER UP THE STEPS TO THE next level and turned right. His presence made this dreary, broken down place bearable — without him, its emptiness, gloom, and dilapidation might have crushed her. She swept her light over the walls, which had been stained by water and time, and noted several small cracks. Bits of debris that had fallen from the walls and ceiling lay scattered on the floor.

While the lower level's edge was lined with thick mooring posts that were spanned by heavy chains in some places, the second tier had a waist-high guardrail that blended seamlessly with the railing of the two bridges. Aymee glanced over her shoulder; for a fleeting instant, she imagined some huge watercraft anchored there, its metal-and-plastic hull gleaming under long-dead lights.

They stopped and turned toward a pitch-black corridor to their left. Aymee shined her light onto the wall over it. Like everything else here, the words were worn, but remained legible.

AUTHORIZED PERSONNEL ONLY.

"Turn off your light," Arkon said.

They both clicked off their flashlights.

"There is a light at the end of the hallway," he said.

"I don't see anything."

"It's very small. Very faint. A single point of red..."

"Has it always been on?"

"I do not know. I have never noticed it before." Without releasing her hand, he moved ahead of her into the corridor, switching his light on again.

She turned her light on and followed him.

Though she'd seen construction like this in The Watch — at least one or two of the old concrete structures had hallways like this — there was something oppressive about this space despite it only being three or four meters deep. Perhaps it was instinctual claustrophobia, but the walls and ceiling felt too close after the relatively open area of the bay, where the ceiling was so high she'd yet to see it through the cloying shadows.

They passed two large metal doors — one on each side, both with small keypads built into their frames — as they moved. Arkon held his light on the door at the end of the corridor. It looked like the others at first glance, but Arkon gestured to its keypad.

"There."

They shifted their lights away, and she saw what he'd noticed from the other end of the hallway — a small red light on the upper corner of the keypad.

"The other keypads are dark," Arkon said.

"So, this is the only one working?"

"Maybe. It could be the only one with functioning power. This would be the spot to try, I'd guess."

Aymee straightened and considered the keypad, running her fingers over the flat numbers. "You said there was a keypad to enter the Facility. Did you try the code here?"

Arkon extended a hand and entered a sequence of numbers. The red light flashed and returned to its dull, constant glow.

"How did Macy's suit allow her access?"

"She said it asked her when she drew near. Perhaps if you activate the suit, the system will recognize its location and do the same?"

Adjusting her hold on the flashlight, Aymee felt along the suit until she found the wrist piece. She traced her fingers along its shallow grooves. Light flared from it, as intense as that cast by their flashlights, and formed into a glowing orb.

"Hello!" The hologram pulsed as it spoke. "I am your system assistant and monitor, Sam. How may I be of service?"

Aymee glanced at Arkon. The blue glow cast deep shadows on his cheeks, and his pupils were thin lines as he stared at the hologram.

"Sam, can you grant us access?" Aymee asked.

The hologram flickered and was silent for a moment. "You are standing at the IDC Personnel Entry Door. Is this what you require access to?"

"Yes."

"This facility has been placed on emergency standby power." There was a heavy click from the door. "The lock has been disengaged, but the door's automated opening mechanism is currently inoperative. Please open manually for entry."

Aymee stared at the door; the excitement of discovery faded suddenly, giving over to uncertainty. This place had been abandoned for hundreds of years. What would they find on the other side of this door? If the huge room behind them felt lonely and stifling, how would the interior chambers feel?

"Sam, can you power on the facility?"

The hologram pulsed for several seconds. "Manual override for emergency standby power has been engaged. It will need to be released physically to restore power."

"How do we accomplish that, Sam?" Arkon asked.

"The power override switch is in the control room. Turn counterclockwise to deactivate standby mode."

Aymee took a deep breath and reached for the door handle.

Arkon settled a hand on her forearm, gently guiding her arm down, and moved in front of her. "I do not believe there to be anything dangerous on the other side, Aymee, but I would rather stay between you and the unknown all the same."

She stepped back with a nod. Arkon grasped the hand and pulled; the door groaned, and he leaned his weight to one side, muscles tensing.

If *he* had to strain to open it, she would never have managed.

Finally, metal scraped against metal, and the door slid aside. A gust of cool, clean air hit Aymee. The corridor beyond the threshold was lit by a faint red glow from above, just enough to cast everything in deep shadow.

Arkon straightened, and they turned their flashlights forward.

Though crafted from the same slate gray concrete as the rest of the building, the walls inside were cleaner and showed little of the wear evident in the exterior. The corridor led first to an intersection, where another hallway bisected it, and ended at a door some fifteen meters beyond that.

She followed Arkon inside.

He stopped at the intersection and Aymee glanced up at the

red overhead lights. Though they were solid, they all seemed to flow from the ends of their respective corridors to this meeting place, from which they led to the entry door.

She raised her flashlight to look past Arkon, down the center hall. The small sign beside the door at the end read CONTROL ROOM.

"There," she said.

They moved toward it, passing more doors on either side.

"Control room lock has been disengaged," Sam said. Aymee started at his voice; it had been amplified by the concrete.

Arkon grasped the handle and pulled, nearly falling into the wall — this door slid smoothly, and he'd likely put too much force into it. Arkon met her eyes when she chuckled.

"Everything in here has been protected from the moisture and salt outside," she said.

"Well, it is nice to hear you laugh, even if it's at my expense, in this case."

Smiling, she turned her attention to the control room. It was lit with the same dim glow as the hallways, but movement ahead caught her attention — a blinking red light. The beam of her flashlight revealed a control console, atop which the light blinked beside a handle. Both were set within a square of striped red paint.

"That must be it!" Aymee stepped into the room, wrapped her fingers around the handle, and turned it counterclockwise.

There was a low rumbling in the floor. Instruments flickered on along the console, and holographic projections of screens materialized in the air.

"Primary power restored," a female voice said from overhead.

"That is the voice of the Computer in the Facility," Arkon said from beside Aymee.

The red emergency lights went out, replaced by bright white illumination an instant later. Aymee squinted against its intensity. She turned off the flashlight and placed both it and the suit atop the console.

"Performing diagnostic scan," the computer said. "Structural damage detected in submarine pen. Rerouting power from damaged lighting. Communications array non-operational. Submarine pen ventilation system operating at thirty-five percent efficiency. All other systems operational."

Aymee turned to glance behind her. "And we now have li—" She shrieked as she caught sight of something in the corner of her eye and leapt back against Arkon.

He encircled her with his arms and turned her away, shielding her with his body. The tenseness in his muscles quickly faded.

"It is all right, Aymee," he said gently.

Heart pounding, Aymee peered around him.

A skeleton lay face up on the floor. Bones yellow with age, its empty eye sockets stared blankly at Arkon and Aymee, and its dislocated jaw hung open in an awful grin. Its uniform, though intact, was filthy, and the floor beneath it was stained dark. One of the skeleton's arms was outstretched, fingers curled over the grip of a pistol.

Slowly, Aymee crept from behind Arkon and walked around the skeleton, gingerly avoiding the stain — she knew it was blood, even if it wasn't the right color anymore. By the uneven lay of the skull, she guessed the back had been shattered by an exit wound.

"He killed himself," she said.

Arkon clicked off his flashlight and set it on the console beside hers. He lowered himself near the remains and reached out with a hand, delicately turning the skull to get a better look. "Is that normal for humans to do?"

Aymee pressed her lips together and furrowed her brows. "Sometimes..."

He lifted his gaze to her, tilting his head to the side. "Why?"

"I mean, it isn't *normal*. Self-harm is often a result of mental illness, distress, or extreme fear..." She glanced around the room before her eyes settled back on the skeleton. "Do...the kraken know of this place?"

"Jax, Dracchus, and myself, but only the main chamber. If our people knew of it before, that knowledge was lost before I was born." Arkon rose. "Is there... something we should do?"

Aymee shook her head. "For now, no. We can take him to sea later...and hope there are not others."

"Your people give your dead to the sea, also?" Despite the morbidity of the situation, there was unmasked curiosity in his voice.

She carefully returned to Arkon's side. "We do. Families take their loved ones out for their final goodbyes."

"We do not have families in the same manner you do, but the hunters carry our dead away from the Facility to be reclaimed by the sea. It is symbolic of the cycle of life — the sea provides for us and sustains us, and in the end, it claims us all."

Aymee took his hand and traced a fingertip over his knuckles and down to the webbing between his fingers. "I wonder what things would be like now, had our people lived together peacefully."

"No one can say with any certainty." He raised a tentacle and brushed its tip across the back of her hand. "But, selfish as it may be, I would not wish to change any of that history."

Aymee tipped her head back to look up at him. "Why?"

Arkon smoothed his palm over her hair. "Because I would not want to place the chances of us meeting in jeopardy."

Warmth blossomed in her chest as she stared into his otherworldly violet eyes; they were layered with color and emotion, and she wasn't sure there were enough shades of purple to encompass their depth.

Her hand tightened over his. Perhaps her earlier fears were unfounded; how could he say such things if he didn't desire her? He showed it in his every gesture, his every touch, word, and glance. Whatever had happened between them that morning on the beach, there'd been good reason for his retreat. Arkon would never purposely hurt her.

She stood her toes and placed a light kiss on his lips. "Me too." Smiling, she released his hand and stepped back. "Let's see what we can find on the console."

"Yes," he said distractedly.

Aymee touched the main screen. The projection presented a variety of choices; she perused them slowly, not sure what she was looking for. *Maintenance, Temperature Control, Core Monitoring, Surveillance, Personnel Records.* She tapped *Operations Logs.*

"Please enter your access code to—" the computer said, and then the screen — and all the others around it — flickered. "Computer security systems have been rebooted. Welcome back, Captain Wright. Please create a new access code."

Aymee looked at Arkon.

He leaned forward and entered a series of numbers. "Zero eight one three zero five," he said.

"Access code reset." The projection displayed a series of still images, each with numbers at its bottom, arranged in neat rows — five across and five down, with an arrow at the bottom indicating more. All the images were of the same man, though the background and his clothing differed in some of them.

"That is the same code we use to enter the Facility," Arkon said. "I didn't know what any of these symbols were until Macy taught me."

"The kraken can't read?" Aymee asked.

"In the beginning, I believe at least a handful knew how. But it was not a skill that was passed down through the generations."

"And the code was all you knew?"

"We learned by the pattern." He smiled to himself, and moved his finger in the air, pantomiming entry of the code. "Always the same buttons in the same order. Jax and I later realized that we recognized the symbols on the buttons, though they held no meaning to us."

"I'm glad she was able to teach you." She turned her attention back to the screens. "Do you think that's him?"

He glanced over his shoulder at the skeleton. "I do not see a particular resemblance, but it's possible."

Aymee stared at him. She waited for the hint of a smile on his lips, for a glint of humor in his eyes, but his expression remained serious.

Arkon furrowed his brow. "What?"

Unable to hold it in, she laughed. As horrible as she felt about it — that had been a living human being, however long ago — it was liberating to find some humor in the situation. "I can't believe you said that."

"But...it is true. Isn't it?"

"Yes, but of *course* there'd be no resemblance *now*."

"Hmm." He glanced at the remains again. "You're right. Though the bone structure influences a person's facial features, it is difficult to picture without the overlying musculature and—"

He paused when he saw the smile on her face.

"I think I understand," Arkon said. "You were amused by the absurdity of my initial response?"

Aymee chuckled and brushed her fingers over his arm. "You're adorable."

His skin took on a faint purple tinge. "I do have a tendency to overthink things."

"I don't mind, Arkon. It's what makes you you." She turned back to the console and swiped her finger down, scrolling through the stills. The numbers on each one, she realized, were dates and times. "These are all marked in Standard Galactic Year. That hasn't been used on Halora for at least three hundred years."

Arkon leaned closer to study the numbers on one of the images. "How can you tell?"

"The colonists keep the year based on when our ancestors first landed, three hundred and sixty-one years ago. I think they switched sometime after we stopped receiving supplies from off-world. The only time I've seen dates marked like this have been on old medical records and holos from before the colonization."

"What is the purpose of these images? Are they meant as a record of how this man aged during his time here?"

"No. Some people used holo logs to record information. My father, and many doctors before him, used holos to document new medicines, toxins, and diseases they encountered on Halora. It's our most reliable means of passing information from one generation to the next, though we've had to start writing more and more of it down by hand as the old technology fails."

She continued to scroll down, then paused and swiped back up. The dates had been spaced out with weeks between them in the beginning, but the more recent ones were recorded closer together — daily entries, sometimes more than one on a single day, and the man's appearance grew more haggard with each one.

Aymee tapped on the first of the daily logs.

The hologram expanded into a three-dimensional image — it was like looking through a window into the control room, with the man from the image positioned close to the hologram's edge, his body cut off from the chest down. He was clean-cut, dark brown hair slicked back and his face shaved. He wore a dark blue uniform with silver buttons and trim.

The clothes on the skeleton might have looked the same once, long ago.

"This is Captain James Wright of the Interstellar Defense Coalition, officer number one-five-three-bravo-six," the man said, "in command of Darrow Nautical Outpost. The date is August twenty-third, SGY 2509.

"Four days ago, we received a series of communications from the offshore underwater facility, Pontus Alpha, indicating a massive security breach. The limited information I have received regarding that incident is detailed in my log dated August nineteenth.

"We have received no further communications from Pontus Alpha since then. Today, at eleven hundred hours, one of the submersibles, the *Nautilus*, appeared on the tracker for thirteen minutes and disappeared. We received a distress message from the crew during that window. I...am currently under official orders not to discuss the contents of said message."

Wright's features were strained, and there was a far-off gleam in his eyes — he'd seen something disturbing. Aymee suspected it was humans being killed by kraken. Had he known of their existence before seeing his men slaughtered?

"Since that message, we have been unable to establish further contact. There are no vessels remaining at this location, and therefore I was unable to dispatch a search party.

"At twelve hundred hours, we received official orders from Central Command in Fort Culver. We have been instructed to hold the line against anything that might come and defend the colonists to the last man. Due to the simultaneous declarations of war in eight separate star systems earlier this year, the IDC will not send additional troops or equipment to reinforce our positions. The sensitive nature of the situation at Pontus Alpha has left me unable to brief my soldiers on our enemy and their potential capabilities.

"Central does not want panic to spread through the populace. Our directive is to hold this facility at all costs and maintain a base of operations for any future underwater endeavors. We are not to send any communication to Watchpoint Echo, which is the base closest to Pontus Alpha."

"Watchpoint Echo?" Aymee asked quietly, brows drawn. "Does he mean The Watch?"

"I will record another log as soon as there is more information relevant to the situation. Captain Wright, signing off."

The holo flickered out, reverting to the collection of still images.

Aymee glanced at the skeletal remains on the floor. She crouched and extended a hand, carefully adjusting the worn, dingy material. A name had been embroidered on the coat, hidden beneath a crease — *WRIGHT*.

"Computer, what is Watchpoint Echo?" Aymee asked as she stood, wiping her fingers on her skirt.

"Watchpoint Echo is a military outpost established as a drop-point for supplies delivered from space and a shipping hub for seaborne materials on this side of the Halorian mainland. Civilian settlement was permitted three years after Watchpoint Echo's establishment."

A three-dimensional map appeared in the air. Though she'd never seen it from that angle, the land it depicted was familiar to Aymee. All the old buildings were there — the most prominent being the lighthouse on the cape. It was The Watch as it had looked hundreds of years ago.

"That's your home," Arkon said. He pointed to a spot to the west of the settlement. "This is the beach we met on for the exchanges, isn't it?"

"It is."

"The technology your people once commanded is fascinating."

"So much of it has broken down or stopped working over the years that we've learned to do without. I can't say things wouldn't be easier if we had access to some of it again, though." Aymee tilted her head, staring at the map. "Computer, why did the deliveries to Watchpoint Echo stop?"

"Halora was declared too remote and unstable for continued support from the Interstellar Defense Coalition after war began in 2509 SGY. The final shipment was dropped in April of the same year."

Aymee looked at Arkon. "They abandoned everyone."

She shouldn't have felt any emotional attachment to the

event; it was a wrong done by people she'd never heard of to people she'd never known hundreds of years before her birth. Anger flashed through her, nonetheless. The people who were supposed to protect the colonists had turned their backs and left the settlers to their fates with little care for their chances of survival.

However, had reinforcements been dispatched, Arkon and the kraken would likely have been wiped out.

It was a sobering thought.

The people of Halora — human and kraken alike — had persevered through abandonment, and Aymee had met Arkon because of it.

"It is talking about...about things beyond this world?" Arkon asked.

"You mean space?"

"Space. That is the darkness between the stars, is it not? Where your people originally came from?"

"Yes. Humans originally came from a planet called Earth, though we visited many other planets and solar systems before we came to Halora. We had huge ships that flew through space, from world to world."

He turned his attention back to the map, which slowly rotated to display the topography of The Watch from different angles. "Even with all I've learned, with all I know to be true, that seems so unlikely. So impossible."

"Creating a being from two different species seems impossible, too," she said gently.

Arkon smiled and spread his arms slightly, glancing down at himself. "Not so to me, when I have the proof right here all the time."

Aymee's eyes trailed from his broad shoulders down to his

narrow waist and beyond, drinking in every detail of his form. Beneath these lights, his skin was more cerulean than blue-gray, the color of the sea on a sunny day.

"It is jarring when I recall that our people are so closely related, given the violence and hostility between them in the past," he said, calling her gaze back to his.

"If only they'd seen what Macy and I do when we look at you. Physical differences aside, we really are the same." Aymee sighed and faced the console. She swiped the map away. Captain James Wright filled the screen. "Looking at the past and a lot of the present, it's hard to envision a peaceful future between our people."

"It can be achieved. Even if it's only one...or two...people at a time."

She smiled at him and took his hand again before tapping the next image.

They viewed the logs in silence, one after another, and found each more harrowing than the last despite the lack of new information presented. After the first few had played, Arkon curled a tentacle around Aymee's waist and drew her close. She slipped her arms around him. His presence and quiet strength provided her only comfort.

Though many of the logs were mundane and uneventful, some lasting less than a minute, Captain Wright grew increasingly distressed with each passing day. His frustration became evident as his repeated declarations of having received no new orders or information from Central Command were delivered with progressively less emotion, while the unhealthy gleam in his eyes conversely intensified.

He detailed many of their normal operations, mentioning the base only had nineteen personnel apart from himself, as it had never entered full operation. His early note that they were well provisioned eventually turned into detailed weekly inventories of their stores. After the first few weeks, the Captain stopped shaving.

The formality of his introductions lapsed as the entries continued, but he maintained a calm demeanor through most of it, never seeming to communicate the scathing opinions belied by his expression.

Until the log he made on the one hundred and fourteenth day.

"Our provisions are lower than projected. Six soldiers violated standing orders, raided the stores and armory, and exited the facility during the night. Privates Thompson, Harris, Brown, and Everett—" Aymee started at the name, thinking of James and Maris, "—along with Corporal Jennings and Sergeant Brick." His face contorted with rage, and he growled through his teeth. "These men swore an oath, and they have broken that oath by deserting their posts and stealing IDC property. I have sent word to the other bases that they are to be shot on sight, but I haven't received any responses."

Captain Wright dipped his head and dragged a hand over his haggard face. "We may be all that is left."

Aymee and Arkon continued watching. Two weeks after the first desertion, Wright reported another — seven more men, gone during the night. Wright's anger was far more pronounced, now, and he seemed to have aged years since the first log Aymee had selected. His cheeks were gaunt beneath his scraggly beard, his skin sickly-pale.

"I had sealed the armory and the storeroom," he said in the log five days later, head bowed, and face lost in shadow, "to keep the men from helping themselves. Without order...none of this works. So, my second-in-command, the man I should have been able to trust until the end, led a group of them into both rooms, using the clearance granted by his rank, stocked them with food and weapons, and deserted."

He sat in silence, his head shifting from side to side as though searching for something on the floor.

"The one man I thought I could trust. The one man I thought valued his honor and duty above everything else, the way a soldier should. Just another fucking rat." He slammed his hand down; Aymee jumped at the loud bang. "If he shows his face here again, I will shoot him. I will unload every round from my service pistol into his fake smile, and then I will walk to the armory, reload my firearm, and empty it into him again.

"Only Lindholm and Warren are left. They're the only two who are man enough to stick to their duty. Maybe the only two decent soldiers on this entire God-forsaken planet. And I can't trust them. I don't know why they haven't left yet, but I know they're just waiting for an opportunity.

"I left the armory and storeroom unlocked after the most recent desertion. I think...I need to watch the cameras. Hold this facility at all costs. We need to hold it. *I* need to hold it."

Aymee's finger hovered over the final log. She turned her head and stared at the remains on the floor. All he'd gone through had chipped away at his mind, leaving only blind rage and paranoia by the end. She knew what the last file would contain.

She opened it.

Captain Wright leaned on the console, one hand in his short-cropped hair and the other holding a familiar pistol. He was silent for a long while — the timer ticked away three minutes and twenty-two seconds before he spoke.

"Sergeant Lindholm and...and Private Warren. They have been executed under provision one-nineteen-charlie of the Interstellar Defense Coalition Judicial Code for attempted desertion of post. Provisions have run out. There are no supplies coming. No word. No word from anyone, anywhere."

He shook his head, the gesture taking on an almost violent energy. "They were in the armory. Taking weapons against my orders. Arming themselves, maybe to...maybe to kill me? I detonated an incendiary device within the armory to prevent the stored weaponry from falling into enemy hands...tentacles...

"What the *fuck* are those things? They were on the *Nautilus*, and they..."

Suddenly, he stood up. He was wearing the dark blue and silver uniform; it looked surprisingly clean and crisp, and he'd shaved for the first time in months.

"Captain James Wright, officer number one-five-three-bravo-six. This is my final report. I have held my post for as long as is possible. I have engaged all the security doors and will be shifting the facility into emergency power to keep it as intact as possible when IDC forces reclaim it."

He shifted his pistol to his left hand and saluted with his right.

Lowering his hand, he stepped forward, back straight, and reached for something on the console.

The hologram flickered, and static distortions ran through it. The bright light shifted to the same dim red glow that had illuminated the place when Aymee and Arkon first arrived.

"Manual emergency standby power switch engaged," the computer said. "Shifting to standby power in five seconds. Five...four...three..."

"Captain Wright, signing off." Though his figure was shadowed, Aymee saw him lift the gun to his mouth.

"Two...one..."

There was a boom and a flash of light, burning the image of Captain Wright with his head snapping backward into Aymee's mind, and then the hologram dissipated.

CHAPTER 14

GOLDEN SHAFTS OF MORNING SUNLIGHT STREAMED THROUGH THE water as Arkon swam away from the Broken Cavern, creating contrasting patches of light and shadow on the seafloor. His gaze drifted over rocks encrusted with sedentary creatures of a hundred different colors and beds of seagrass swaying hypnotically in the current. He tracked the movement of long, sleek, shimmering fish and scuttling, hard-shelled creatures. The sparkling surface overhead gave way to the endless, varied blue of the distant ocean on the fringes of his vision.

It was beauty he longed to share with Aymee.

After watching the logs, they'd explored the Darrow Nautical Outpost, and discovered a few useful chambers — foremost being a kitchen like the one in the Facility and a room filled with thirty-two narrow beds. They'd pushed three of the beds together to create a space large enough to lie in side by side. Aymee had slept in Arkon's embrace and hadn't moved away from him once during the night.

He'd slept little; he knew she'd been more troubled by Wright's final log than she admitted.

Aymee was still sleeping when he'd awoken, though she stirred when he slipped out of bed. She'd muttered a question — more a sound than a word — and grunted her understanding when he explained he was going hunting. Sound sleep had claimed her again within seconds.

She could have come — they had the diving suit he'd brought and had located several more in one of the chambers — but Arkon wanted her to rest. The last few days had been harrowing for Aymee, and even if she hadn't physically exerted herself, the toll on her emotions was immense. She needed time to adjust, to recover, to find her joy again.

He'd delayed only long enough to gather Captain Wright's remains as he left, so he could bring them out to sea.

While he took in the beauty of his surroundings — he was certain Aymee could perfectly capture the unique essence of morning light in the ocean through her painting — he kept watch for both predators and prey.

Though Aymee could survive on plants alone if necessary, they both needed meat to remain strong and healthy. As Aymee's provider and protector, he refused to allow *any* of her needs to go unmet.

He drifted farther than he'd originally intended, into unfamiliar waters, and felt a small thrill at the prospect. This had been Jax's experience for years — always pushing beyond the boundaries a little at a time, always seeking the unknown to discover it, break it, master it.

Of course, Jax himself had likely swum these waters long before, and a short hunting trip was hardly pushing any limits, but it was a taste of his friend's normal experience. Strangely,

Arkon had never shared Jax's thirst for exploration, despite his insatiable curiosity. It had taken Aymee to open him up to new possibilities, to enable him to view the world through different eyes.

Was this what Macy had meant when she spoke about finally feeling alive after being numb for so long?

He realized suddenly that he'd been swimming for some time — long enough to notice a change in the angle of the sunlight. It may have been a quarter of an hour, perhaps twice that, but it was too far from Aymee either way. He didn't want her alone for long, especially after she woke; the Broken Cavern's isolating, restrictive ambience would not ease her already strained emotions.

He was about to turn around when a flash of pure blue from up ahead caught his attention. As he moved, the light did, too — it was a reflection.

Arkon pushed on. When the source finally became apparent, he halted and stared in wonder.

A portion of the coastal cliffside had collapsed. The rubble — chunks of rock in all sizes, globs of dark mud, and dead plants from the surface — lay piled at the base of the cliff. The rockslide had torn open the stone to reveal hundreds of halorium shards embedded within. More pieces were mixed into the debris.

The halorium gave off its own glow, most pronounced where it was shadowed, but rays of sunlight still caught the edges of the shards to produce blue-tinged reflections.

Arkon swam closer. He'd seen halorium on the seafloor many times, usually in small clusters, but he'd never found so much all at once. The surrounding water hummed with the halorium's collective energy. Though it was safe to handle according to both the knowledge passed down through generations of kraken and the human records in the Facility, its power was undeniable, especially in such a concentration.

His skin tingled, and waves of energy slowly worked over his body. This material, these gem-like shards, had driven the creation of Arkon's people. He imagined the kraken of old working here, sifting through the rubble for tiny glowing bits and prying larger pieces from the cliffside, stowing it all in shielded containers for transport.

The kraken owed everything to halorium. Because of it, they *existed*. Because of it, their home was secure and largely functional.

And, having listened to the Computer's accounts of Halorian history, he knew halorium was the main reason for Aymee's presence, too. Humans were not likely to have colonized the planet were it not for the discovery of halorium.

Arkon tilted his head; the sea was in constant motion, even if that motion was not always apparent. The shafts of sunlight danced with the surface's movement, and barely perceptible impurities whirled in the current, but something else had floated through his vision.

He focused his gaze on the water between the light, and wonder overcame him.

Tiny particles drifted between the shafts of light, each emitting its own pale blue glow, too faint to perceive in the direct sun. They floated up from the halorium shards by countless thousands, as innumerable as the stars in the night sky, and were swept landward by the current in flowing, twisting streams.

Lost in his curiosity, he followed their path. The particles spread as they moved farther from their source, making them difficult to track, but they eventually led to a stretch of pale beach. Arkon lifted his head above the surface and looked toward the shore.

With the sun shining on the sand, it was impossible to tell whether the particles persisted on land — until a cresting wave cast a shadow beneath itself at the perfect angle. For an instant, points of blue light glowed in the shadow. Then they were swallowed up by the water.

I must bring Aymee here and show her this.

The thought of Aymee reminded Arkon abruptly of his reasons for coming out here. He looked skyward. Based on the position of the sun, he'd been gone at least an hour, and he hadn't even attempted to make a catch. Heat spread over his skin — disappointment, frustration, and worry gnawed at him. He had to hurry. It wasn't fair to leave her alone for so long.

His mind raced as he dove under, mentally sorting the easiest prey to obtain without the aid of tools.

ARKON BROKE the surface in the sub pen and glanced up. With the sky having mostly cleared, sunlight poured through the hole in the ceiling, overpowering the closest man-made lights, many of which had come on after the power was restored. He'd paused that morning as he left to hunt and stared at the stained, worn walls and ceiling. Somehow, despite the brightness, the pen felt more desolate now than ever before.

Before the power had been restored, the ceiling and walls were always dominated by shadow, even when the sun was shining; it had granted the massive chamber an air of mystery as intriguing as it was ominous. The effect had created a certain beauty, allowing the sunlight and its reflections on the water to highlight some of the precise edges and lines while leaving everything else to the imagination.

It reminded him of what Aymee had said about the mind filling in the details; perhaps Arkon's mental image was simply more appealing than the truth.

The artificial lights left nothing hidden — even the water was illuminated from within by lights in the walls and floor. The precision of this place's construction was impressive, but apart from the painting on the wall, it seemed largely uninspired. Years of damage and wear only made it seem dreary and lonely.

He swam to the ladder and climbed up to the platform. Aymee was nowhere to be seen; was she still asleep?

After taking a few minutes to fill a container with seawater and store the single fish he'd caught inside — the fish was large enough to provide them both a single meal, at least — he went up the steps to the second level and entered the short hallway. The door at the end slid open with a groan after he punched in the number sequence.

He moved through the threshold and along the corridor, allowing his eyes to wander, and found himself comparing it to home — *Pontus Alpha*, as Captain Wright had called it. The interior of this place was cleaner, but the higher ceilings and concrete walls made it feel colder, even though the climate control systems kept the air comfortable. The contours and lines in the Facility were sleeker and smoother, which dulled the edge of heartless precision that seemed to have gone into constructing such locations.

He turned down one of the intersecting corridors and was heading toward the room they'd slept in when the door ahead slid open. Aymee emerged, wearing her diving suit with a mask tucked under her arm. Her long, curly hair was pulled back from her face; he'd never seen her wear it that way before. The suit accentuated her long, graceful limbs and molded itself to her every curve.

Arousal stirred within him, a dull heat in his lower abdomen that spread throughout his loins. His gaze fixed on the V between her legs. The heat intensified, and his shaft pulsed. He forced his eyes back up as she neared.

She smiled at him. Though the bruise on her cheek was already fading, its presence rekindled his anger; he'd seen her come to harm and had been unable to prevent it.

"How was your hunt?" she asked.

"It was not quite as fruitful as I had intended, but we will have some meat for today, at least."

"Then it was a success." She kissed his cheek and caught his hand as she walked past. He followed her lead. "Let's go swimming. I want to try out the suit. I've already gone through the tutorial with Sam."

Arkon's gaze dipped. The suit cupped her swaying backside, leaving little to his imagination.

He fought a surprisingly strong urge to reach forward, clutch her hips, and draw her back against him.

"Macy never went into detail on everything these suits are capable of," she said as she led him toward the submarine pen. "I can't wait to try it out in the open sea."

Her words reminded Arkon of the beauty he'd witnessed during his hunt. Aymee would have appreciated it immensely, but there'd be future opportunities to take her.

"It is for the best that you learn its functions here, where the dangers are minimal."

The door to the submarine pen opened and they moved through it. Aymee walked him to the railing and didn't release his hand as she looked at him, smiling. "I suppose I should be honest and tell you that I'm not a strong swimmer."

Arkon couldn't help but smile back at her; the hint of guilt in her expression was endearing. "The suit is meant to help that. And I will be nearby the entire time."

"I know." She squeezed his hand and released it, peering over the rail. "Since the storm's let up, I thought now would be good. The water is calm."

"Perhaps that will lend itself well to a lesson. Even when the sea appears calm on the surface, there are currents running below, out of sight, and they will carry you away if you are not ready for them." He gently took her wrist and raised it, indicating the white piece attached to the suit. "This will help you immensely, but you cannot allow yourself to grow complacent because of it."

"I won't."

Arkon nodded. It required a surprising amount of willpower to stop himself from listing all the potential dangers; *he* was the one who'd said life was meaningless without risk, and there was no controlling the fickleness of chance.

"Come." He led her down the steps to the lower platform.

"Macy said Sarina is already swimming."

"She is. Kraken can essentially swim immediately following birth, though it is not the most graceful sight."

"It's amazing. Our newborns are helpless. It takes them months to get strong enough to move themselves around. When do kraken learn to walk? It is walking, isn't it?"

Arkon glanced down at his tentacles. He'd never really thought about it before; *walk* was one of many words the kraken rarely used, as it had never seemed applicable to them. "*Dragging* may be more accurate. Because of the way my people typically handle the raising of our young, I have not spent much time with children until recently, so I cannot answer you with any certainty. I know only that it does not come as naturally to us as swimming, and it involves using our muscles in ways we are typically unused to. Our skeletal structure does not extend below our waists, so our stability outside the water is a matter of the musculature in our tentacles."

They stopped half a body length from the edge of the platform. Aymee slipped her wrist from his grasp, set her mask down, then placed her hands on his sides from behind. Arkon stiffened, eyes widening.

"I never considered that you wouldn't have bones in your tentacles," she said thoughtfully. Her fingers slid toward his spine, pressing firmly. Though it wasn't her flesh meeting his, it was still her touch, and it was enough to reignite the fire within him. She traced his spine first up then back down, past his last vertebrae. "That you stand and move like this on land is an amazing show of strength."

Against his will, Arkon's skin shifted toward violet. The same sort of fascination he so often felt was plain on her face and in her voice, but it was her closeness and the familiarity of her touch that caused his body to react so powerfully.

She flattened her hand and ran it along a tentacle. "I've seen you turn this color before, and red a few times. What does it mean?"

He released a long, slow breath. "Red is anger or aggression, though the nuanced meaning varies depending on the particular shade."

"And violet?" She withdrew her hands and bent to collect her mask.

He dropped his gaze. "Embarrassment."

Aymee's face fell. "Oh." She looked away from him, but not before he saw a flash of guilt in her eyes. "I'm sorry if I made you feel uncomfortable. I don't think sometimes, and I let my curiosity get the better of me."

"No." Forcing his skin to its normal color, he lifted his head, settled his palms on her hips, and drew her closer. "You've no need to apologize. I am unused to such contact, but it is *not* uncomfortable."

She pressed a hand against his chest, and he again wished it was her skin on his. "The kraken don't touch?"

"We share a home, but most of us live alone. There have always been some conflicting instincts within my kind that push us to both exist as a tightknit society and satisfy a need for solitude. Many forms of physical contact can be taken as a challenge amongst the kraken...an invasion of the space we consider private."

She tilted her head. "Do I challenge you?"

Arkon smiled. "In many ways."

Aymee chuckled, sliding her hand to his shoulder.

"While Jax was in The Watch, I observed the humans working on the dock every day," he said, leaning his head down to press his forehead to hers. "I saw them share touches, and the warmth between them, the familiarity...I wondered what that felt like. Part of me longed to know. Macy has taught me much about the expression of friendship through touch in the time since, has shown me how it can strengthen a bond between two people."

"And when I touch you?"

He closed his eyes and inhaled her scent, hands dipping to her backside. "When you touch me, I know I have had only the merest taste of what is possible, and I hunger for more."

AYMEE'S BREATH QUICKENED, and she curled her fingers to keep from grabbing on and pulling him against her. This...this was a different Arkon. His touch was bold, confident. His words flowed through her, heightening her awareness of him, and her body craved more contact.

What had begun as fascination had grown into something deep and powerful. She'd been drawn to Arkon from the start, intrigued by the contradictory nature of his features — at once human and alien — but her curiosity had quickly extended beyond his appearance.

He'd become her friend. She could talk to him about anything, she related to his passions and doubts, and she trusted him unconditionally.

She also respected him and wouldn't push toward anything he wasn't ready for. No matter how much she wanted him, she would go slowly.

Aymee tilted her chin up and softly kissed the corner of his mouth, his jaw, his neck. His fingers tightened on her ass.

Lifting her head, she smiled up at him. "Let's go swimming."

She stepped away before he could react. It was one of the hardest things she'd ever done. His hands remained in place, as though still holding her rather than the empty air in which she'd stood a moment before.

Pulling up her hood, she tucked her hair beneath it and moved the mask into place. It automatically sealed, and a soft internal glow lit her face.

"Sam, could you turn the mask light off?" she asked. It blinked out.

She flashed Arkon a smile and walked toward the ladder, carefully lowering herself onto the top rung.

"In this particular instance," Arkon said, moving to stand on the edge of the platform beside the ladder, "I think it is acceptable to forgo the usual caution."

Without awaiting her reply, he leapt off the platform and hit the water with a splash.

Aymee laughed, watching him move underwater. "Easy to say when you live in the water."

Facing forward, she took a deep breath and let go.

The water swallowed her, blinding her for a moment, and she waited fearfully for it to flood her mask.

"Your heart rate has accelerated," Sam said. "Do you require assistance?"

She took a measured breath, then another. "No. I'm okay."

Something curled around her waist. Aymee's hand dropped to it as she was gently turned to face Arkon. She smiled at him. "Thank you."

He shook his head and pointed to his ear.

"Oh. You can't hear me." She pointed up, and they surfaced together.

"How does it feel?" Arkon asked.

"Strange. I can feel the water, but not. It's like there's almost no resistance when I move, and it's not even cold. It's like...flying."

His tentacles — save for the one around her waist — glided through the water around her as he kept himself afloat. "Macy has said much the same."

"I bet she was absolutely thrilled the first time she used this."
She inhaled deeply. "Okay, I'm ready."

"I will be with you the whole time." Arkon released his hold
on her.

She allowed herself to sink and gazed around her. Rows of
lights embedded in the concrete walls and floor illuminated the
water; several were inactive, and many were clouded with age
or overgrown with sea life, but they granted a full view of the
pen below the surface.

Her eyes were drawn to the massive chunks of stone that
had fallen from the ceiling, which lay in the shaft of sunlight
streaming through the ceiling. They — and the twisted remains
of the walkway they'd crushed in their fall — were covered with
small plants and immobile sea creatures in a variety of colors;
bright yellows, rich reds and purples, deep blues and vibrant
greens. Fish with iridescent scales swam in and out of the gaps
in the debris, and spindly-legged creatures slowly walked over
the rubble, feeding on the plants.

She swam to the mound of rubble, feeling like a flailing
toddler as she moved, and sank until her feet touched the
bottom. Reaching out, she touched one of the plants. It folded in
on itself, and Aymee flinched away with a laugh. She tilted her
head back. Rays of sunlight penetrated the water from above as
though through imperfect glass — the light was bent, altered,
and amplified, creating an ethereal glow.

Carefully climbing the rock, she followed one of the spindly-
legged creatures until it ducked out of sight. A shadow passed
over her. She glanced up to see Arkon drifting nearby, his eyes
fixed on her and a warm smile upon his lips. She returned it.

She spent time asking Sam questions and exploring the suit's
features and capabilities. Any new displays were seamlessly

introduced into her view through the mask — she could monitor depth, water temperature, pressure, currents and their speeds, and track living creatures, and she knew that was only scratching the surface.

Whether ahead or behind, above or below, Arkon remained close all the while.

Eventually, she caught Arkon's attention, and they resurfaced.

"This is amazing!" she exclaimed as soon as her head was above water. "It's so different down there, and we're not even out *there*." She waved toward the tunnel leading out to the sea. "I wouldn't even know what to begin painting."

"Is there anything that moves you more than all the rest?"

Aymee grinned. "You."

There was sudden intensity in his eyes. He *saw* her, *all* of her, and sought to claim her with his gaze.

He wants me. He's wanted me since the first time we met, he just didn't know how to express it.

At that moment, all she wanted to do was touch him. Kiss him. Love him.

"Sam, release the mask."

"All right. Field generator deactivated," Sam said. The seal broke with a soft hiss.

She reached up and took hold of the mask, pulled it away, and tugged her hood back.

A loud crack from the ceiling echoed through the chamber. Dirt and bits of rock rained into the water from overhead.

Aymee looked up to see a huge piece of the ceiling directly above her tremble and fall.

Arkon slammed into her with startling speed, enfolding her

in his arms. They plunged underwater. Stinging seawater filled her nose and mouth.

There was an immense sound behind them — the deep, resonating bass of a massive rock breaking the surface — and Aymee and Arkon were thrust forward on a wave of displaced water. Her head came up. She sputtered and gasped for air. Arkon twisted as they crashed into the wall, taking the impact on his back; the force of it rattled into Aymee.

He shifted his hold on her, raising his arms to keep her above the surface as they came back down. Her hair, free of its tie, covered her face, and she coughed up water, but she didn't go under again. Water lashed at them angrily and pulled away several times. Arkon kept them locked in place until the waves calmed.

Aymee coughed a few times to clear her throat and swept her hair back, looking up. Bits of debris tumbled from the hole in the ceiling, which had expanded by at least half of its original size.

"Ark—"

He yanked her into a crushing embrace with arms and tentacles. One of his hands cupped the back of her head, guiding her face to his shoulder. His breath was ragged, and faint tremors rippled through him.

Aymee slipped her arms around him. "Arkon?"

"I'm such a fool," he muttered. "I should have known the rain would... I almost lost you, Aymee."

"I'm okay." She rubbed her hands up and down his back. His trembling didn't cease.

"Are you sure?" A pair of his tentacles moved over her back, mimicking the motions of her hands.

"You saved me." She kissed his shoulder, ignoring the thundering of her pulse. "I'm fine."

Taking gentle hold of her hair, he lifted her head back. His eyes were rounded, pupils dilated to huge, black pits. For a moment, he just stared at her.

Then he leaned forward and pressed his lips to hers in a desperate, claiming kiss.

Aymee's eyes widened only to flutter shut as she opened to him. Her body molded to his, held tight in his quivering embrace. He stole her breath as he took from her mouth, his lips caressing, sucking, nipping, and filled her once more with the breath of life. She tasted him on her tongue and craved more.

Heat suffused her. Her breasts ached, and her nipples tightened, frustratingly confined by the suit; all she wanted was to feel his skin on hers.

His hand slid from her hair to her neck, gently tipping her head back to deepen the kiss before his mouth trailed from hers and caressed her jaw.

"Arkon," she sighed. Setting her hands on his chest, she gave him a little shove.

He drew back and blinked, his pupils contracting. "I am sorry, Aymee. I did not—"

Aymee covered his mouth once more in a kiss, silencing his words, before pulling back with a smile. "Don't be sorry. You have nothing to be sorry about." She rubbed her cheek against his. "Loosen your hold, Arkon," she said softly. "I'm not going anywhere."

Arkon eased his grip reluctantly, tentacles sliding over the suit at her waist, hips, and thighs as he uncoiled them. She parted her legs once they were released, and the throbbing between them intensified.

"Take us to the ladder," she said, wrapping her arms around his neck.

He held her gaze as he swam. His trembling had ceased, but now a different sort of energy radiated from him.

Anticipation.

When they reached the ladder, he grasped one of the rungs overhead, anchoring them in place.

She kissed the small hollow at the base of his throat. "Wrap a tentacle around my waist and raise us up out of the water."

When he obeyed, pulling up so their pelvises were exposed, she smoothed her palm down his arm, clasped his wrist, and guided his other hand to the ladder rung. "Keep your hands here."

Arkon tilted his head, the curiosity in his gaze — which had become delightfully familiar to her — bolstered by intense longing.

"Why?" he rasped.

"Because I want you to trust me." She brushed her nose over his cheek and kissed the corner of his mouth. Bringing her hand to her chest, she slid her fingertips around the suit's circular chest piece. The suit loosened, gaping open in the back. Cool air brushed her skin.

"I trust you, Aymee." The tentacle around her waist tightened infinitesimally.

She straightened, allowing him to take her weight, and pulled her arms free of the suit. She peeled the material farther down, exposing her breasts.

He lowered his gaze, and his pupils expanded once more. She touched a hand to his chest; his hearts beat rapidly against her palm, and he released a shuddering breath.

Aymee smiled and curled her other arm around his neck,

leaning in to kiss him. He returned the kiss and his muscles tensed.

Her nipples rasped against his skin, the pressure increased with each of their heavy breaths, and jolts of pleasure shot straight to her core. She hooked a leg around his waist and drew them closer together, but that would be all — this was about *him*.

His mouth tasted of salt and something wholly Arkon. She slid her hand down his chest, over ridges of muscle, past his lean stomach, and halted it at his pelvis. He swayed his hips into her palm and gasped against her mouth. Something hard bulged beneath his skin, and he stilled as her fingers dipped lower.

"Aymee, I...I don't know..."

She lifted her head and met his gaze. Apprehension and desire warred in his eyes.

"Trust me, Arkon."

He nodded, tipped his head back, and closed his eyes. "Always."

Aymee watched his face as she explored with her hand, searching until the tips of her fingers touched upon his slit. Gently, she stroked along its length.

Arkon's shaft pushed out against her palm; she grasped it.

The ladder rungs groaned as he tightened his grip and hissed through his teeth. The cords stood out on his neck, and his brow creased.

He was hard and slick, and her hand glided over his length easily. Only when she reached his base, and something brushed over her skin, did she lower her gaze.

His cock was darker than his normal skin at its tip and darker still at its base, where four thin, two-centimeter-long feelers writhed. Moisture glistened from his shaft. She lifted her hand and rubbed her fingers together.

He produced his own lubricant.

"Aymee."

She looked up. Arkon had tipped his chin down to look at her with uncertainty in his eyes.

Aymee smiled, replaced her hand, and curled her fingers around his girth. He was hot and thick, velvet over steel. Her gaze locked with his as she stroked him, setting an easy rhythm.

"You're beautiful," she said.

Arkon groaned. Two of his tentacles slid along her legs, up the backs of her thighs, and over her ass to caress the bare skin of her back.

Aymee trailed her lips over his chest and up his throat until their mouths met once more. He kissed her deeply, desperate with need, and she gave all she could. His tentacles moved around her sides to caress the undersides of her breasts. She moaned into his mouth, grinding her pelvis against him as she tightened her leg around his waist.

His hips rocked, and his stomach quivered. His motions grew more hurried, frenzied, seeking. She squeezed, quickening her strokes.

Arkon tore his mouth from hers with a growl. He threw his head back, expression drawn, teeth clenched. His shaft thickened, growing impossibly harder before a loud groan of pleasure burst from him. His body trembled and jerked as he came. Aymee didn't relent until he sagged forward, shivering in the aftermath.

She moved her hand to the base of his shaft and pressed a fingertip to his pulsing feelers. Her core clenched as she realized where they'd touch once Arkon was inside her.

His shoulders rose and fell with his deep, ragged breaths. "That was... I... I do not have the words."

Aymee chuckled and flattened her palm on his chest. His hearts pounded.

Releasing the ladder, he pulled her against him and fell backward into the water. He floated on the surface with her laying atop him and ran the tips of his tentacles along her spine. His bare skin, despite the solid muscle beneath, was soft. She laid her cheek on his chest and listened to the sound of his heartbeats, content as they drifted. Occasionally, his tentacles moved in the water, directing them well away from the broken ceiling.

"Thank you," he finally said, awe in his voice.

Aymee laughed, lifting her head to look at him. Her hair fell forward. "It was my pleasure."

CHAPTER 15

A LOW RUMBLING ROUSED ARKON FROM SLUMBER. HE OPENED HIS eyes and listened as the sound built to a peak and faded away. He could feel it, too, but only barely.

The overhead lights were off, and the lights along the bases of the walls were dim, leaving the room in relative darkness. With Aymee — dressed only in a long-sleeved shirt — snuggled against him in bed, her bare legs tangled with his tentacles, it was a comforting darkness.

Only her slow, gentle breaths broke the ensuing silence. He turned his head toward her. She looked younger while she slept, her features softer despite the shadows cast upon her face. Perhaps it was the absence of the sorrow he too often saw in her eyes. Aymee was doing better than she had been the night he'd brought her here, but she was still healing.

He understood — Aymee was a doctor, expected to display calm and confidence to soothe others in dire situations. But she had Arkon, now. He would be her strength when she felt weak. She didn't have to pretend for him.

The rumbling came again, louder this time. Aymee inhaled and shifted, pressing her face deeper into his shoulder as her hand moved from his chest to his stomach.

The slide of her palm over his skin heated his blood, and his thoughts returned to the day before. Whether due to his people's general avoidance of it or his own inexperience, he'd never imagined physical contact could be so staggeringly powerful.

Not any *physical contact,* he corrected. Aymee was the key. *Her* touch affected him.

They had floated in the water for some time after she'd pleasured him, and once his hearts had finally slowed and the euphoria of her touch had faded, he'd wanted to explore more of her. His glimpse of her breasts had left him craving, and the fleeting brush of his tentacles over them had been taste enough to become addicted. Aymee had only laughed and pulled her suit back into place when he tried to touch her after climbing out of the water.

"This was about you," she'd said with a soft smile before kissing him.

Aymee had taken enjoyment from making him feel good. He couldn't deny his lack of understanding at the concept. She'd done it *to* him, and he'd felt it all. How could the pleasure have been hers? He wanted to learn her body, her taste, every tiny aspect of her; he wanted to learn how to make her cry out in ecstasy. But, somehow, she'd found satisfaction through his release.

That went against all he'd known about females before meeting Aymee. He'd been told kraken females took pleasure for themselves. What concern had they for the males they mated with? Thanks to the way the kraken were designed, there'd always been plenty of males ready to please and provide for the relatively few females.

It was a male's duty, after all, to attempt to father the next generation of kraken. Personal desire or contentment was nothing compared to the survival of their people.

Not so with Aymee. She wanted to make Arkon happy. More than that, she derived her own happiness from his.

He lightly combed his claws through her hair, careful of the tangles.

On a rational level, Arkon knew that the ways of his people did not apply to humans. Their physiology, history, and societies were very different, shaped by unique challenges and necessities. Choosing a mate did not have the same meaning to humans as it did to kraken. It did not have the same implications.

Still, he couldn't help but feel Aymee had chosen him. It was likely she'd done so after their night together on the beach, but he'd been too startled by his body's reactions to recognize the significance of what she'd offered — *herself*. Her actions today had expanded his understanding of the way humans viewed such matters; Aymee had placed Arkon's contentment before her own, had chosen his satisfaction, had chosen *him* despite their multitude of differences.

Absently, he trailed the tip of a tentacle down her leg.

"Is it morning already?" Aymee asked, voice husky with sleep.

"No, it is not," he replied. The base's lights — at least in this room — were set on some sort of timing mechanism. They came on fully only for a few hours around sunrise and sunset. Aymee had theorized it was because the people who'd worked here had slept in shifts.

"Then why are you awake?"

As though in answer to her question, the rumbling returned, drawn out over several seconds.

"Another storm?" She buried her face between his neck and shoulder and slid an arm around him. "Can you hear the storms when you're below?"

"Not in the Facility, no. But in the water, those sounds sometimes seem to go on forever. There is a certain feeling in the sea when a storm begins. It is difficult to define or describe..."

"What kind of feeling?"

"It feels like...the water is *charged*. It's tension, anticipation, fear. The currents are disrupted and can become violent, and much of the sea life seeks shelter."

"Is it dangerous?" Her breath was warm against his neck and sent tingles across his skin.

"Hunts are ended when such storms begin, and most of us remain home." As his awareness of her body against his heightened, it became more difficult to hold onto his thoughts. "I've never known a kraken to be killed by lightning, but the sea is dangerous enough without the complications introduced during bad weather."

Her hand returned to his chest, resting above his hearts. "Must be difficult during the wet season, then." She rubbed her thumb across his skin. "Do you miss it? Home?"

Arkon slid his tentacle back up her leg slowly. "I miss Jax, Macy, and Sarina. Even Dracchus, if I am honest. I know there is still so much information to delve through with the Computer. It is the only home I have ever known...but I do not miss it. I am content."

Her hand stilled, and she fell silent; Arkon wondered if she'd fallen asleep.

"Thank you for being here with me," she finally said.

He shifted, propping himself up on an elbow, and turned to look down at her. She moved onto her back, hair fanning out over the bedding.

"There's nowhere else I would rather be," he said, cupping her cheek in his palm.

She peered up at him, a soft smile on her lips, and cradled his jaw in her hand. "Me too."

After a moment, his gaze trailed downward, sliding over her body. Human and kraken anatomy bore many similarities, at least on the surface, but she should have appeared alien to him. She should've been little more than a passing curiosity, easily sated and subsequently forgotten. Yet she tantalized him. Aroused him.

She was beautiful in every line and curve, and he cherished every smile she gifted him.

Her arm fell to rest beside her head. "Do you want to see me, Arkon?"

Hearts stilling, he stared down at her; had he heard correctly? Her legs parted as she slid a foot along his tentacles.

Arkon swallowed. "Yes."

Aymee raised her hands to the collar of her shirt, unfastening the top button and allowing the fabric to billow open before moving down. Arkon watched, enrapt, as she revealed her skin little by little. His breath quickened when her fingers hovered over her stomach, and his claws dug into the bedding when she touched the final button.

Once it was undone, she grasped the edges of the shirt and drew it slowly apart.

Arkon's breath fled, and heat suffused him.

She lay bare before him. Her breasts were small but full,

tipped with dark nipples, and her flat stomach dipped before meeting the flare of her hips; farther down, an enticing patch of black hair. With one knee bent, she parted her thighs, allowing him a glimpse of the pink flesh between her legs.

His pulsating shaft pressed to the inside of his slit. His tentacles — sliding restlessly, hungrily, along her legs — tasted her growing arousal in the air, and it sent a shudder through him.

"I see you, Aymee," he rasped, "and long to do more."

"You can touch me, Arkon," she beckoned.

He settled a trembling hand on her stomach and slowly trailed it up, brushing between curves of her breasts with his fingers. Her skin was warm, soft, and responsive. When he covered a breast with his palm, she closed her eyes and arched into his touch.

Shifting his tentacles, Arkon lifted his torso and held himself over her. He placed his free hand on her other breast and stroked her beaded nipples with the pads of his thumbs. She released a soft sigh.

"You can kiss them." She smiled. "I'm yours to do with as you please, Arkon. Touch me, kiss me, taste me. Anything."

Something tightened in his lower abdomen. He absently ran his tongue along the points of his teeth, more mindful than ever of the delicateness of her skin, and lowered his head. She caught his face with her hands and forced his gaze to hers. Her eyes were deep, dark pools, and he tumbled into them.

She lifted her head and skimmed her lips over his mouth. "Love me, Arkon," she whispered, then released him.

Love...

He'd longed for Aymee's love, but he hadn't realized it could go both ways — that he would come to love her, too. It seemed an immense oversight, a sign that he had indeed lost his wits.

Somewhere along the way, his fascination had evolved into something more. Into something that existed independently of her feelings for him, though it was in many ways fueled by them. Something as simultaneously simple and complex as the word that impossibly encompassed it.

Love.

Arkon lowered his mouth over one of her nipples and did as she'd said — he kissed. But that fleeting contact, that tiny taste, wasn't enough. He encircled it with his lips and flicked his tongue over the tip. She inhaled sharply and lifted her chest. Urged on by her reactions, he sucked her nipple into his mouth while caressing the other with his palm and the pads of his fingers.

Aymee's hands flew to his head and pulled him closer. Her moan flowed through him like a strong current through the ocean, and her scent strengthened, pushing his desire to a new, unimaginable peak.

Despite his thrill in her reactions, he released her nipple and trailed his lips down her body; he *needed* to experience the source of that scent, that *taste!*

Her stomach quivered as his lips brushed over it. He glanced up to find her watching him, her lips parted with her soft panting.

When he came to the small patch of hair at her pelvis, he ran the backs of his fingers through it. It felt different than the hair upon her head, coarser, and was heavily perfumed with arousal. Coiling a tentacle around each of her thighs, he spread them wide.

She was beautiful. The petals of her sex were slick, unfurled and ready to receive him, and here her scent was at its strongest.

His mouth watered.

He angled his hand to slide his finger along her folds but stopped before doing so; her flesh here was surely even more sensitive and fragile than elsewhere, and he couldn't forgive himself were he to cause her harm.

"Arkon?" she asked.

Raising his hand to his mouth, he bit the claws off his first two fingers and spit them to the floor.

"Why did you—" Her words came to an abrupt halt when Arkon touched her; he slid his fingers along her sex, coating them in her oils. Maddening heat radiated from her core.

He lifted his hand away and slipped his fingers into his mouth, sucking off her moisture. He'd had slight, fleeting tastes of her through his suction cups, but they had not prepared him for her true flavor. Aymee's sweetness flooded him.

Arkon's shaft throbbed with the pressure of his restraint; her taste on his tongue eroded what little self-control he'd maintained. He extruded fully, and in the same instant he dropped his head between her thighs and licked her sex.

Aymee gasped. Her legs trembled, muscles tensing, but he held them wide with his tentacles — he'd not relinquish what she'd so temptingly gifted him. He flattened a hand on her stomach to hold her down while pressing his other hand to her inner thigh.

He slid his tongue between her folds, exploring her from top to bottom, and when he brushed a nub of flesh near her sex's peak, her moaning intensified, and her hips jerked. Intrigued, he glanced up; her face was turned aside, eyes squeezed shut, bottom lip caught between her teeth. He licked again. Another tremor coursed through her.

Arkon closed his lips over the nub and took it into his mouth. He sucked.

Her back arched, body stiffening as she screamed his name. Moisture flowed from her, and Arkon drank greedily, unwilling to allow a single drop to escape. He didn't relent until her shudders subsided and she gently urged him up with her hands.

He raised his head. Aymee's tousled hair framed her face, and her eyes were hooded.

"Lie back for me, Arkon," she said, caressing his cheek.

He rolled away and lowered himself onto his back beside her. Smiling, she ran a hand along one of his tentacles and disentangled it from her leg. She rose onto her knees and guided the same tentacle to her waist, and Arkon wrapped it around her.

His hearts nearly stopped when she threw a leg over him.

She straddled his abdomen, hair a dark curtain around her face as she gazed down at him. Her breasts rose and fell with every breath, nipples hard, and he longed for another taste of them. The scent of her arousal enveloped him, and he could see the pink of her parted sex, feel the brush of her backside along his straining cock.

This was Aymee. Beautiful, wild, sensual Aymee.

His Aymee.

She leaned forward and their eyes locked. She skimmed her nose along his cheek, brushed her lips over his, and slipped a hand between their bodies to grasp his shaft. Arkon released a shuddering breath. Aymee lifted her hips, pressed the head of his cock to her opening, and lowered herself, taking him into her body.

Heat; incredible heat surrounded him. It spread into his core, intensifying that needful ache to an unbearable degree. He clawed at the bedding and his tentacles curled. Pressure built within him, immediate and irresistible, but somehow, he held his tenuous control.

As she flattened her hands on his chest, Arkon's eyes drifted to the point of their connection, watching her rise and fall, taking him deeper and deeper. His shaft glistened with their combined oils.

There was something primal about their bodies joining, something that touched upon previously unknown instincts. The pleasure was immense, but the connection was more than physical — this was mating, it was possession, it was *love*.

She suddenly thrust down, taking him to the hilt. Her sex clenched. The tendrils at his base slid over her, smelling and tasting, brushing her soft skin.

Arkon took hold of her hips and coiled his tentacles around her calves. He bared his teeth and bucked his pelvis, pressing further into her, on the verge of an explosion that would tear him apart from within.

Aymee gasped. Her fingers flexed, and she raked her nails over his chest. Shutting her eyes, she threw her head back in abandon and ground her sex upon him. Her inner walls tightened.

Arkon released a tortured groan.

Her hips undulated, body moving up and down, breasts jutting out with the arch of her back. The pressure inside him built as pleasure raked his insides, seeking release. Aymee moved over him like the rolling waters of the ocean; Arkon found her rhythm and matched it, dropping his hips when she rose and meeting her downward thrusts, pushing harder, deeper.

Her features strained and soon her tempo faltered. She

panted, her moans loud but musical in the otherwise silent room. He was determined to hear her cries once more. To feel her release around him.

Aymee fell forward, catching herself with her hands on either side of his head. Her movements quickened.

"I've wanted you for a long time," she breathed against his mouth, eyelids heavy with desire. "And now you're mine."

She squeezed her eyes closed and cried out. Her body locked, sex clamping around his cock and quivering as she reached her peak.

She has claimed me.

Arkon moved his hands to Aymee's backside and slammed her down on him, pushing himself beyond anything he'd thought possible. The pressure burst, and her name escaped him in a roar, her words echoing in his mind. A wave of pleasure stole his breath and tensed every muscle in his body, sweeping away conscious thought like driftwood on the surf. Her cries punctuated his thrusts, which ended when neither of them had anything left to give.

Aymee lay upon him, a welcome weight, her breath tickling his neck. She cradled his head with one hand, brushing her thumb against his skin. He realized only then that his tentacles were tangled around her legs and waist; he loosened his hold but was in no hurry to release her.

And now you're mine.

"I am yours, Aymee," he said, smoothing a palm over her hair. There was a tightness in his chest that had nothing to do with his labored breathing.

She inhaled deeply and rubbed her cheek against him before placing a kiss at the base of his throat. Lifting her head, she shifted her hands to cup his jaw and kissed his lips before resting her forehead against his. She closed her eyes, and the peacefulness on her face belied the sudden tension in her body.

"I love you, Arkon," Aymee whispered. When he opened his mouth to speak, she pressed a finger to his lips. "Someone once told me to take what I wanted. To take it all and never hesitate because it could all be gone in the blink of an eye, without any warning." Her arms slipped around him. "No matter what happens, or what our future might hold, I have this. This moment with you, where you are mine, and I am yours. Where we *loved*. And I will never regret it."

Arkon gently slipped his fingers into her hair and raised her head. There was a troubled gleam in her eyes, an unfamiliar vulnerability.

"I did not know what love was, not very long ago," he said. "I knew the idea of it, but it was only a word. As I learned, I came to crave it, longed to know it myself...but I've never truly felt it until you. I love you, Aymee. Always and without regret."

Aymee's body eased atop his. Her smile in that moment was the most radiant thing in all the universe. She kissed him, and Arkon embraced her. When she shifted her hips, he was reminded that he was still buried deep inside her body; he groaned, and she laughed.

"Love me some more, Arkon."

He rolled her onto her back and propped himself over her on his hands. She moaned, canting her hips to take him deeper. He grinned down at her. The sated exhaustion that had filled him a moment before fast faded, replaced by the rekindled heat of desire.

"As much as you wish."

CHAPTER 16

THE STORM LASTED THREE DAYS; THREE DAYS OF THUNDER, howling winds, and torrents of rain pouring through the hole in the submarine pen's ceiling.

Aymee sat on the edge of the platform, arms folded over the lower rail, watching lightning streak across the gray sky. She bit into her last apple.

Despite being away from home, she was happier than ever. Unfortunately, that didn't leave her immune to boredom; she wasn't used to inactivity, to staring at the same drab walls day in and day out, without a taste of open air or the inherent variety of her normal duties.

It was too dangerous to venture out during the storm, so they remained inside.

Arkon had spent some time in the control room, as he was now, speaking to the computer, learning about the history of this base and the Halorian colonies. Aymee preferred not to go in there.

Though he'd removed the body, the room was uncomfortable, oppressive. While she stood within, the sound of a single gunshot echoed ceaselessly through her memory. Arkon admitted he didn't understand why she felt that way but didn't press her on the matter — understanding and acceptance were not mutually exclusive concepts to him, and she loved him more for it.

Whenever he emerged, he'd tell her of what he learned. Based on the records he had accessed, the settlements — of which there were twelve on the Halorian mainland — were only meant as the beginning. They'd chosen varied locations with access to unique resources to serve as the foundation of a thriving, continent-wide colony, and had planned to land more settlers and supplies at regular intervals.

Arkon had even uncovered preliminary plans for entire underwater cities. He said they appeared similar to the place his people lived; it was obviously strange for him to think about such structures scattered across the seafloor, larger and more populated than either of them could imagine. The limited information available failed to answer the primary question they'd both asked: why? There was abundant land for human use, and it wouldn't have required such complex, sophisticated construction to utilize.

This base, the Darrow Nautical Outpost, had been constructed with dual purposes in mind — first to ferry personnel and supplies to Pontus Alpha, where the kraken now lived, and secondly to house underwater craft for civilian use. It had been operating at a fraction of its intended capacity when everything fell apart and had never come close to fulfilling its secondary function.

Thunder boomed overhead, and Aymee watched bits of the ceiling crumble and fall in the downpour.

How long until the entire roof came down?

Aymee finished her apple and tossed the core. It disappeared in the churning water below.

"I never realized just how much water there could be outside the ocean," Arkon said from behind her. She heard him set something down, and then one of his tentacles slipped around her waist and another beneath her legs. He lifted her, turned her to face him, and embraced her.

Aymee wrapped her arms around him and laughed. Since they'd made love, he'd grown increasingly more comfortable with physical contact, and — at times — seemed unable to keep from touching her.

"It's why we call it the wet season." She pulled back. "Missed me, did you?"

"I am sorry I took so long. Time seems to lose meaning when I dig through those archives. It is unfair to you."

"Don't be. But now that you're out here, are you hungry?" She motioned to the food set out on a piece of cloth on the floor and grinned sheepishly. "I attempted to cook fish again, and I didn't burn it this time."

Give her a broken arm, and she could set it with her eyes closed. Give her a piece of meat to cook, and she'd somehow reduce it to a lump of charcoal almost every time. It seemed such a simple skill to master, but competence in the kitchen had always eluded Aymee. Her mother had tried to teach her on many occasions, but those attempts always ended with Jeanctte shooing Aymee out of the kitchen before the whole house went up in flames.

Aymee had ruined the first fish Arkon caught for them. By the time she was through, the outside of the meat was a charred, blackened mess, while the inside remained raw.

Regardless, he'd eaten it with a smile and thanked her when he'd finished.

She'd loved him a little more at that moment.

"I am hungry, yes." He released her and eased down beside the cloth, plucking up a piece of fish and slipping it into his mouth.

She returned to her spot on the floor, placing her back against the rail, and ate with him. When they finished the food, Arkon reached behind him with a tentacle and grabbed what he'd been carrying — one of the many sturdy plastic bins they'd found scattered throughout the base.

Aymee leaned forward, bracing herself on her hands. "What's in there?"

"I wanted to make up for the time I have spent in that room," he said. "Would you like to paint with me?" He tipped the bin toward her, revealing the brushes and jars of paint she'd given him.

She leapt up and threw her arms around him. He swayed with the force of her sudden embrace, and the jars rattled softly. She'd forgotten he had brought them. Aymee had never gone so long without an outlet for her creativity. "Yes!"

"I hoped you would say *yes*, but I underestimated the enthusiasm you'd show." He turned his face into her neck and kissed her.

Aymee laughed. "If we have to stare at these walls, we might as well make them easier on the eyes." She pulled away, placed the jars on the floor, and carried the now-empty bin to the lower platform. "Where do you want to begin?" she called, leaning down to fill the bin with water.

"You are the artist, Aymee. I trust your judgment in the choice of canvas."

She climbed the stairs slowly, doing her best not to slosh water everywhere, and set the bin down in front of the wall near the hallway. There'd been no murals painted here — it was a blank canvas, limited only by their imaginations.

"Bring those closer, please," she said.

Using both hands and tentacles, he gathered up all the paint jars and brushes and carried them to her. She helped him arrange them on the floor.

"Have you used them yet?" she asked as she opened the lids.

"No. I wasn't sure how. I would've asked you during one of our meetings...but obviously, other events did not allow that."

"Here." She held up a brush.

He accepted it, taking it awkwardly between forefinger and thumb.

"I hold it like this," she said, reaching forward to adjust his grip on the brush. Heat stirred between her legs when her fingertip ran over one of the claws he'd bitten away. His pupils expanded as though he knew where her thoughts had gone. She cleared her throat. "If it's not comfortable or the rest of your hand gets in the way, adjust your grip to whatever feels right."

Arkon nodded. On the lower edge of Aymee's vision, his tentacles shifted restlessly over the floor, narrowly avoiding the open paints. His eyes remained fixed on her, like she was all that existed for him.

Aymee smiled, closed the space between them, and kissed him. When she drew away, he nearly followed; he stopped himself by shutting his eyes and taking a deep breath.

"We'll have plenty of time for that later, Arkon." Tempted as she was to toss the brushes aside and have his hands on her again, she hadn't painted in days, and this was another first for him she could share in. Another lifelong memory to create.

"Let's keep it simple for now," she continued. "I know you have a talent for patterns, so we can work with that." She gestured down at the paints. "There's no wrong way. Just experiment."

His eyes slid from side to side as he looked over the paints, and she could almost see the possibilities forming in his mind. He looked at her. "You are painting too, are you not?"

"Yes." Picking up a brush, she dipped it into the green paint and turned to the wall. She began a simple base — a long stem with sprouting leaves. At the edge of her vision, Arkon jabbed his brush into one of the jars.

She laughed as he raised his hand; paint dripped from the tips of his fingers and covered most of the brush's handle. "I guess I should've told you to only dip the bristles. You can rinse it all off in the water."

His skin tinged violet while he moved to the bin, plunged his hand in, and scrubbed. The water clouded red.

"Can we say I was slightly over enthusiastic and forget this mishap?" He lifted his hand from the bin and shook off the excess water.

"Forget what?"

"What just hap—" A slow smile spread across his lips. "I understand. I shall now make my *first* attempt."

He reached down with exaggerated delicacy, easing the tip of the brush into the jar of red paint. His attention shifted to the wall, where he painted — with equal concentration — a triangle. His lines were surprisingly straight, though he applied the paint somewhat unevenly.

She watched from her periphery as he lost himself in the activity; he built on that first triangle, positioning more around it at varying angles and colors, only allowing shapes of the same color to come into contact at their corners. Both his concentration and his excitement strengthened as the pieces came together, though he still managed to cover his hands in paint.

He asked a few questions as he worked. Aymee showed him how to mix colors to create new ones, and the process brought a look of wonderment to his face. His early attempts were less than appealing, but he quickly learned the relationships between the colors and grew better able to predict what the combinations would produce.

They painted until a section of wall at least three meters across was covered in shapes and images, blotches of color and lines.

Aymee turned her head toward him and grinned; his intense focus was endearing. She stepped closer and ran her brush down his arm, creating a blue line a few shades darker than his skin.

He paused and looked down at his arm, brow furrowing. "Are we not meant to be painting the wall?"

"I've decided to paint you." With a few flowing motions, she painted a series of spirals and lines on his chest.

"I do not believe I make a very good canvas," he said, and his skin changed to match the color of the paint, making it disappear.

Aymee laughed as she rinsed her brush, dipped it into the white paint, and created another design on his abdomen.

Arkon smiled and leaned down to dip his brush into the jar of orange paint. "I've no desire to ruin your clothing. Will you remove it...or shall I?"

Immediate desire flooded her. "Which would you prefer?" she asked.

One of his tentacles reached forward, encircled her waist,

and drew her close. "I prefer to have my hands on you." He passed the brush to another tentacle and carefully unbuttoned her shirt with his fingertips and claws. His skin changed again as he did so, making the paint on his arm and torso stand out against its rich maroon.

"What does that color mean?" she asked as he pushed her shirt aside, baring her breasts. She let the garment fall to the floor along with her paintbrush.

He ran his palms down her sides, trailing paint over her skin, and hooked the waistband of her pants with his fingers. "It means I am *very* interested in my new canvas."

The tips of his claws lightly grazed her legs as he slid her pants down; though heat suffused her, she shivered when she stepped out of them.

"And what will you paint on your new canvas?"

He dipped his chin, moving his gaze down her body. "Now that I look upon it in full, I find it too beautiful to mar with my amateur attempts."

Aymee's breath quickened, her nipples tightened, and she squeezed her thighs against the ache growing between them. His words, paired with his gaze, brought her body to life.

Arkon's eyes darkened, violet irises eclipsed by the black of his pupils.

He advanced, and Aymee retreated until her back hit the wall. Pressing his palms to the surface on either side of her, he leaned in close. His tentacles slid up along her bare legs, caressing, and she willingly parted them for him. Suction cups lightly kissed and tasted her flesh.

She placed a hand on his stomach. The muscles beneath her palm rippled as she slid it down. His slit parted when she teased it with her fingers, and his glistening shaft thrust out. Aymee curled her fingers around him.

He growled, baring his teeth, and tilted his head toward her. A shudder coursed through him, and he covered her mouth with his. His arms remained anchored to either side, but his tentacles moved, brushing her thighs, her breasts, her hips; the tip of one slid along her sex.

She gasped against his mouth and he deepened the kiss, his tongue beckoning hers to join in a sensual dance. The tentacle between her legs spread her nether lips and stroked the sensitive bud hidden there. Aymee moaned and rocked her hips, wanting — *needing* — more. Her arms looped around his neck and she drew herself closer, pressing her breasts to his chest. Fire spread through her as she moved against him. Her breasts ached and her core clenched.

"Arkon," Aymee begged, tearing her mouth from his. She undulated on his tentacle, panting out the words as she climbed to a peak. "Please. I need you."

He dropped his hands to her ass and lifted her suddenly. His tentacles forced her legs around his waist. She clutched at him as he lowered her onto his waiting cock, seating her fully upon him with one powerful thrust, filling her, stretching her.

It was too much. It wasn't enough.

The feelers at his base found her clit and stroked.

She broke with a crescendo of cries.

Waves of pleasure swept through her, and she was caught in their current. Aymee squeezed his sides with her legs, digging her heels into his back, and clawed his shoulders with her nails. Warmth pervaded her, and her sex tightened around him, inner muscles quivering and drawing him in deeper.

Arkon held her through all of it. He hissed softly into her ear until he finally pulled back and pushed into her again. His tentacles worshipped her skin; his claws grazed her backside in his desperate but surprisingly gentle grip. Though his rhythm remained consistent, his pace increased, and their moans mingled with the sounds of the raging storm.

The fires inside her rose into an inferno, blazing through her from head to toe and dominating her entire being. It was pain; it was pleasure; it encompassed her entirely.

She came again with a scream and clung to him — her life-line — as he sped his pace, pistoning in and out of her, pushing deeper with every thrust. Violent tremors wracked her. Seeking relief, she bit his shoulder.

Arkon threw his head back and roared. The sound vibrated through Aymee. She felt him thicken, stretching her further, and then he exploded within her, flooding her ravenous body with his hot seed.

He pinned her to the wall. Aymee writhed as the feelers at the base of his cock flicked and stroked her swollen, sensitive clit. She panted and ground against him.

Breathing heavily, Arkon leaned back and covered her breasts with his hands, kneading her flesh. His tentacles and pelvis held her in place, and he watched with hungry eyes while he pushed her to the edge again.

"Arkon," she rasped when her body's quaking subsided.

"You're beautiful." He moved his hands from her breasts to settle upon her hips. One corner of his mouth lifted. "Though I do prefer your natural color."

Aymee glanced down. Whorls of color were smeared all over her body, and she knew her back had left proof of their love-making on the wall behind her. She laughed, and the slight motion reminded her of their lingering physical connection. His grip on her tightened.

"Did you enjoy painting?" She grinned. Streaks of paint were smudged over his cheeks, shoulders, and chest.

"More than I had imagined possible," he replied with a grin of his own. There was a reluctance in his movement as he pulled back from her, finally severing their connection, but he soon scooped her up into his arms. "Perhaps now is an appropriate time for another new experience. I've yet to have a shower. Will you show me?"

She slipped her arms around his neck and smiled. "Gladly."

CHAPTER 17

SOMETHING BRUSHED ALONG THE SOLE OF AYMEE'S FOOT. BROWS furrowed, she jerked her foot back, tucked it safely beneath the covers, and nuzzled her cheek into the pillow to go back to sleep.

The same gentle touch trailed over her cheek. She scrunched her nose and turned her face away, inhaling deeply. Even half-asleep she recognized Arkon's scent — a hint of the sea, a taste of the rain, and something indescribably, utterly *him*. Its comforting familiarity enveloped her.

The touch moved to her neck and changed, becoming the caress of lips over her sensitive skin. She moaned and reached up, her hand encountering something solid — the side of Arkon's head.

"Wake up, Aymee," he said.

"Mmm…" She ran her hand along his jaw then down his neck. "Is it morning already?"

"Already? The sun rose two hours ago, at least."

"Then the sun woke up too early," she muttered. She sank back into the bedding, curling up under the blanket.

Arkon made no reply; for several, blissful seconds, Aymee drifted closer to slumber. Then his arms slid beneath her, and he lifted her out of the bed, blanket and all.

"Arkon!" She flailed until she looped her arms around his neck. Shoving aside the tangled blanket, she blew hair out of her face and met his gaze.

"You have talked several times over the last few days about how you felt caged-in here," he said. "The day dawned clear, which means we can go out. You are wasting daylight."

"The storm's moved on?"

"Yes, but who is to say when the next will come?" He set her gently on her feet. "We need more meat. Would you like to join me on a hunt?"

"Yes! Why didn't you just say so?" Excitement thrummed through her, and she hurried away, dropping the blanket. The air chilled her bare skin as she retrieved the diving suit from the open chest at the foot of the bed.

"I tried. You didn't even stir."

She walked toward the bathroom, suit draped over an arm, and glanced over her shoulder. "You should talk louder next time."

Though she'd never seen him wear this particular expression — a brow arched and one corner of his mouth raised — she knew it meant something like *you're kidding, right?*

Laughing, she entered the bathroom. After relieving herself, she washed her face, scrubbed her teeth, and pulled the suit on. She tied her hair back as she stepped into the barracks again and retrieved her mask. Arkon remained where she'd left him.

She beamed at him. "Let's go!"

He caught her arm before she rushed out, commanding her attention.

"We're not going to be able to speak to each other while we're under, Aymee."

"Oh." She'd forgotten about that.

"I need you to stay close at all times, and if I separate from you at any point, remain where I indicate."

She nodded, hating the fact that she wouldn't be able to communicate with him. Her mind leapt back to her first meeting with Arkon — it had been initiated because of a gesture Jax had taught Aymee, a signal.

"What about signs?" she asked. "Hand gestures?"

"There are very few that you would be able to accurately recreate," he said, "so we will keep it simple." He extended a single finger and pointed down. "Stay here."

Aymee stared at him blankly.

He turned his hand palm-up and beckoned with his fingers. "Come. I think those will serve as a good starting point."

She offered an *are you kidding me* look of her own, but grinned when his lips twitched.

"What about danger?" she asked.

Arkon flashed his skin yellow.

"A sign *I* can make."

"Why don't you create a gesture now, and that is what it will mean to the two of us?"

Aymee scrunched her mouth to the side in thought. She opened her hand, fingers together, and waved it in front of her chest.

Arkon nodded and mimicked her motion. "So it will be."

They went to the submarine pen together, and Arkon kissed her — a deep, lingering kiss — before she raised her hood and put on the mask. Aymee dove into the water after Arkon, and when he guided her to take hold of him, she wrapped her arms and legs around his torso. Smiling up at him, she rested her head on his shoulder.

He ducked underwater and propelled them forward. Aymee thrilled at his agility as they sped through the concrete tunnel and entered open water. She was torn between appreciating the beauty of the surrounding ocean — which only increased as they neared the bottom — and watching the graceful, hypnotic rhythm of his tentacles as they flared out and came together.

When they reached the seafloor, Arkon slowed and ran his hands along her thighs. Desire rushed through her. With a grin, she unlocked her ankles and lowered her legs, feet coming down on the uneven rock of the bottom. Arkon only released her fully when she'd found her balance.

The submarine pen had granted a tiny glimpse of the sea as a whole; being here now, on the bottom, with endless blue stretching in all directions, was overwhelming. Sunlight glittered on the surface far overhead, casting thin, ever-shifting shadows on the sand and rock at her feet. Sea plants of countless varieties grew all around — patches of waving grass; green and purple stalks covered in bulbous, floating pods; masses of branch-like plants resembling bushes without leaves.

Creatures of many shapes and sizes moved around and through it all. Their colors spanned the rainbow, and their patterns varied; shimmering scales and sleek skin, stone-like hard shells, opalescent carapaces that shifted hue as they were hit by light from different angles. She slowly swept her gaze across it all and stored the images to memory for later paintings.

She looked at Arkon and smiled.

He returned the smile and motioned for her to follow as he swam toward one of the larger rock formations jutting up from the bottom. Many of the creatures scattered, but as Aymee and Arkon slowed their movement, the creatures resumed their normal behavior. She was content to simply watch as they scuttled and swam in and out of holes and through plants, each following its own survival instinct.

Arkon pointed at the ground. Aymee rolled her eyes, but his expression remained stern, and she let herself sink to the bottom.

Her feet touched down on the edge of the rock formation, just before it gave way to a large patch of sand which was broken only by a few smaller rocks and sparse vegetation.

As he swam away from her, Arkon shifted his color to match that of the water. The effect didn't leave him invisible, but it broke up his silhouette, making his form difficult to distinguish from the surrounding blue. He floated near the rocks about twenty meters away, at the far edge of the sand, directing himself with only the smallest movements of his tentacles. The nearby sea creatures seemed not to notice him.

A shadow passed over Aymee. She twisted, looking up to find its source, and her heart stilled.

A boat.

Turning, she searched frantically for Arkon. It took her a few panicked seconds to pick out his shape. She waved her hand over her chest.

Danger. Danger!

But his back was to her.

"Damnit!" Her gaze flicked back up to the boat as it continued its course.

It was likely nothing — just a fishing boat from The Watch,

perhaps with Macy's father on board. But she couldn't see any nets or fishing lines trailing in the water behind it.

"Your heart rate has accelerated," Sam said, startling her. "Do you require assistance?"

"No. Nothing you can help with, Sam." Aymee searched for Arkon again, tapping her foot on the ground in indecision. He'd told her to stay put, but what if they needed to leave? What if there were hunters on that boat, searching for them? Arkon still hadn't looked her way.

She needed to reposition herself to catch his attention.

Aymee stepped off the rock and walked across the sand, careful to avoid the small, swaying plants. She glanced up and finally caught Arkon's gaze when the ground beneath her moved.

His eyes widened, and his skin flared yellow.

Danger!

The sand under Aymee burst upward, and something huge rose out of it. She tumbled backward, only for the thing to slam into her and send her spinning, annihilating her sense of direction. Fear spiked through her. A cloud of sand obscured the water all around, offering only a glimpse of the beast that had emerged.

The small of her back came down on the edge of the rock formation. Pain arced along her spine. The surrounding water moved in a torrent, and Sam said something, but she couldn't understand his words over her own rasping breaths. Aymee scrambled away, shoving herself along the bottom, as the creature charged.

It was fully in her view for only a moment, but that was long enough for it to be forever burned into her memory. Wide mandibles extended to either side of its mouth, likely acting as funnels to direct food toward the rows of razor-sharp teeth at the middle, and thick, paddle-like fins pumped along its belly. The hump on its hard-shelled top resembled the surrounding rocks. Its small, black eyes — six of them arranged over the toothy part of its mouth — were directed at her.

In a surge of motion, Arkon slammed into the creature's belly. His momentum threw off its course, and it spun aside, thrashing to right itself. Aymee's breath caught in her throat.

Sam's voice seemed to contain a hint of alarm, but she still couldn't decipher his words; all her attention was on the struggle before her, leaving room for nothing else.

Arkon latched onto the beast — which was at least as long as him and almost twice as wide — wrapped his tentacles around it, and jabbed its belly repeatedly with his claws. It bucked and kicked its fins to dislodge the kraken, but Arkon didn't relent. His tentacles coiled tighter. Cracks appeared in the beast's shell.

Blood clouded the water, mingling with the still-settling sand.

Don't let him be hurt!

The creature came down on its back, slamming into the rock hard enough for Aymee to feel the vibration of its impact. She scrabbled away, heart in her throat. She couldn't take her eyes off Arkon.

Bending, the creature waved its mandibles to catch hold of Arkon. He brought both his hands down on its chin, burying his claws in the soft flesh of its underside. More blood flowed as he forced its head down into the rock. Keeping it pinned with one arm, he drew the other back and struck, over and over.

The beast's frantic thrashing kicked up more sand, impeding Aymee's vision for a moment.

When the cloud cleared, the creature was still, and Arkon's

siphons flared. There were several wounds on his torso and arms from which trickles of blood drifted into the water. He turned his head, met Aymee's eyes, and suddenly released the beast, rushing to her.

Arkon grasped her upper arms and ran his eyes over her. Then he drew her into a tight embrace. His tentacles slid around her, and the two of them sank to the bottom, but he didn't let go.

"Do you require assistance?" Sam asked, his voice finally breaking through as her panic eased. "Would you like me to send a distress signal?"

"I'm fine." Aymee wrapped her arms around Arkon, holding him just as tightly. She waited until her heart settled and her trembling subsided before she guided Arkon to lean back.

"I'm okay, Arkon." He couldn't hear her, but she hoped he'd understand. She placed a hand on his jaw and stroked his cheek. His eyes were dilated, possessing a fearful gleam. Red mist drifted through the water between them. Aymee frowned, dropping her gaze to the various wounds on his chest, shoulders, and arms.

She didn't know as much about the ocean as Macy, but Aymee knew blood attracted predators. "We need to go, Arkon." She motioned to his wounds.

He glanced down and frowned but didn't seem concerned. His hold on her didn't relent.

"Arkon." He didn't look up, so she cupped his face and directed his eyes back to her. "We need to go. It's too dangerous, and you need to get those taken care of." To illustrate her point, she gestured to his injuries, then back to the creature he'd just killed, and finally in the direction of the base.

Turning his head, he looked over his shoulder at the beast.

When he looked back to Aymee, he drew her against him, tentacles guiding her legs up and around his waist.

Sighing in relief, Aymee tightened her hold on him, crossing her ankles at his back. He kept an arm around her as he swam. With his free hand, he grabbed the dead creature's tail and dragged it alongside them.

THE BASE'S infirmary was much smaller than the one in the Facility — this place had three examination tables rather than beds, all of them adjustable in a variety of ways and possessing numerous attachments for tools Arkon couldn't identify, and several storage cabinets along one wall. Despite its age, everything in the room exuded newness, as though none of it had ever been used; understandable, as the base had never entered full operation. That sense was heightened by the pure white of the overhead lights.

"This isn't necess—" Arkon bit off his words with a hiss as Aymee dabbed more of the pungent liquid onto one of his wounds. It hurt worse than when the cut had been opened. The ends of his tentacles writhed over the floor.

"How is it not necessary? Some of these look like they need stitches, Arkon!"

Aymee had insisted on bringing him to the infirmary to tend his wounds. He'd delayed, more concerned with taking care of the meat once he confirmed she was unharmed apart from the bruise on her back. They'd hauled the sandseeker out of the water with ropes and hooks, and he'd cut as much meat as he could from it; Aymee glared at him until after he'd stored everything in the freezer.

"I will heal, Aymee," he replied. "My wounds are minor."

She gestured to one of the deeper cuts, then carefully cleaned the blood oozing from around it. "This is not minor."

He winced, muscles tensing.

Better myself than her.

Though they were at least an hour beyond the attack, Arkon's nerves had little settled. His memory insisted upon reviewing those terrifying moments repeatedly. Fear kept his blood cold, and his hearts thumped. The first time he'd taken her out, and his stupidity had nearly cost Aymee her life.

"I am not human, Aymee," he said through his teeth, too harshly. "Your standards do not fit me, in most cases."

Aymee flinched and lowered the cloth. "No, you're not. Sometimes I forget how different we really are." She pressed her lips into a thin line, averting her eyes. "But you *are* wounded and bleeding. I've seen people die from cuts smaller than this."

"And I watched you nearly get killed!" He lashed out with a tentacle, knocking the metal cart — and the medical supplies upon it — to the floor. "If my blood is the price to keep you safe, I will gladly pay it again and again. But if I had been as attentive as I should have you would never have been in danger to begin with." His shoulders heaved as he breathed through clenched teeth. Had such anger ever flowed through him? Such disappointment in himself?

She'd chosen him as her mate, as her lover. And he had proven himself, at best, an incompetent protector.

She stared at him silently, though her eyes softened, and some of his anger dissipated. "Wasn't it me who didn't obey?" Aymee knelt, righted the cart, and replaced the items that had fallen from its top. When she stood up, she dabbed his arm with a fresh cloth.

"You moved to signal me of danger, didn't you? Do you think I can fault you for that?"

"No." She set the cloth aside and frowned as her eyes roamed over his numerous wounds.

"I brought you into my world, and I failed to keep you safe."

"I'm here, Arkon, and so are you. That is not failure."

"My inattentiveness put you at risk!"

"You once told me that life has little meaning without risks."

Arkon dropped his gaze and clenched his fists at his sides. Having his own words thrown at him was like a physical blow; though he'd spoken them only a couple weeks before, they'd been uttered during another life. Before he had something too valuable to lose.

He inhaled deeply and took her hands in his, meeting her eyes. "And now life would have little meaning without you, Aymee."

She stepped closer, tucking her head under his chin. He wrapped his arms around her; his Aymee was here, with him, whole.

"I was aware of the danger, just like you knew how dangerous it was for you every time we met on that beach. You're worth the risk, Arkon." Her breath was warm against his throat.

Frowning, he slid a hand into her hair and cupped the back of her head, holding her closer. She kissed his neck, and he closed his eyes. Now he understood how Jax must have felt when Macy was attacked by a razorback — the sense of helplessness, the gut-wrenching terror. He tried to push those emotions aside, to calm his frayed nerves, but a lump of dread lingered in his stomach.

"If you weren't aware of the sandseeker, why were you

trying to get my attention?" he asked, combing his claws through her hair. It was an oddly soothing action; a simple, concrete reassurance of her presence, of her wellbeing.

"I saw a boat."

His hand stilled. Tumultuous thoughts roiled through his mind, a hundred questions and a thousand possible explanations, all lacking any semblance of certainty.

"A fishing boat?"

"I don't know. I didn't see nets or lines."

Perhaps they simply hadn't reached their desired location. That was the logical conclusion, but something inside Arkon said logic might be a hindrance in this situation — what if the hunters were closing in while he attempted to rationalize all this? "Is it normal for them to come to this area?"

Aymee sighed and lifted her head. "I'm not sure. It's possible, but I never had much to do with it. Macy would probably know."

If it had been the hunters in that boat — no, they couldn't afford *ifs* now, they had to assume it *was* the hunters — then this place was at risk of being discovered. The chances of it being spotted by someone hugging the coastline were strong, though it depended on the angle of their approach.

"I think it best we have the computer shut down all the lights in the submarine pen and leave them off. If they find this place, we want them to think it is abandoned," he said.

"I agree." She stepped back, and Arkon loosened his hold on her. "Are you sure your wounds are okay?"

He was tempted to pull her close again, but he refrained. "They will be, yes. Most of them will heal by tomorrow."

She nodded, cupped his face, and tugged him down for a kiss. "I suppose you won't need to hunt for a while then?"

"So long as you enjoy the sandseeker meat." He smiled and kissed her again.

Aymee chuckled and caressed his face. "I'm in no position to be picky. Besides, you killed that thing to save me. I'm sure it will be the most succulent meat I've ever had." Her lips spread into a grin. "So long as I'm not cooking it."

CHAPTER 18

ARKON'S SIPHON TWITCHED ENOUGH TO DRAW HIM FROM THE depths of sleep into murky awareness. Without opening his eyes, he turned his head away.

Something touched him near his nostrils, tickling his skin. Confusion suffused the groggy haze that had settled over his mind. He lifted a hand and brushed his palm over his face.

Another tickle, this time on one of his tentacles. His muscles tightened as the limb reflexively curled away, and Arkon finally opened his eyes.

Laughter filled his ears — Aymee's laughter.

"I finally woke up before you!" Aymee grinned down at him. "I've been waiting three days to get you back."

He furrowed his brow and tilted his head, staring up at her. The barrack's overhead lights were off; it was very early morning, but Aymee was wide awake. Arkon smiled. Joy and humor brightened her face, and he couldn't think of a more beautiful image to wake to.

It didn't hurt that she'd not yet dressed for the day.

Thrusting out his tentacles, he caught her around the waist and dragged her down atop him. She shrieked with laughter, hands landing on either side of his head and hair falling around their faces. Her breasts pressed against his chest and desire stirred within him.

"Well, now you have me, what do you plan to do with me?" she asked.

He brushed the hair back from one side of her face and studied her features. It seemed there was something new to be found in them every day, something more to appreciate.

"I will allow my imagination no limits in deciding that."

The glee in her expression softened, giving way to sudden solemnity. She cupped his jaw, running her thumb over his cheek. "I feel like I've waited for you my whole life." Her gentle touch moved to his lower lip. "I didn't know it then, but that moment on the beach, the first time we spoke to each other, I felt...something. A connection. I thought it was simple fascination. You were so different, so extraordinary, so...beautiful.

"I anticipated every glimpse of you, cherished every gift. We never spoke except for that short encounter, but I could almost *feel* you. And then you finally came to me. Our friendship was so easy. It was as though we'd always known each other. Does that make it fate?" she asked. "When I had to make the choice to part ways, it devastated me, but not as much as the thought of losing you irrevocably."

He covered her hand with his. "I cannot tell you whether it is fate or not, Aymee. That is a word which holds little meaning to my people. The kraken have simply survived. We were made, and we exist, and that was as far as most of us seem to have considered it.

"But the chances of you and I ever meeting, of ever knowing

of one another's existence, were so tiny, so improbable, that it should never have been. I have spent most of my life searching out something I could never define, pushing to express thoughts and emotions I did not — or could not — understand, and when I finally saw you for the first time...the rest of it didn't matter anymore."

His chest swelled with the emotions she'd woken in him; even now, he could not express himself in a way that did his feelings justice. But Aymee understood. From the beginning, she'd understood.

She turned her face and kissed his hand, smiling. "I love you, Arkon."

"And I love you, Aymee."

Aymee pressed her lips to his before laying her head on his shoulder. They remained in that position for a time, enjoying the mutual embrace. He closed his eyes and focused on the steady beat of her heart.

"We should make the most of the early hours," she eventually said, slipping from his arms. "We've been cooped up for days." She grabbed her suit and grinned at him. "Take me swimming, and when we get back, you can have your wicked way with me."

He watched her walk away, appreciating the play of muscle in her lithe legs and the sensual sway of her hips and backside. Once she was out of sight, he turned his gaze upward.

If Jax had wandered the seas in a physical search, Arkon had navigated tangled paths of thought, hoping to find meaning, to find purpose. To find something beyond mere survival. He'd been restless in his own fashion.

Now, he'd found contentment. He was still curious, still inquisitive, still thirsted for knowledge, but he was content with Aymee. He was *happy*. Though he couldn't pretend to understand the changes he'd undergone, he couldn't deny them. She filled in a piece of him that had been missing.

She was his muse, his centerpiece, the jewel that belonged at the heart of his life.

His tentacles shifted over the bedding, picking up hints of her taste on the fabric.

His Aymee.

"I'm ready!" she called.

Arkon turned his head to see her emerge from the bathroom. She picked up her mask from one of the nearby bunks and moved toward the door leading into the corridor. He rolled off the bed and accompanied her.

They hurried through the corridors, sped by her excitement. Aymee was the first through the door to the submarine pen.

"—mee? Arkon?" a voice called, echoing through the chamber.

"Is that..." Aymee stepped forward, looking over the rail. "Macy!"

He hurried to the railing beside her. Macy stood on the lower platform, water dripping from her diving suit, flanked by Jax and Dracchus.

Macy tilted her head back and beamed up at them before she and Aymee simultaneously raced for the stairs.

Arkon followed her, turning toward the stairwell as Macy and Aymee met on the center steps and embraced one another.

"I missed you so much!" Aymee exclaimed.

"I was worried when we came in here and didn't see either of you!" Macy grinned at Arkon. "I've missed you, too."

"It is good to see you," he said, and shifted his gaze to the two kraken at the base of the stairs. "All of you."

Aymee pulled back. "Not that I'm not happy to see you, but why are you here, Mace?"

"They wanted to check on you two, so I demanded they bring me along."

"Macy demanded to see you *before* she knew we were coming," Jax said, his half-smile belying his serious tone. "She said she would go by herself if I didn't take her."

"I knew he wouldn't let that happen." Macy's gaze was warm as it met Jax's. "And it worked, right?"

"Where's baby Sarina?" Aymee asked.

"Rhea has her with the other females and younglings. They'll protect her from anything. Even Dracchus wouldn't cross those women."

Dracchus grunted. "They will not keep me from my...what was your word, Macy? *Niece?*"

"I thought she was *my* niece." Arkon looked at Macy and lifted his brows in question. On the surface, human familial relationships seemed simple, but perhaps they were more complicated than he'd assumed.

Macy chuckled. "You're *both* her uncles, and she's got the best uncles in all of Halora."

Arkon was reminded of how much he missed these people — not the kraken in general, but his *family*. Only Sarina was related to anyone else by blood, but that didn't matter. Their bonds had formed in different ways.

And now Aymee was part of his family, too.

He turned to look down at Jax and Dracchus. "There is something I must speak to the two of you about."

"Come on, Aymee," Macy said, hooking Aymee's arm with her own, "show me where you've been staying. I felt like I was calling your names *forever* before you came out."

"Sure. There's actually a lot for me to tell you." Aymee walked alongside her up the stairs and toward the interior of the base.

Jax moved up the steps to watch the females disappear into the short hallway. A few moments later, the metallic groan of the opening door echoed through the submarine pen.

"It opened?" Jax asked, surprise on his features.

The groan repeated as the door closed.

"The suit I brought for Aymee interfaced with the computer in this base, just like Macy's had at the Facility. It opened the door for us."

"What is beyond it?" Jax swung his attention toward the hallway again.

"Let us talk first. Then you can explore until your curiosity is sated."

Nodding, Jax followed Arkon down to the lower platform, stopping near Dracchus.

"You and Aymee are well?" Jax asked.

"Yes. We had an unplanned run-in with a sandseeker a few days ago, but apart from that, we have been comfortable. We've...made good use of our time together."

"You mated with her?" Dracchus asked.

Arkon straightened his back and rose slightly higher. "Yes. We have claimed one another."

"I am glad for you." Jax lifted a hand and settled it on Arkon's shoulder for a moment before dropping it away. The contact was surprising but welcome; the warmth and good nature of the gesture were clear.

"In many ways, I owe it to you, Jax." Arkon met his friend's eyes. "Had you not rescued Macy... I would ask more of you, though. Both of you."

"What do you require?"

"Your support. We are mated, and our current situation, while viable, is not ideal... I want to bring Aymee to the Facility. To stay."

Dracchus and Jax exchanged a glance, and more meaning and understanding seemed to pass between the two kraken in that moment than Arkon had ever thought possible.

"You have my support, no matter what," Jax said. "Just as you gave me yours."

"We have seen boats during the last few hunts." Dracchus tilted his head back and ran his eyes over the shadowed walls and ceiling. "They do not appear to be fishing. We must assume the danger is growing, and the humans are searching for us."

"What does that have to do with taking Aymee to the Facility?" Arkon asked.

"It is no longer safe here. If Aymee is your mate, you must bring her among our people," Dracchus replied.

"And Kronus? I will not tolerate so much as an implication of intent to harm her." Arkon's skin took on a faint red tint; he swallowed his anger but could not put it aside.

"Kronus has been suspicious of your absence since the news about the human hunters." Jax moved to one of the mooring posts at the edge of the platform and leaned against it, curling a tentacle around its base. "He has not eased, nor have his followers. But we will keep them at bay, together."

"I will put him down as many times as necessary. I do not fear facing him." There was no aggression in Dracchus's voice, only cold, unshakeable confidence.

"I have not spoken to Aymee about this yet. I want the choice to be hers. This is something—"

Arkon snapped his mouth shut, and all three kraken turned

their heads toward the tunnel that led to the sea. The sound of gentle waves lapping against the concrete walls had changed; something was moving through the water.

A hushed voice echoed from the darkness.

A *human* voice.

Arkon's hearts stilled. There was a chance it was simply some curious fishermen from The Watch, but that seemed as probable as he and Aymee meeting one another in the first place.

"The females," Jax whispered.

"They are safe," Arkon replied. "The door automatically locks."

The sound of something breaking the water drew nearer. Arkon quickly signaled to the others.

To the dark. No water.

The kraken separated, moving quickly and silently to the deepest shadows in the pen. Arkon flattened himself in a corner and altered his skin to match his surroundings. His hearts thumped. Jax and Dracchus slipped into their own positions and faded into the environment; even Arkon, who knew what to look for, had difficulty discerning their forms.

From his vantage, Arkon watched the water. Whispers floated from the tunnel, more distinct than before.

A boat coasted into the pen. It was undoubtedly from The Watch — riding on a shallow draft, it was as long as three or four kraken stretched head-to-tentacle, its single sail bundled up. Six human males manned the craft; two on each side propelled it forward with oars, and two more were at the front.

Randall sat on the foremost bench. Cyrus stood near the prow.

"The hell is this place?" asked Joel from his position at the oars.

"Ain't no cave," Cyrus replied. "Bring us in over by that ladder. We'll tie off there."

"Look at that ceiling," another man said. "Should we even be in here?"

"Been up for this long," Cyrus said.

The boat, save for the mast, exited Arkon's vision as it neared the wall. There was the sound of movement from inside the vessel, and the mast bobbed and rocked as two of the men climbed onto the platform. Both had long guns slung over their shoulders. They knelt and swung the weapons into their hands, watching opposite directions, as Joel climbed the ladder and tied a rope around the nearest mooring post.

"Think anyone at The Watch knows about this place?" one of the other men asked.

"Think it'd be empty if they did, Chad? No one has been here in years from the looks of it," another said.

"Even if they knew about it, what use would they have for this place?" The voice was Randall's; a moment later, he hauled himself onto the platform with one arm. His face was pale, and his left arm was bundled against his chest. "The roof could collapse at any moment."

Cyrus climbed up last. His face was a patchwork of light green and yellow bruises, and there were scabs on his cheek and lips. "Animals don't care about that shit. That's what we're hunting, boys. Animals."

Randall scowled, glaring at Cyrus. "Quick sweep. I don't want us here any longer than necessary. Some of that roof fell recently."

"And how can you tell that, Randy?" Cyrus grinned,

displaying a black space where a tooth had been knocked out. Arkon felt a small pleasure in that.

"Because, Ranger, some of that debris is not overgrown like the rest. You all know what to do."

The humans split up, most of them holding their long guns across their chests, fingers near the triggers, and began their search.

"What do you think this place was for?" one of the men called out, his voice echoing loudly.

"Keep it down, Ward!" Chad hissed.

Cyrus and Joel walked up the steps to the second level, out of sight.

Arkon's chest tightened. The door would not open for these men — he was certain of it. But what if Macy and Aymee came out before the hunters left?

"Well damn. Hey Randy!" Cyrus called. "Best head up here and look at this."

Randall — who had remained near the boat, peering at the other side of the pen through the morning gloom — turned and went up the steps to join the others. Within a few moments, all the humans were on the second level.

"Got a short hallway leading deeper into the base, and next to it... Looks like your fish girl's paintings." Cyrus's smirk was apparent in his voice.

A chill swept through Arkon's body, stilling everything inside him and building to an unbearable, heavy dread. Though he'd stopped to admire their paintings on the wall upstairs almost every time he'd passed by, he hadn't realized it was clear evidence of their presence.

"Could've been done by anyone," Randall said.

"Oh? So you can paint like this, too, Randy? Damn shame I left my brushes back home, or I'd have you show me."

"This looks recent," Joel said.

"It could've been in the last few days or the last few months," Randall said. "This wall wouldn't get any sun, so the paint won't fade."

"You still trying to protect her?" Cyrus demanded. "She *shot* you, kid. Pretty cut and dry, that relationship."

"I'm being practical. I'm not any happier about this situation than you are, Cyrus, but it is what it is. We've gone up and down this coast and haven't found a single sign of them."

"*This* is a damned sign! It's the same shit she painted on the side of her house, and it's right here next to three closed doors. Going to call that a coincidence? Hell, they're probably living back there!"

"Those doors aren't likely to be functional," Randall said.

Arkon looked toward Jax and Dracchus's hiding places and flashed yellow. Jax leaned off the wall, glancing toward the steps, and signaled.

They know.

"There's a little light flashing at that door," Joel's voice was hushed.

The scraping of metal echoed through the pen. The hunters went quiet after the whisper of footsteps.

"Wait until Jax sees it," Macy said.

"Get back inside!" Jax yelled.

"Wha—" Aymee's words were drowned out by a scuffling of boots and shouts from the hunters.

Macy's scream was cut off, and Aymee's angry exclamation silenced.

"Months ago, huh, Randy?" Cyrus laughed. "This must be that girl who left to live with the fish."

Someone growled — Macy.

Jax moved to climb onto the second level, but Dracchus caught him and held him down before he exposed himself.

"What are you doing?" Randall demanded.

"What you don't have the balls to do," Cyrus replied. "You ask the fishermen back in town, they'll tell you — a hook needs to be baited if you want to catch a fish. We just found our bait."

"We're not hunting humans, Cyrus. Let them go — both of you. We have no right to harm these women."

"Once we bag what we came for. Though I have something to settle with this bitch."

Aymee cried out sharply.

Fury crashed through Arkon like waves lashing the shore during a storm. It filled his limbs with anxious, overwhelming energy, and everything in him screamed to charge to the upper platform and tear into the hunters. To protect Aymee. To avenge her pain. His nostrils flared. He'd never craved the spilling of blood as he did in that moment, had never longed for the satisfaction of breaking another creature. The fire in his veins urged him to violence.

Muscles tense, he crept forward.

A flash of yellow in the distance called his attention to the other kraken; Jax's eyes were filled with rage, and his skin was crimson. Dracchus met Arkon's gaze and shook his head firmly.

Calm. Keep to the dark, Dracchus signaled. *Keep quiet.*

"We heard you," Cyrus called. "Might as well come out if you don't want these two hurt. Blondie's quite a looker. Be a damn shame to mess that up."

"Don't touch her," Aymee grated.

Clenching his teeth, Arkon halted. *Calm. Quiet.* He'd seen the hunters' weapons. A headlong attack would only expose him to their gunfire and would do Aymee no good. He forced his breath to slow, but his tension did not ease.

He reached up and grasped the ledge, rising just enough to peer over it to the second level. The humans were just outside the hallway in a ring; Joel held Macy, his hand covering her mouth, and Aymee was bent forward, one of Cyrus's hands fisted in her hair. He held a pistol in his other hand.

Randall stepped toward Cyrus. "Cyrus Taylor, I am hereby—"

"Shut it already, kid. You want to go by the book?" Cyrus fired his gun from the hip. The sound of it was thunderous as it bounced off the concrete walls. "We're going by the *original* book."

Aymee and Macy screamed. Randall stumbled backward and collapsed on the floor.

"What the fuck, Cyrus?" Chad shouted.

"Randall Laster has been relieved of command," Cyrus replied.

"We never talked about shooting him!" one of the others said.

"He chose his side, Hassan, and it was going to come down to this either way. We bag these fucking fishmen, and Randy's sacrifice will have been worth it. We'll tell his father he died in the hunt. That's more than he deserves."

"We're not supposed to kill our own, Cyrus!"

"The fuck you think the Culver Hunters started out doing? We hunted traitors and deserters, kiddies. When that wasn't a thing anymore, we moved to bounty hunting — running down anyone who pissed off the wrong people. Shit, you haven't *lived* until you've hunted a human. Nothing like it...but these fish-men are pretty damned close. Don't know why the hell we stopped."

Cyrus moved closer to the railing, dragging Aymee along with him. She clawed at his wrist. He shook her forcefully, and she returned her hands to her hair as though to relieve the pressure. "After what this bitch did to me, I have zero issue with putting a slug in her gut. You come on up here and talk to us, or we lay her out next to Randy and come down there."

Arkon's fingers flexed; brittle concrete crumbled beneath them.

Calm, he reminded himself, but the word possessed no immediate meaning to him. Aymee was in danger, her life was at risk, and he wasn't there with her. He might lose her forever. If he moved quickly enough, he could get to Cyrus and strike a mortal blow before...

"You're a monster," Aymee said.

"I'm the only thing standing between you and the monsters," Cyrus growled.

Monsters...

Arkon wouldn't give them the monster they wanted to slay.

He lowered himself. Perhaps he might have compared Cyrus to Kronus, once, but there was a stark difference — Cyrus was not held in check by fear, or honor, or anything of the sort. He'd been left battered and bloodied, and it had only pushed him toward *this*.

Arkon looked to his companions; Jax — whose expression was a jumble of terror and fury, of helplessness and desperation, mirroring Arkon's emotions — was still restrained by Dracchus.

Arkon could not lose Aymee. Would not.

A hook needs to be baited if you want to catch a fish.

He knew then what he had to do.

Go around, Arkon signed.

Confusion flicked over Jax's features, but he nodded. Dracchus released him, and together the two kraken crept along the wall, toward the far steps.

Arkon drew in a deep breath, filling his lungs. Life had no meaning without risks. *Everything* he cared about was at risk now. Almost everyone he loved. At least Sarina was safe.

"I am coming up," Arkon called. "There is no need to harm the females."

"Arkon, no!" Aymee yelled.

"And here part of me thought you'd dive into that water and swim as far away as you could," Cyrus said.

"Fuck!" Joel exclaimed. "She bit me!"

"Don't come!" Macy shouted.

"Damn it, Joel, you're twice her size! Handle your shit."

"What do you want me to do?" he demanded.

"Hit the bitch. Shut her up. The adults are trying to talk."

"You're going to regret th—"

A *thwap* — flesh against flesh — silenced Macy.

Arkon moved to the steps, forcing his skin to its normal color — doing so had never been so difficult. He kept low, shielding himself from the hunters' lines of sight. "I am coming. I told you there's no need to do them harm."

"Guess you're just taking too long," Cyrus said.

"Lay down your weapons. There's no reason we cannot all leave here in peace."

"Arkon, he isn't—"

Cyrus's shout cut off Aymee's words. "Shut your mouth!"

Clenching his jaw, Arkon climbed the stairs. Cyrus wore his broken-toothed grin. Macy was on hands and knees at Joel's feet, lip bloody. Randall lay where he'd fallen. The other three hunters pointed their long guns toward Arkon, eyes wide with shock and fear.

Beyond the humans, Jax and Dracchus were dark shapes creeping across the floor.

"You're even uglier than I remember," Cyrus said.

"As are you," Arkon replied. "I'd hate to have to make it worse if we cannot work this out."

"I'm not giving you that chance this time."

Cyrus raised his arm and fired three times in rapid succession.

"No!" Aymee screamed.

The breath fled Arkon's lungs; it felt like three blows from Dracchus impacting his abdomen at once. He looked down to see blood oozing from three holes, and piercing, burning pain spread across his stomach.

When he lifted his gaze, Aymee was staring at him, her eyes round with terror, their whites pronounced. His limbs trembled, and his head spun. Her face blurred as his vision clouded.

CHAPTER 19

Aymee's heart stopped.

For a moment, everything fell away and time slowed. She stared in horror at the dark blood dripping down Arkon's abdomen. Her lungs burned; she was suffocating but couldn't draw breath. The fear of losing him was too much. She lifted her gaze to his.

Arkon's features were drawn with pain and startlement, his eyes glassy. He swayed but remained upright.

There was a whisper of movement behind, and someone released an agonized gurgle. Cyrus yanked hard on Aymee's hair as he swung around. Through the curls that fell into her face, she saw two large, dark figures overpowering the pair of rangers who'd been behind Cyrus.

Jax and Dracchus. The blood spurting from the humans' wounds was lost against the kraken's crimson skin.

"More of them?" Cyrus tightened his grip on Aymee's hair. There was an undercurrent of uncertainty in his voice. He raised his gun.

Aymee gritted her teeth against the agony in her scalp and covered a fist with her other hand. She twisted, pushing with all her strength, and slammed her elbow into Cyrus's groin.

He grunted and doubled over. His hand tugged back on her hair, forcing her gaze up before his fingers slipped away.

Jax hurtled past, landing atop Joel. The kraken wrapped his tentacles around the ranger and squeezed. Bones cracked. Chad, the only other ranger standing, settled the butt of his rifle against his shoulder and aimed at Jax.

A shot rang out. Chad's body jerked as a bullet hit his arm, and his weapon fell from his hand. Dracchus was there an instant later, wrapping a huge hand around Chad's neck. There was a wet crunch.

Chad's limp body sagged to the floor.

Aymee flicked her eyes toward the source of the shot; Randall was propped against the wall, pistol trembling in a bloody hand, a trail of crimson smeared beneath him. His arm fell, gun slipping from his grip. He held his other hand to his gut.

Free of Cyrus's hold, Aymee kicked the gun from his grip. It skittered across the concrete floor.

"You bitch!" he wheezed. He swung his arm, and Aymee braced for impact.

A roar echoed through the pen.

Before Cyrus's blow connected, Arkon — his skin a furious red — slammed into him. They hit the floor hard in a tangle of limbs. Arkon reared up over the man, his back turned to Aymee, and struck Cyrus quickly, repeatedly, savagely.

She couldn't see the damage, but she heard it. Saw the blood dripping from Arkon's arms.

Aymee backed away from them and searched out Macy. She

stood in Jax's embrace; his skin was still crimson, and his shoulders rose and fell with heavy, ragged breaths. Macy brushed her thumb over his cheek soothingly.

Dracchus stalked toward Randall; the other rangers were dead.

"Stop!" Aymee yelled, inserting herself between Dracchus and Randall. She held her hands out in front of her, backed up until she was standing over the surviving ranger, and glanced at him over her shoulder.

Randall looked up at her. His face was pale, his eyes glazed, his hands covered in blood. "Shouldn't have let it come to this. Sorry."

"I tried to tell you," Aymee said, returning her attention to Dracchus.

"He is one of them," Dracchus said.

"He helped us. He stopped one of them from shooting Jax."

Dracchus turned his head, glancing over his shoulder toward Chad's body. He seemed to consider it for several seconds before finally grunting. "Will he live?"

Aymee stepped over Randall, crouched beside him, and gently pulled his hand away from his wound. It didn't look as though anything serious had been hit, but she couldn't be sure without further examination. She removed his sling and folded it, pressing it to the wound. "If we can get the bleeding to stop, yes." She looked up. "Macy, I need you."

Macy nodded and spoke softly to Jax. He hesitated before releasing her and followed directly on her heels as she approached Aymee.

"Keep pressure here, Mace."

Once Macy had pressed her hand over the bloodied cloth on Randall's stomach, Aymee stood and went to Arkon.

Pushing up off Cyrus, Arkon swayed backward unsteadily. Blood and gore dripped from his hands. He turned and met Aymee's gaze, chest moving rapidly with short, shallow breaths. His skin reverted to its normal color and then paled. She couldn't tell how much of the blood on his torso was his own.

She ran to him, catching him before he fell. His weight bore down on her, his body slick with blood.

"Dracchus!" she cried, then lowered her voice, fighting tears. "Don't you dare die on me, Arkon."

"Not dying. Just...dizzy."

Within a second, Dracchus was beside Arkon. He took hold of Arkon's arm and slung it over his shoulders, relieving Aymee of the weight.

"We need to get him to the infirmary. Both of them. Jax, can you take Randall?"

"Yes," Jax replied.

"Macy, keep pressure on his wound," Aymee said, then moved ahead of Dracchus, leading him into the hall. Hurriedly, she entered the code. The door groaned open.

Knowing Dracchus was right behind her, she raced through the hallway, turning right at the intersection, and slapped the button to open the infirmary doors.

"Lay them on the tables." She ran to the cabinets, thankful she'd taken time to familiarize herself with the supplies on hand.

Her hands shook as she opened the cabinets. She paused and drew in several deep breaths.

Calm.

Panicking or crying wouldn't help Arkon. She needed to distance herself from her emotions, from the pain in her heart, and focus on her knowledge. These weren't the first bullet wounds she'd dealt with.

Releasing the seal on her suit, she tugged her arms out — she'd need her hands unrestricted to work properly — and tied the sleeves behind her back to keep her chest covered. She brushed the tears from her eyes, scrubbed her hands at the small sink, and gathered the tools and supplies she'd need to remove the bullets and seal the wounds, placing them on a cart.

When she turned back toward the room, Arkon and Randall were already stretched out on the tables. Macy kept her hands over Randall's wound, and Dracchus and Jax stood beside Arkon, Jax's hands on his friend's abdomen to staunch the bleeding.

Wheeling the tray to Arkon, Aymee grabbed the scanner hanging overhead and directed it over his abdomen. "Lift your hands, Jax." She pressed the button on the side of the device.

It hummed to life. Beams of light bathed Arkon, illuminating the blood vessels beneath his skin with a soft red glow. This was far more sophisticated than the scanners they had in The Watch — those displayed through a screen, rather than directly on the patient. Her fingers fumbled over the touch panel on the scanner until she found the depth adjustment and used it to view deeper inside his body.

The differences and similarities in their anatomy were apparent. His three hearts beat weakly, pumping blood through large arteries. The scanner picked out the bullets and high-lighted them as non-organic objects; she ran her eyes over his abdomen, studying it closely, and finally breathed a small sigh of relief.

No major arteries had been hit, and the damage to his internal organs appeared minimal.

Aymee wiped away the blood and bits of carnage from his stomach with a towel and cleaned around the wounds with antiseptic. She picked up the anesthetic injector and dialed up the dosage slightly; there was an entire science behind determining the proper dosage, but such anesthetics weren't common in The Watch, and she didn't have time.

"If this does its job, you're going to be nice and numb, okay?" she said as she pressed the gun to his neck and injected him.

"I will heal," Arkon slurred.

Aymee glanced up; his eyes were closed, his features drawn in discomfort, but there was a hint of a smile on his lips. Despite his attempt to comfort her, he was far too pale for Aymee's liking.

"You will," she replied, "but you don't have a choice this time. I'm helping you along."

She bit her lip and watched his face as she pressed a finger into one of his wounds; he made no reaction.

"Jax, be ready to clear blood away for me." Aymee took up her tools and, using the scanner to guide her, removed the bullets one by one. Jax mopped up the blood as she worked, and she couldn't help but notice the strangely washed-out cast of his skin; he was worried for his friend.

"How are you doing, Randall?" she called as she worked.

"Tired. Of getting shot." His voice was strained and weak.

A pang of guilt rose in her chest. She swept it aside; no room for emotion, now.

Once the last bullet was out, she used another tool to seal the internal damage and close his wounds. Despite the room's climate control, sweat trickled down her face and back. She wiped her forehead with the back of her hand and set the tool down.

She cupped Arkon's cheek. He didn't respond to her touch.

"Rest," she said, pressing a kiss to his lips. "And remember, you're *not* allowed to go."

One more patient to treat.

AN HOUR HAD PASSED in relative silence since Aymee finished tending Randall's wound. She sat beside Arkon as he slept, and Macy remained nearby, her presence providing a bit of comfort. Jax and Dracchus had left to search for more boats once they'd been told they could do nothing more for Arkon.

Aymee held Arkon's hand, brushing her thumb over his. She hated this. Hated not knowing.

He'd lost so much blood. Kraken were tougher than humans, but to what extent? How much damage was too much, when did their bodies reach their limits? She'd done everything in her power. Now, idleness had invited her fears back in.

The door slid open; Dracchus and Jax entered.

"How is he?" Jax asked.

"Stable. Sleeping," Aymee replied.

"Were there any more boats?" Macy asked.

"Nothing nearby."

"We need to leave this place," Dracchus said.

"Arkon needs to rest," Aymee said, looking at Dracchus, "and I'm not leaving Randall behind again."

"We will bring the other human. It is too great a risk to allow him to return to your people."

"Will you hurt him?" she asked carefully.

"He acted in defense of Jax," Dracchus replied. "I have no reason to do him harm."

"We only have two suits," Macy said.

"There are more in a room near the barracks." Aymee settled her hand on Arkon's chest. His heartbeats were steady, but still distressingly weak. "Arkon and I found them when we explored this place."

Dracchus moved toward Randall and stared down at him. "Then we need to go. We will carry them if we must."

With no other choice, Aymee left the infirmary to retrieve a suit, bringing two extra masks — one for her and one for Macy. Randall woke as she was tugging off his pants.

"I knew I'd win you over eventually," he mumbled. Though his eyes were closed, he smirked.

Aymee chuckled. "You'd be surprised how many men I've undressed. It doesn't make you special."

"Could've let me pretend for a little while longer." He was quiet for a time as she finished removing his clothing. "Did I ever stand a chance?"

Aymee glanced up, but Randall's eyes were still closed. "Had I not already met Arkon, you might have."

"Not sure if that makes me feel better or worse." He swallowed thickly.

"I'm sorry."

"Don't be." Randall finally opened his eyes and lifted his head, glancing from Aymee to Jax, who stood on the opposite side of the bed. "What's going on?"

"We're leaving. We need to get you in a PDS."

"A what?"

"A diving suit."

Randall's brow creased. "Why would I need a diving suit?"

"Because you would die otherwise," Jax said.

When Randall swung his gaze from Jax to Aymee, his expression was troubled and his eyes questioning.

"They're taking us with them," she said.

He inhaled deeply and reverted to a calm, neutral expression. "What does that mean for me?"

"You will be under our protection," Jax replied.

"A prisoner?"

"You saved a kraken from harm," Dracchus said, "but we cannot allow you to return to your people. You know too much about us, now."

"One of the rangers is already on his way back to Fort Culver," Randall said.

"There was another?" Dracchus demanded.

How hadn't Aymee realized it yet? Seven of them had been on the stage in the town hall. Only six had come to the submarine pen.

Randall let his head fall back and sighed. "Cyrus sent Jon Mason to Fort Culver after we were brought back into town. Did it while Aymee's father was patching me up, so I couldn't stop him. Wanted to make sure my father knew the kraken were real."

Skin flashing crimson, Dracchus darted toward Randall, lashing out with an arm; Jax intervened, blocking him. Randall lifted his head, eyes gleaming — but not with fear.

"What does that mean for my people?" Dracchus growled.

"It means more hunters will come," Randall said. It was shame in his voice, in his eyes. "I should have stopped this sooner. I should have done more. But I failed my rangers; I failed The Watch. I failed Aymee and your people."

"All of us have made mistakes." Jax locked eyes with Dracchus's. "He is trying to make it right. Should we not allow him that opportunity?"

Dracchus bared his teeth, swung his gaze to Macy and Aymee, and backed away. "You will have our protection, human. That will not extend to any of your hunters, should they come for us."

"I understand." Randall squeezed his eyes shut.

"I'm sorry, Randall," Aymee said.

"You're protecting the people you care about. Never feel shame for that. It's what I was supposed to have been doing all along."

"You did what you thought was right. You had no reason to believe me."

"Don't need to make excuses for me." He sat up, features strained and face paling with the exertion. Aymee hurried to help him. "I can dress myself," he said, but his voice was weak.

"Don't be difficult. The skin is still tender over the wound, and we don't want to reopen it."

Aymee and Jax helped Randall get into his suit; he insisted upon taking over once the sleeves were high enough for his arms, but when he moved his shoulder, he groaned in pain and finally gave in to their assistance.

Macy and Aymee supported Randall on his slow walk out.

Jax and Dracchus lifted Arkon and followed.

He stirred as they moved him. The color hadn't yet returned to his skin, and for a moment he appeared disoriented. His pupils shrank to slits against the overhead lights. "We are leaving?" he asked softly.

"We are going home, Arkon," Jax said.

"Aymee? She is safe?"

"I'm here," Aymee said.

"She is just ahead of us," Jax said. "Rest. You'll be there soon, with Aymee by your side."

They entered the submarine pen. The blood splattered, smeared, and pooled on the concrete was still wet, but the kraken had removed the bodies. Aymee should have felt *something* about that — lingering anger, satisfaction, relief, horror at the memory of the slaughter. All she had now was her love and concern for Arkon. She'd think about the rest after he healed.

Descending to the lower platform, Aymee helped Randall secure his mask, put on her own, and leapt off the edge. She and Macy helped Randall ease down the ladder while Jax and Dracchus lowered Arkon into the water.

Jax came and took hold of Randall. "I will swim with him."

"We need to take it easy on them, or their wounds may reopen," Aymee said.

"Stay close," Jax said to Macy, brushing a hand over her shoulder.

"I will," she replied with a smile.

To Aymee, the swim was an eternity. She had no idea how far they traveled; once the coastline was no longer visible behind them, she lost all sense of direction. Sam might have been able to tell her, but it wasn't important, and she was too preoccupied with monitoring Arkon and Randall to ask.

Aymee had discovered she could speak to Macy and Randall through the masks soon after submerging, but they remained quiet as they swam, especially when the surrounding ocean became nothing but impenetrable blue in all directions.

A faint light in the gloom was the first sign of the place Captain Wright had called *Pontus Alpha* and the kraken called the Facility.

"We're here," Macy said.

Aymee's gaze swept over the Facility. It had been here for hundreds of years, and no one on land had known.

"What the hell is this place?" Randall asked with wonder in his voice.

"Their home," Macy replied, turning her head to look at him. "Our home. It was built by humans before the first colonist ship arrived. It's where they made the kraken."

"*They*? You mean humans... We *made* them?"

"As slaves."

"They revolted against the humans," Aymee said, swimming alongside Dracchus to watch Arkon. His eyes remained closed, and he was limp in the larger male's hold. "Humans were the villains of kraken history. It's why they've kept to themselves all this time."

Macy led them past a pair of freestanding lights and to a door on the front of the large central building. There was a red light over the doorframe.

"Do you require entry?" Sam asked.

"Yes, Sam," Macy replied.

The light over the door turned green, and it slid open.

"How many of them live here?" Randall asked.

"I don't know," Macy said, swimming into the open chamber. "A lot."

Aymee hurried in after, turning as Dracchus carefully entered with Arkon.

Macy pressed a button once everyone was inside, and the door closed.

"Re-pressurization sequence initiated," Sam said.

The room seemed to hum around them. The water level steadily dropped, and Aymee's feet settled on the floor. Her awareness of her own weight returned slowly. It was an odd sensation. When the water was gone, the light over the interior door turned green.

"Pressurization complete," said a feminine voice from somewhere overhead. "Welcome back, divers two-zero-five, five-nine-one, and eight-six-six."

Macy, Aymee, and Randall removed their masks. The air was surprisingly clean, with only a faint seawater smell.

Together, Aymee and Macy moved into position to support Randall while Jax helped Dracchus lift Arkon, whose head lolled gently from side to side. Aymee looked at him with worry; he'd been unconscious for most of the journey.

Macy reached forward and activated the door switch, opening the way into a long, metal corridor.

"Melaina!" a female voice called.

A small kraken turned the corner and hurried toward them. "Macy! I saw you coming through a window!" she called, face bright. She held an even smaller kraken in her arms.

Aymee's eyes shifted to the baby. "Is that...?"

"Sarina," Macy said.

Melaina stopped suddenly, eyes widening as she looked from Aymee to Randall. She clutched Sarina closer. "Who... Are you...Aymee?" she asked, then her gaze shifted to Arkon, and her eyes rounded further. "Arkon's hurt!"

"Melaina!" A larger kraken turned into the hall. Bare breasts, delicate features, and lighter build marked her as a female. Several more kraken followed behind, all with similarly feminine traits.

"Holy shit," Randall said breathlessly.

"We cannot stand here forever," Dracchus grumbled.

"You brought humans," one of the females said, frowning.

"They are friends," Jax called. The humans stepped through the door and stood aside to allow the kraken males through.

"Rhea, this is Aymee," Macy said, nodding toward Aymee.

Rhea — the female in front of the group — looked at Aymee and smiled. "I have heard much." Her smile faded when she glanced at Arkon. "Come."

"Melaina," Macy said, "I need you to watch Sarina for me, okay?"

The little girl nodded.

Randall looked from Macy to Sarina and back again. "That's... She's your…"

Macy met Randall's gaze, and her eyes hardened as though awaiting either an insult or a threat. He staggered slightly, leaning more heavily upon the women, and shook his head. He said nothing.

"We need to go. Now." Aymee moved down the corridor behind the males, who themselves followed the kraken females.

They turned into another long hallway, passing open door-ways. She didn't look into any of the rooms, didn't stare at the walls in wonder; only Arkon mattered. She needed him stabilized, needed him in a place he could rest for as long as it took to heal, needed access to the right tools to care for him.

The group stopped suddenly, and Aymee peered around Dracchus. The females ahead growled as they were forced apart by another group of male kraken. Aymee nearly growled herself; the corridor was too small for so many bodies, and they needed to get to the infirmary!

"We have been looking for y—" The kraken in the lead came to an abrupt stop. "What is this?"

"Stand aside, Kronus," Jax demanded.

"What happened to him?"

"Aside, now!"

Kronus pressed his lips together and shifted, as did the males behind him, allowing Dracchus and Jax to pass with Arkon. When his eyes fell on Aymee and Randall, they widened before narrowing. His skin turned crimson.

"Humans!" he snarled, raising his claws.

"Don't you dare!" Macy shouted.

If Aymee had stopped to think, she might have acted differently; Kronus wasn't as large as Dracchus, but all the adult kraken were taller and more powerfully built than most humans. She followed her instinct. Stepping forward, she rammed her fist into Kronus's jaw, twisting her hip to put as much force into it as she could.

"Get back!" she yelled, glaring at him. "Arkon needs help!"

Kronus's head snapped aside, but his expression was one of shock rather than pain. Rage quickly overcame that shock. His muscles tensed as though to strike.

A huge black arm wrapped around Kronus's neck from behind. Dracchus swung the other kraken around and slammed him face-first into the wall. The structure itself seemed to shake.

"These humans are under *my* protection," Dracchus growled, glaring at Kronus's companions. "They are our people now. Do you understand?"

Kronus spat something that sounded like a muffled *yes*, and his companions nodded.

Dracchus held Kronus in place as the women hurried past with Randall, who leaned on them a bit more with each step. They passed Jax; Rhea was helping him support Arkon.

They reached the infirmary after one more turn, and Aymee's hand was throbbing by the time they entered. With

Macy's help, Aymee guided Randall into a bed, removed his suit, and inspected his stomach and shoulder to ensure the wounds hadn't torn open. Macy retrieved a blanket and laid it over him.

As Dracchus and Jax carried Arkon into the infirmary, Aymee pulled her arms free of the suit and tied it off as she had earlier.

She moved to Arkon's side after they lifted him onto a bed and checked his wounds. They'd remained sealed during the journey, but his skin was pale and cold.

"We need to cover him up, too. He lost a lot of blood, and his body's going to need all the help it can get to recover," she said.

Macy settled a blanket over Arkon, and Aymee reached beneath to take hold of his hand. Several kraken lingered in her peripheral vision. They watched in silence, male and female alike, until Dracchus made them leave; only he, Jax, and Rhea lingered.

"He'll be okay," Macy said, wrapping her arms around Aymee's shoulders. The worry in her voice was overpowered by a practical optimism. Aymee drew strength from it.

"This is a human male?" Rhea asked.

"Last I checked," Randall replied, slurring slightly.

"Hmm." She tilted her head as she studied him, then lifted the blanket to look beneath. Her eyes widened. "He is extruding."

Macy laughed, pulling her arms away from Aymee as she straightened.

"Two women in one day," Randall said.

"What does he mean?" Rhea asked Macy.

"People seem awfully interested in getting a glimpse of me, lately," he replied.

Rhea's attention returned to Randall. "He is not unattractive, for a human."

"I'll take that as a victory." Randall's voice trailed off as he succumbed to his weariness.

Macy brought a chair closer to Arkon's bed. Aymee thanked her and sat down.

"Jax and I are going to check on Sarina. We'll be right back, and I'll bring you a change of clothes. Do you need anything else?"

Aymee shook her head. "No. Thanks, Mace."

Dracchus and Rhea followed Jax and Macy out.

Sitting on the edge of the chair, Aymee slipped an arm around Arkon, laid her head on his chest, and closed her eyes. His hearts thumped beneath her ear, steady but weak. She squeezed him tight.

Exhaustion settled over her. Her body felt leaden, her eyelids heavy, but she kept her gaze on Arkon's sleeping face. As much as he needed his rest, she wished he'd wake so she could see the vibrant violet of his irises.

I nearly lost him.

Tears rolled down her cheek to wet the blanket beneath her.

The emotions she'd pushed aside rushed back, and all she could do was hold onto him as she cried.

"Don't leave me," she whispered, clutching the blanket against the pain in her heart.

Macy returned with Rhea shortly after, carrying clothing and food. Aymee stripped out of the diving suit and pulled on a shirt and a pair of loose pants. She didn't touch the food, and Macy' didn't push it on her. They sat in silence, watching over the males, Rhea helping Randall sip water whenever possible.

The same wouldn't work for Arkon — the kraken hydrated

naturally by being in water. After some searching, Dracchus and Jax brought in a large basin filled with seawater. They set Arkon into it as gently as possible, positioning him so his head was underwater, and he breathed through his siphons.

When there was nothing left to do but wait, Aymee sank to the floor, keeping a palm on his chest. Each beat of his hearts was a pulse of reassurance.

CHAPTER 20

ARKON OPENED HIS EYES. THE OVERHEAD LIGHT STUNG, AND HE squinted against it. Everything was a white blur until his vision adjusted.

The lights weren't bright at all; they were dimmed. He knew the ceiling overhead, but his mind could not reconcile its presence.

He'd been in the Broken Cavern — the Darrow Nautical Outpost — not the Facility.

Something warm and scratchy was laid over him. He lifted his head, wincing as his neck cramped, to see a heavy blanket draped over him. Aymee's arm was atop the blanket; she lay against him in the narrow space between Arkon and the bed rail.

"Arkon?"

He turned his head. Jax stood beside the bed, the shock in his expression quickly giving way to relief.

"You are okay," Jax said. "Your color had been improving,

and Aymee was outwardly optimistic, but none of us were sure..."

"How... You will forgive me, Jax, but..." Grunting softly, Arkon lowered his head. His entire body ached, now that he'd woken fully, making it more difficult to work through his confusion. "How did we get here?"

"You were badly injured. After Aymee closed your wounds, we brought you here to recover. This seemed the only safe place."

The hunters. *Cyrus.* Echoes of pain rippled across Arkon's abdomen, and he shifted a hand to the gunshot wounds. His fingertips brushed over hard scar tissue.

"No one else was hurt? Aymee wasn't hurt?" Arkon's hearts thumped; the events were fuzzy in his recollection, and Aymee was here, next to him, but had she come to harm?

"Only Randall. It seems he might have saved my life. We brought him with us." Jax gestured to the other side of the room.

Arkon lifted his head again to see Randall in the bed directly across from him, covered by a similar blanket. His eyes widened when he realized Rhea was at Randall's bedside, eyes closed and head resting on her crossed arms atop the blanket, back rising and falling in a slow, peaceful rhythm.

He looked at Jax and raised his brow in question.

Jax smiled and shrugged. "She has been helping Macy and Aymee care for the both of you over the last two days. They have had little rest in that time. Rhea seems to have taken an interest in him."

Arkon studied his friend's face; the gleam of surprise and relief had faded from Jax's eyes, leaving only weariness. "What of you?"

"Now, I may finally join my mate and youngling in our den."

He placed a hand on Arkon's shoulder. "I am glad you are well, Arkon."

"Go to them and rest, Jax. I will take vigil. I have slept enough for now, I think."

Jax departed quietly, and Arkon settled back down onto the bed, his unfocused gaze directed at the ceiling. Aymee's scent drifted to his nostrils; he inhaled deeply and sighed. Moving slowly, he slipped an arm out from beneath the blanket and wrapped it around her, drawing her closer against him.

She groaned, stirred, and moved her hand to rest on his chest. She exhaled softly.

He uncovered his other arm and placed his hand over hers.

Aymee tensed. "Arkon?"

"I didn't want to wake you. I am sorry."

She lifted her head. Her thick curls were in disarray, one strand endearingly hanging over her eye. "You're awake," she breathed.

"I am. But you should not—"

Aymee fell upon him, grabbing his face and pressing her mouth to his. She kissed him long and deep, then several more times in quick succession before wrapping her arms around him. "You came back to me."

He embraced her and marveled in her feel, her warmth, her energy. "I will always come back to you. I gave myself to you, Aymee. It is not my life to lose."

"And I won't ever give it up." She raised her head and met his gaze, eyes bright with tears.

He brushed the moisture from her cheek.

"How do you feel?" she asked.

"Like I have not moved in days."

She laughed, and it was the loveliest sound he'd ever heard. "That'd be about right."

"Now that you are here... Will you share my den, Aymee?"

She lowered her head and ran her nose over his cheek before kissing the corner of his mouth. "Yes. That and more. I want to join with you, Arkon."

Warmth blossomed in his chest and flowed to the tips of his fingers and tentacles.

After a moment, Aymee chuckled. "I don't think I made the best first impression on some of the kraken here, though."

Arkon furrowed his brow. "What do you mean?"

"I punched Kronus in the face."

He lifted his head to look at her. She was serious. A dozen emotions flickered through him — pride, concern, anger. "What did he do?"

"He was standing in our way and threatened us."

"What threat did he make?"

"Well, he raised his claws and said *humans*, and I *needed* to get you here, so I punched him."

"Kronus said a single word to you, and you struck him?"

"He was in the way, Arkon."

Arkon pressed his lips to hers in a lingering kiss. When he broke away, he touched his forehead to hers and grinned. "I love you, Aymee."

She smiled. "I love you, too."

"And I can hear you," Randall said. "Trying to sleep over here."

"Be silent and rest, human," Rhea commanded.

Arkon and Aymee stared at each other, smiles widening.

"Be silent and rest, human," Arkon whispered to her.

Aymee laughed and rolled off him. He raised the blanket.

She slipped under it and curled against him as he took her in his arms, twining his tentacles with her legs.

Arkon closed his eyes.

His Aymee was beside him, he was home, and he finally felt complete. Finally knew contentment. Aymee was the center-piece of his life. His heart.

His jewel.

EPILOGUE

AYMEE CLUNG TO ARKON AS HE PROPELLED THEM THROUGH THE depths. His body glowed, a beacon in the dark, and she couldn't help but run her hands over him. Her fascination never waned; he was a thing of beauty, a creation that had surpassed its creators.

And she'd come so close to losing him.

It'd been four weeks since their run-in with the Culver Hunters. Arkon had recovered within four days. His skin reverted to its healthy blue-gray, his strength returned, and if not for the three scars on his abdomen, Aymee might have believed she'd dreamed the whole encounter.

Tightening her hold, she rested her head on his shoulder. She couldn't see anything beyond the soft glow he emitted. The ocean was as dark and endless as the night sky.

Arkon had told her there was something he wanted to show her. He wouldn't say what it was, only that it was a surprise. The kraken hadn't seen much of anything apart from the usual fishing boats, which remained near the coast and didn't venture far from The Watch, so he'd decided it was safe enough. Aymee was also antsy to be back on land after weeks in the Facility. The rooms were comfortable — more spacious and accommodating than anything back home — but she needed open air every now and then.

He angled them upward, and his light went out.

Only the barest hint of illumination touched the surface of the water overhead. This was so far removed from the feel of the sea during the day — all the vibrant colors and sea life gone, leaving infinite black — that she felt like they'd traveled to an unknown, unforgiving world.

There was a faint speck of light ahead. She squinted, wondering if it was a trick of her eyes, but it was joined by more blue flecks.

They broke the surface a few moments later. The sky was partly clouded — patches of black dotted with twinkling stars were visible over the land to Aymee's right, but it was only bleak, dark gray over the sea apart from two spots where the obscured moons backlit the clouds.

Arkon released his hold on her and guided her to his back. As he swam forward, Aymee's eyes settled on the reflection of the stars upon the surface of the water. They were a bright blue, thousands or millions of them, moving with the gentle motion of the waves.

But the stars aren't visible over the ocean now.

Arkon carried them amidst the tiny blue points of light, which flowed in a wide stream toward land. Aymee stared in awe and reached a hand out. Several of the flecks, most no larger than a grain of sand, flared as they flowed between her fingers, returning to their prior brightness once they'd moved away.

"Halorium fields detected," Sam said. Something resembling a map with spots of blue color, varying in thickness, blinked across the mask. "Interference is currently minimal, but it is suggested that you turn back and avoid further exposure."

Aymee frowned. "What will the exposure do, Sam?"

"My systems may be compromised by the energy fields emitted by halorium, which could result in failure of life support."

"Is the halorium dangerous?"

"Only for its potential effects on your PDS."

An unfamiliar thrum pulsed over her skin; she knew the suit created some sort of invisible buffer between itself and its wearer, but this was the first time she'd felt it.

"It does not have any known adverse effects on living creatures," Arkon said. The tiny spheres bathed his face in a soft glow, making his smile even gentler.

"Is this what you wanted to show me?" she asked.

"Yes. But we're not quite where I intended yet."

"The concentration of the halorium radiation is increasing," Sam said, a hint of static in his voice. The vibrations in the suit increased.

"Sam, release the mask."

The seal broke with a hiss and the thrumming ceased. Aymee removed the mask and tugged off her hood. Relaxing against Arkon's back, she kept her arms around him as he continued forward, smiling when one of his hands brushed her arm.

The blue flecks thickened around them until it looked as though they were swimming through a clear night sky. Waves of blue flared, rippling out around them.

"The color reminds me of your glow," Aymee said.

"I do not think it is an accident," he replied. "Many native sea creatures have similar bioluminescence."

Arkon took them toward a stretch of beach. The sand was pale against the dark, imposing forms of the cliffs backing it, but even from a distance, she could tell it was covered with the little flecks of light. As soon as the water was shallow enough, she released her hold and walked alongside Arkon onto land.

She turned to face the ocean, water skimming past her ankles, and her breath caught at the beauty of it. Waves rolled ashore, and the flecks they disturbed pulsed like lightning crackling in the clouds. Kneeling, she ran her hand over the water's surface, watching it come to life, and when she lifted her hand, particles sparkled on her suit.

"This is incredible!" she exclaimed, looking up at Arkon.

His eyes were upon her. "It is."

Warmth flooded her. The combination of his words and intense expression made her heart pound. She looked back down. "Why isn't it like this everywhere?"

"I do not know," he replied, moving closer. "But this — this place, at this moment — is just for the two of us."

Aymee tilted her head back and smiled. She stood up, running a finger from the center of his waist to his chest. "What should the two of us do in such a place?"

"Anything we want."

Stepping away from him, Aymee moved up the beach until she was a safe distance from the water. She tossed the mask into the sand and turned to face Arkon. Wrapping her hand around the suit's centerpiece, she twisted her fingers, and the fabric separated at her back.

"And what do you want, Arkon?" she asked, peeling the sleeves off her arms.

He approached slowly, the glowing surf sweeping around his tentacles, gaze fixed upon her. "I want you. Only you. Forever, you."

Aymee's heart raced. His voice, deep and filled with desire, enveloped her. She slipped the suit down her body until she was able to kick it aside. Her breasts ached, and her nipples tightened, begging for his touch, and a throb of arousal slickened her inner thighs. She held her arms out to him.

"You have me."

He slipped an arm around her waist, and she looped hers around his neck. He eased her onto the sand and held himself over her. Tiny glowing orbs clung to his skin, granting him an ethereal visage.

Arkon leaned down and slanted his mouth over hers. His kiss was equal amounts love and lust, tenderness and passion, possessiveness and surrender. Her hands roamed over his chest and shoulders to cup his face as she returned the kiss with everything she had to give.

He tore his mouth from hers with a growl and ran his lips down her neck, grazing his teeth along her skin. His hands framed her ribs, thumbs brushing the undersides of her breasts. Aymee tilted her head back with a moan that turned into a gasp when the heat of his mouth covered her nipple, and he sucked, sending jolts of sensation straight to her core. She spread her thighs to welcome his weight between them.

Arkon moved further down her body, sliding his palms to her hips. His shoulders forced her thighs wider. Cool air struck her heated sex. She shivered. Opening her eyes, she gazed down the length of her body. It was the most erotic thing she'd ever seen — Arkon there, between her legs, his gaze locked with hers.

He lowered his mouth without looking away from her and kissed her clit. Aymee's hips bucked, but he held her down. She panted, unable to look away as his tongue slipped out to lick at her folds and flick against her sensitive bud. Liquid heat flooded her, and he drank greedily.

She watched him with hooded eyes, biting her lip to muffle her cries until she was unable to withstand the powerful sensations. Her head fell back, hips undulating against his mouth.

Pleasure built within her like the gathering clouds of a storm, and her skin tingled, every nerve lighting up.

"Arkon!" she screamed as the storm broke. She writhed, but he didn't relent.

He growled, the vibrations prolonging her release. His grip on her tightened, and he lifted her hips, lapping at her until she was spent.

His hands slid back up her sides as he moved over her. She felt the slick hardness of his shaft against her thigh, felt his tentacles coil around her legs and lift them until they wrapped around his hips, felt the soft caress of his suction cups as they tasted her skin. Such strength, yet he was always so gentle with her.

Arkon pressed his mouth to hers, and she opened to him, tasting herself upon his lips. Her hands gripped his arms. It didn't matter that she'd already reached her peak. She craved more of him, *all* of him.

"Now," she breathed against his mouth, tilting her hips. His tip pressed against her opening, and then he thrust in, sinking deep. Her body clenched.

His forehead pressed against hers. "Each moment I am with you is more breathtaking than the moment before."

Aymee slid her hands to his back. The feelers at the base of his shaft tickled and stroked her sex and clit. She was beyond words. Arkon withdrew, and she moaned at the loss of fullness until he pumped forward again. He didn't stop, setting a rhythm that was both satisfying and maddening. He filled her, stretched her, stroked her, pushed deeper and deeper.

His lips and tentacles caressed her skin, and she clawed at him, needing more.

Growling, Arkon settled his hands on her hips and quickened his pace. The tips of his claws pressed against her skin, producing pricks of pain that added to the sensations building within her.

Her body shuddered, tightening around him, and her panting gasps turned into keens of pleasure as she came apart.

Arkon reared back, muscles tensing, and yanked her onto him, pinning her sex to his, grinding as his fire filled her. He turned his face skyward and roared.

As they descended from their climaxes, their connection was no less powerful. Aymee stared up at Arkon, nearly bursting with happiness. She pressed a hand to his chest, feeling the strong, steady beats of his hearts, and smiled.

He gazed down at her, eyes dark and half-lidded with lingering desire and adoration, shoulders rising and falling with heavy breaths.

"Glow for me," she said.

His skin lit up, casting its glow on her. She trailed her palm down his abdomen, pausing to touch the round scars.

He covered her hand with his. "It is in the past, Aymee. We must look ahead."

She took his wrist and guided his hand to her stomach. "To our future."

He tilted his head to the side, brow furrowing as his gaze

335

dipped. His eyes suddenly rounded, and his lips parted in wonder. "You mean…?"

"You're going to be a father."

The smile that spread across his face was slow, but when it formed fully it was more beautiful than the starlit sky and held all the joy in the world. Arkon leaned down and pressed a gentle kiss to her stomach. Aymee closed her eyes and rested her hands on his head.

"Our future," he whispered.

ALSO BY TIFFANY ROBERTS

Tiffany Roberts - Unleashed

VENYS NEEDS MEN COLLABORATION

Tiffany Roberts - To Tame a Dragon

Tiffany Roberts – To Love a Dragon

ABOUT THE AUTHOR

Tiffany Roberts is the pseudonym for Tiffany and Robert Freund, a husband and wife writing duo. Tiffany was born and bred in Idaho, and Robert was a native of New York City before moving across the country to be with her. The two have always shared a passion for reading and writing, and it was their dream to combine their mighty powers to create the sorts of books they want to read. They write character driven sci-fi and fantasy romance, creating happily-ever-afters for the alien and unknown.

Sign up for our Newsletter!
Check out our social media sites and more!

Made in United States
Troutdale, OR
01/16/2024

16960875R00213